THE GUIDED TOUR
BY
MAGGIE BROOKE

THE GUIDED TOUR

ISBN: 978-1-905091-60-7
Paperback Version
© 2011 by Maggie Brooke

Published in the United Kingdom by Logical-Lust Publications 2011
www.ll-publications.com
57 Blair Avenue
Hurlford
Scotland
KA1 5AZ

Edited by Zetta Brown
Proofreading by Billye Johnson
Book layout and typesetting by jimandzetta.com
Cover art and design by James Keefer www.jameskeefer.net © 2011

Printed in the UK, USA, and Australia

DEDICATION

For all the men that I have loved...and for every "Mary" who has helped me while I was working in the Outback.

ACKNOWLEDGEMENTS

A big thank you to Zetta for all her help, patience, and belief in my story, and also to the Mackay Book Club, the first to read and critique it.

CHAPTER ONE

ONCE I FINALLY FELL ASLEEP, I dreamt I was in Hell. When I woke up, I found that it was true. I really was in Hell. Grabbing at my watch to shut off the obnoxious dinging of its alarm, I opened my right eyelid about one millimetre, just enough to recognize the same stained, sagging ceiling was still above my bed. My hand tentatively touched the grimy sheet covering the quarter inch of brittle foam rubber that they called a mattress here. I leaned cautiously over the edge of the top bunk and confirmed my fear; I was surrounded by five gargoyles that appeared dead. The smells emanating from their bodies approximated three-day-old road kill, but they weren't, in fact, as dead as they looked unless the deceased have taken to drooling, snoring, farting, and scratching their balls. The overhead fan, close enough to decapitate me if I sat up, blew dust, hot air, and odours while sweat coursed down my cheeks like tears. It was 5:30 a.m. but the already warm light of day could do little to penetrate the gloom of this room. Yes, I was in Hell and it was called Darwin! Funny that a place where evolution clearly stopped several ice ages ago would name itself after the guy who first formulated the theory.

Brushing damp curls, which now stank as badly as the mattress, from my burning, swollen eyelids, I collapsed back onto the thin pillow and briefly pondered my fate and my future.

How, you might well ask, did *I*, Louisa Mayflower Smith (yes, my ancestors were on the Mayflower, but that was another country, another century and, most definitely, another religion. I've been called many things but never, ever, has "Puritan" been one of them!), a beautiful, wealthy, privileged, educated—did I mention beautiful?—twenty-three-year-old woman on the cusp of life from Sydney's North Shore, ever end up in the Goanna's Grunt Backpackers in Darwin? I'd been asking myself that question every hour of every day for almost a week now. The answer, still as evasive as ever, limped its way into my tired brain.

Suffice it to say that the arrest warrant precluded my catching the return flight home. There was stuff-all accommodation in this hole and, more to the point, Daddy had insisted on cancelling all my credit cards until he had the full, unbiased story of my criminal record, which I obviously couldn't give him until I got home, so I was forced to survive here on my good looks and pocket money. Plenty of good looks, of course, but here in Darwin I'm sure that all you needed to be considered beautiful were a full set of teeth. I thought I'd outgrown hating my father but this blatant lack of trust in his errant offspring caused me to regress.

"You've been *what*?" he'd shouted down the phone, obviously thinking that the lines were hollow up here in the Top End. "You've been *arrested* and you're ringing from *prison*?" The gasping sounds as he tried to catch his breath made me wonder if he was having a heart attack, but he recovered quickly.

"Not prison, just the police station." I tried vainly to placate him. My soothing, if plaintive, voice had no effect.

"No member of the Smith family has been arrested since the Rum Rebellion of 1808! Even our ancestors who came over on the First Fleet—" (Here we go. I knew he was *seriously* displeased when the First Fleet was mentioned.) "—came over as sailors—not as convicts! Louisa Mayflower Smith, what will I tell your mother?"

And then he had obviously told her everything because suddenly she was blubbering down the phone, crying about the example I was setting for my younger sisters and why couldn't I be more like my brother? Just like my dad, her understanding was conspicuous by its absence.

So I'd been stranded in Darwin for the last five days, abandoned by my family, cooling my heels, waiting for my week-long Community Service Order (or "CSO" in the lingo) to begin. Five days of associating with a breed of people known as "backpackers." Five days of walking a waveless beach. Five days of looking for a decent cup of coffee and an intelligent conversation. The woman who ran Goanna's Grunt, obviously a refugee from the '60s whose fly-away grey hair reached very nearly to her bare feet, had cheerfully offered me seven days for the price of six and I had cheerfully laughed in her face. Wilfully choosing to remain an extra two days in this place would have cost more than I could afford in terms of self respect.

Darwin is so strange. Everybody, men, women, and babies, say "mate" every second word. They drink their beer from litre bottles and consider thongs to be suitable footwear whatever the occasion. Sometimes, in pursuit of glamour, women will add rhinestones to the straps of their thongs and men will paint PISS OFF on theirs. The air up here is so humid it's like walking through walls of sweat. Nothing, ever, is completely dry, and fungi grow in places better left unidentified. I sighed as I plucked a mushroom from my left armpit. Even though I was leaving Darwin to fulfil my CSO, I was pretty sure things were just going to get worse.

"Better start moving, Lou." I tried to motivate myself, wiping my face with the damp sheet. I'd booked a cab for 6 a.m.

I couldn't exactly leap out of my bed, uncomfortable though it was. Apart from the guillotine/fan thing, I probably would have broken my leg if I had leapt because, as mentioned, I was on the top bunk and there was no ladder. I peered cautiously over the edge to the bunk below. Only one body–male. The girl he'd been shagging so vigorously last night was gone.

They'd arrived sometime after midnight, whispering, "Be quiet! Don't want to disturb her royal highness" so loudly that, of course, I was disturbed. The bed had begun to rock then, amid giggling and grunting and "Omigod you're so big!"-ing. ("Omigod!" How desperate for a root was this pathetic prima donna?) While hanging on for dear life I managed to pluck small bits of stiff foam from my mattress and lodge them in my ears, but they were of little benefit.

Finally I recognised the "oohs" and "aahs" of a fake orgasm and it must have fooled her Lothario because he gave a moaning thrust that knocked my poor head against the bed frame, and then they lay still. That sexual encounter left me more exhausted than most I've been directly involved in. I fell back asleep, ear foam still *in situ*.

Now I got up, trying to be quiet as I manoeuvred my bags, sheets, and body over and down the conjoined headboards, managing to avoid stepping on the slobbering gargoyle's mattress. By not stepping in his puddle of spittle, however, I managed to get my foot caught in the pair of dirty jocks that he'd hung on the corner post. I flicked them off my foot and they landed on the face of another bearded sleeper. He didn't awaken but plucked the knickers off his face, sniffed them, and then tucked them cosily under his cheek before grunting contentedly and resuming a dream I didn't want to know about. It was *so* past time for me to be out of there. I picked up the sheets I'd dropped during the spelunking endeavour and crept into the hall and down to the communal shower/toilets.

I used half a roll of loo paper to line the seat before I sat, and then half a bar of soap to wash youth hostel bacteria off my body. Removing the yellow crumbs of foam rubber from my ears was not easy and I could only hope, in the end, that all had been evacuated. Any ear infection generated by a youth hostel mattress would surely baffle medical science and the broadest spectrum of its antibiotics. The shower stalls were made from semi-transparent plexiglass and the metal rims were so bent out of shape that none closed properly so the user was always on display in one way or another. Did I mention that these were unisex facilities? Fortunately, there was no-one around to interrupt me at 5:30 on a Monday morning, but I still found it hard to believe that people actually chose to stay in places like this for pleasure. I towelled myself dry, got dressed, and made my way to the kitchen, a room designed to add at least two more layers of incredulity to a thinking person's mind.

It was tiny and ancient but airy since its one small window had been enlarged by white ants. A rusty refrigerator and a freezer without seals were provided for storing perishables (briefly) and the walls were crammed to the gunnels with variously shaped wooden cabinets of different colours. Some of these had louvered doors and some had glass doors but most had no doors at all and were stacked with all sorts of pots, pans, plates, bowls, cutlery, and empty Vegemite jars, all adorned with the requisite sprinkling of cockroach, gecko, and possum poo.

In these hostels (for those of you who don't know and even for those who probably never *wanted* to know) one is expected, even encouraged, to cook one's own food in these communal pots and pans. In the interest of health and safety (mine!), I had relied solely on restaurant food. Most mornings I broke my fast at The Coffee Club—not boutique but at least they could make a decent latté. I did, however, have my own tea bags and a mug that said HANDS OFF! THIS MEANS YOU! because the kettle appeared safe enough and I do like my caffeine in the mornings. I was draining the last of my tea when I heard the taxi arrive.

I guessed that the driver was not a fan of backpackers either since he sat on his horn outside the Goanna's Grunt for the full two minutes it took me to grab my gear, give a last check for anything I might have left behind, dump my dirty bed linen into a cane laundry basket, and exit, gently pulling the door shut behind me. The blaring lasted long enough to wake every sleeping soul in the hostel, most of who had been partying until dawn so I, who had been trying to be quiet, left the building amid a volley of abusive and profane shouts. As a parting gift, I reopened the door and slammed it until the rafters shook. I jumped quickly onto the lawn before the entire, rickety old relic decided to collapse.

"Hey, matey! You the one what's going to the cop shop?" the driver hollered out the window as I approached his clapped-out Corolla.

So maybe it wasn't backpackers but, rather, those involved with the penal system that he didn't care to associate with. I bent down to answer, got a look at the driver, and opted to sit in the back seat.

He was a very special vision first thing in the morning with his cigarette dangling from his lower lip, trapped within a gap caused by missing teeth. His chin stubble was stained a worrisome brown and his body odour had been brewing for a couple of days at least. Where's a good, clean driver who doesn't speak English when you need one?

I opened the back door and climbed in, holding my rucksack in my lap in case I needed to make a speedy exit while clutching my handbag tightly under my arm. I was unfamiliar with these Top End types and hadn't formed anything like a trust base yet. His mouth curled into a leer as he watched me in his rear vision mirror, trying to undress me with his bloodshot eyes. I was very familiar with *that* look.

"You can't do it, fool," I sighed. "You haven't got the imagination or, I'm surmising here, the experience."

"Huh?" he responded predictably. "Why doncha sit up front here, matey?"

"I'll be fine where I am and, yes, I'm going to the police station." It was unbelievable that the man actually thought that I would to sit next to him and give him the chance to put his hairy paws anywhere close to me. He must have been as drunk as he smelled.

With his best "come hither" wink and a moist grunt, he put the car in gear and we were soon driving along the Esplanade. It was not the most direct way to our destination and I nearly said something caustic, but it was the most scenic so instead I stared out the open window. There was a faint scent of Frangipani in the air and I watched the Arafura Sea change from a vast bowl of mercury to a plate of shimmering gold as the morning sun rose quickly over the horizon. Palm trees emerged from silhouette, turning different shades of green, and the sand was dark where the tide had been at its highest. This beach was not without its charm, but it was so terribly different from the southeast coast where I'd grown up. I shook my head and wondered, yet again, how my life had come to this point. Oh, Mama, how I missed my Sydney!

My Sydney of wide streets, green parks, and magnificent trees...of mansions along the North Shore, of concerts and opera and ballet. My Sydney of picturesque coffee shops and quaint cafés where girlfriends wearing Lisa Ho dresses and Prada shoes and carrying briefcases could meet to eat organic brunches during their busy days. My Sydney with its wine bars where the women in Lisa Ho could meet men in Armani suits and wind down at the end of those busy days. My Sydney with its Daylight Saving Time.

I could imagine my closest friends, Suzanne and Claudia, meeting up for an early morning latte and wondering about me. Their skin would be dry and smell of expensive colognes;

their clothes would be crisp and every wayward wisp of hair would have been artistically placed. They'd be talking above the clatter of dishes, the wheeze of the metro buses, and the hustle of people hurrying around them while breathing in the city air, vibrant with the aromas of a life that never stops.

"Poor Louisa," they'd be saying as they gently stirred their espressos. "We tried to warn her. No good ever comes from getting involved in something you don't understand."

"Especially in a foreign country," they would add because there might as well have been an ocean between us. London feels closer to Sydney than Darwin does.

My Sydney, where life is constantly changing and where I never want my life to change. How long was a week? From here it looked as long as a piece of string.

"Christ," I muttered, blinking back the tears, "how many wrong turns can one person make?"

"Whatcha say, love? You accusing me of taking a wrong turn?" the driver asked with phlegm-soaked innocence, the same cigarette still glued to his half-arsed grin. It is not usually my habit to suffer fools but this morning I couldn't be bothered with the effort it would take to respond appropriately. I absent-mindedly flipped him the bird and continued to watch the rolling water.

Here, in this dirty taxi littered with old chips and drink bottles, sat I, a good girl, oozing with breeding and, let's face it, class. I'd gone to a private girls' school in Sydney where the teachers were trendy enough to smoke dope with their students. I'd attended the University of Sydney and taken a degree in chemical engineering while dating (briefly) the head of the Arts Department. I knew people. Hell, I knew people who'd known people like Brett Whitely and Patrick White and Gough Whitlam. I had parents who were on the boards of places like NIDA and the Sydney Opera Company.

(Oops! I better not think about my parents. *How to Get Disinherited in Ten Easy Steps*! I had to be up at least seven by now and this CSO would count for the final three.)

Whenever I travelled, I expected it to be first class and when in the city, wanting to avoid parking fines and damage to my BMW, I preferred to use Daddy's chauffeur-driven town car.

My girlfriends and I met every Friday afternoon at Elizabeth Arden's to get ourselves prepared for the weekend. We shopped at Myers only when we were slumming because everybody knows that if it isn't a boutique, the merchandise isn't worth buying. Hell, even my virginity had come at a price. I lost it in a $500/night suite at the Radisson, bottle of champagne on arrival...

IT WAS THE NIGHT of my high school formal and I wore a sleek, shimmering, Oriental gown, its low cut bodice stitched with real pearls. My heels were soft, silver Moroccan leather, and my jewellery was a diamond pendant with matching earrings that my grandparents had given me for my sixteenth birthday. My date that night, a Grade Twelve-er from the Christian Brothers' College, wore his own tuxedo. We made a beautiful couple and my friends were jealous and that's what it was all about. After the dance, a limousine drove us to the hotel.

Once in the room, however, nothing had gone according to plan. The Grade Twelve-er (what the hell was his name?) was in a hurry. His idea of foreplay was unzipping my gown before ripping it off me and his level of expertise made me suspect that it was his first time as well (not counting the showers in the school gym). I was dry and the condom broke. He finished an hour before I did, and then passed out on top of me, but at least I could say I'd finally "done it."

Frankly, though, I couldn't see what all the fuss was about sex. Except for being sore, I might as well still be a virgin although I'd have to go to a clinic first thing in the morning for the morning after pill and tests. Plenty of tests. He was from a Catholic college, after all.

"And this is what everybody wants to do all the time?" I asked myself as I lay beneath him, listening to his snores. If this was a rite of passage it was no less brutal than what they do to girls in some tribal areas. I was not impressed.

With great effort, and at the expense of two broken nails, I finally managed to get the star of the rugby team off me, and then retired to the sofa to finish what the altar boy had started. Perhaps that's why bad lovers have never worried me much. I've learned to be bloody good on my own. It was quite awhile before I tried it with another person again. But I digress...

BACK TO THE PRESENT. I was stranded in Darwin with a criminal record and just about to start my Community Service Order. For those of you who have never been here, let me try to explain. No. Sorry. I can't. It isn't even fair to say that Darwin is the arsehole of the universe because most people at least care enough about their arseholes to wipe them! Darwin is..., well, Darwin. *I* knew I didn't belong in this place but, there you go; the Law disagreed. The taxi swung into the kerb across the street and half a block away from the Police Station.

"This'll be close enough, matey. That'll be $15. Got a surcharge this early, eh."

"I'll give you $10 for what should have been a $5 ride and, if you've got a grievance, just follow me inside." I dropped the note onto the front passenger's seat and hopped out as quickly as I could.

He gave that moist grunt again, snatched my money, and squealed away, obviously knowing that there were better places to be. I stood in the middle of the road, feeling almost wistful as the taxi disappeared around a corner.

No chance of escape now.

CHAPTER TWO

THE STREET, clean and fresh in the early morning air, was empty and silent under its scrawny eucalyptus trees. The perfume of flowering bushes filled the air and the only sign of life was the open doorway of the cop shop where a fat thing in a khaki uniform stood, knee socks gathered at his ankles, smoking a cigarette, looking like a poster boy for "What happens when Boy Scouts go bad." Why didn't these idiots wear blue like self-respecting coppers the world over? I hoped for his family's sake that his job came with good death benefits. A bus turned into the street a couple of blocks down and the cloud of exhaust obscured my distant glimpse of the sea and its fumes drowned the scent of jasmine.

I shouldered my hand-tooled, soft Italian leather bag, picked up my Paddy Pallin rucksack and looked again at the building I'd have to enter eventually. Might as well get started and get it over and done with. I took a deep breath and crossed the street.

The smoker chose not to step aside to let me in the door so I was forced to squeeze past the grey, hairy belly that stretched his shirt beyond its limits. When my belly-button ring got caught on one of his buttons, he obviously thought all his Christmases had come at once and gave me a grin that could extinguish Rudolph's nose forever. Trying not to sneeze (he'd exhaled a lungful of smoke directly into my face), I freed myself, tucked my own shirt back into my shorts, approached the counter, and slapped my copy of the CSO down on the faux plywood.

"I believe I am expected," I stated caustically, "to go somewhere with somebody and learn my lesson."

The tall, thin policeman standing behind the counter pushed his glasses up his nose, sniffed, placed both palms on the stained, chipped barrier and looked me square in the eye through thick, fly-specked lenses.

"The purpose of this trip, Miss Smith, is to teach you respect for this territory and its people. It will change your life. Trust me."

I got the impression that he was trying to convince himself as well as me that he believed every word he was saying.

"Yeah, right, whatever you say, Officer," I drawled and scratched the armpit where the mushroom had been. When in Rome...

I was so totally without enthusiasm and so totally over Northern Territory coppers trying to control my life. This moron might have taken the course on *How to Get Your Crims On Side* at www.criminology.com, but it was obvious that he'd misread Article 1–where it advised the cop to first find out why the crim had been arrested. He didn't have a clue about the charges against me and I was in no mood to enlighten him. He was so beyond enlightenment and I so didn't care.

"Just tell me what I've got to do or go or sign or whatever. Let me get this over with." I yawned and pulled my sunglasses down from where they'd been balanced precariously on my mildly prominent brow (No, Mother, that is *not* a simian ridge!). There was nothing in this room that I wanted to examine in too much detail. The early morning sun struggled to brighten up the place but it was fighting a losing battle. Sombre blue, dirty grey, and dusty shadows were the colours of the day and they weren't giving up that privilege to cheerful sunlight.

Officer Joe (that's what the badge on his shirt said, swear to God), with his wrinkled shirt and baggy shorts, had the look of someone just coming off night duty but I had it on good authority–the roster white board pinned to the back wall–that he'd only been there thirty minutes. If this was how he started his day, I hated to think how he looked at its close. I hated to think about him at all. He disappeared from view which cheered me up just a little but it turned out that he had only ducked down under the counter to find the ubiquitous "paperwork." The mutterings that were rising from beneath the stained (coffee? tears? blood?) countertop led me to believe he was having difficulty finding what he wanted.

"Maybe if you cleaned your glasses it would be easier to read the forms," I suggested helpfully.

Increased mutterings told me he was not receptive to friendly advice. I sighed, gave my best "only trying to help" shrug, shifted my backpack to the other shoulder, tapped my foot, and continued waiting. And sweating. At this rate, I could complete my entire sentence standing in front of this counter. No such luck. He reappeared, shuffled a worryingly thick stack of papers, pulled a pen from his pocket, and handed them all to me.

Pushing those greasy glasses up his nose again, he bared broken teeth in what was maybe supposed to be a smile. I think he was trying to impress me because he straightened his collar and brushed a freckled hand over a buzz haircut.

"Here. Sign all these forms–there–where it says 'detainee.' You'll have to press hard because they've all got carbons. I suppose you can read them if you want to but they're pretty extensive and you don't have much time."

"Sorry, Joe," I said, taking the pile of papers and flicking my thumb through them, "but this illiterate detainee was taught never to sign anything she hadn't at least tried to read."

Then, just to be difficult, not because I gave a farthing about what any of them said, I carried the stack over to a cracked vinyl chair, sat down, crossed my legs (for Joe's benefit) and read each form, fine print included. It turned out that by signing I would be basically indemnifying the Northern Territory Government in case they, or their minions, happened to kill me–which was highly likely since they were taking me to that place they call "the Outback." Oh, shit. I was getting that panicky feeling again. Maybe it was just low blood sugar since breakfast time had slipped by unnoticed this morning.

I heard the sound of coins dropping into a metal slot and glanced over at Officer Joe, who was now concentrating on extracting a candy bar from the vending machine instead of my response to the forms he'd given me. For a brief instant I thought he was going to offer it to me but he had obviously realized that he didn't have a hope in hell with this crim and stuffed the entire thing into his gob before he'd even finished unwrapping it. I gave up my little protest. I sighed, I signed, I asked no questions. I had the distinct feeling that neither queries nor complaints would get much attention around here.

Tossing the forms onto the counter, I stuffed my copies into my bag, and then looked out the window at the crowd gathering outside. The bus I'd seen earlier was now parked across the street. It wasn't huge, maybe thirty-five seats, and dragged a large white luggage box along behind. Maybe it had been an airport shuttle bus in a former life, but it now had "DELTA TOURS" emblazoned along its side. Like it was proud of that, or something. Then my well-trained eyes zeroed in on the best sight I'd seen all morning.

"Is he coming with us?" I asked Officer Joe, pointing to an extremely handsome Aboriginal man who stood, clipboard in hand, near a bus parked across the street. He looked ever so efficient and that wasn't all.

This guy was a hottie, as my little sisters would say. He had a broad nose, succulent lips and deep-set eyes; his curly black hair reached nearly to his collar and he wore his sunglasses perched on his head. I removed my own sunnies because I definitely wanted to examine him. His light blue shirt stretched across strong, broad shoulders. Tight, dark blue shorts outlined muscular thighs and revealed a promising bulge. He wore the whitest knee socks I'd ever seen and his skin was the colour of milk chocolate. I couldn't help wondering if he tasted as good as he looked. We could have some fun, he and I, comforting each other during this week of open-air imprisonment.

"Yup, he'll be what they call the Tour Leader."

Officer Joe then lost what little interest he'd ever had in the proceedings and poured himself a fresh cup of coffee. It smelled really good but he didn't offer me any of that, either. Instead, he picked up a newspaper and retired to his desk where he could drink his coffee, eat his candy bar (he'd bought another one and it wasn't even 7 o'clock) and read in comfort, unencumbered by pesky detainees. I, with another glance out the window, cheered up a bit. My day had started badly and I was desperate to find any positives I could.

CHAPTER THREE

I LOOKED OVER at the tour leader again. He stuck a hand in his pocket to adjust himself and my panties got slightly damp as naughty thoughts raced around my brain cage. I hadn't even met this guy yet and he was already doing things to me, despite the fact that I was forced to watch through dirty, tape-repaired windows. I needed a closer look. I needed a...Stop it now, Louisa!–I definitely needed to be introduced. I zipped my bag, hoisted my rucksack, and strode outside. Thankfully, the fat copper had left the doorway.

Once I got outside, though, I was forced to notice what else had been happening since the taxi had dropped me off. While I'd been inside reading all my forms, the street had been filling up with some sort of humanity. It was hard to accept, but they must have been members of my group. They looked like nothing but losers, dolts, dweebs, arseholes, and the worst bits of slang my private school vocabulary could come up with. I wished I'd watched more Australian movies; bet there were ripe bits of language in them. About a dozen juvenile thugs milled around looking intent on making life as unpleasant as they could for the few parents who had bothered to show up and the few police who had been unlucky enough to draw the early shift.

A lad in dreadlocks was trying to start a punch-up with a skinhead; a girl with oily, orange hair and John Lennon glasses cried loudly while squeezing a baby who was crying even louder; two middle-aged men in shorts and singlets were yelling at some small children, and a skinny young policewoman was blowing her whistle madly while waving her arms and shouting, "Line up! Stand back! Cut that out!" No-one paid the slightest bit of attention to her orders but a couple of lads imitated her gestures in some distorted form of flirtation.

The teenage boys slouched as if afraid that if they stood up straight their baggy trousers would slide to their feet. Camouflage cargo pants and black denim gangsta shorts were the costume of the day and I couldn't remember ever having seen so many butt cracks at one time. The girls pranced around on elevator shoes and tiny shorts so tight up their fannies they couldn't bend. They all wore tube tops and continually plucked at them, worried that they would slip down and reveal just how little cleavage they actually had. Except one plump girl who was incredibly well-endowed whose top barely fit. She didn't just pluck at it. She held it in place by keeping her shoulders and head hunched forward, as though poor posture was the key to holding it up. I might be forced to give this kid some fashion tips this week, but hopefully I wouldn't have to get that close to her.

No joke, I could practically see the big "L" tattooed on each forehead. It was unbelievable. What was *I* expected to do with this lot? Twisting the strap of my bag tightly around my wrist and holding it close under my arm, I lowered my sunglasses, clenched my teeth, and stepped into the melee. Mistake Number One. Immediately one of the boys sidled up to me and rested a casual hand on my butt.

"Hey, Babe, what say we sit together at the back of the bus? I got some bitchin' weed in my sock."

He was a long, skinny white kid. In fact, he was probably the whitest person I'd ever seen. Despite the weather a black tailcoat hung from his lean frame and I could count the hairs in the sad smudge of whiskers growing under his bottom lip. I picked his offending hand off my bottom and slapped his cheek with it.

"Hey, *Babe*, do I look like I want to smoke your dirty socks? Still, I bet the roll you've got down there is bigger than the one you've got in your jocks." I moved away, feeling contaminated, while the boy stood gobsmacked and slobbering, his mates' yahooing and slapping him on the back.

"Way to go, bro!"

"Looks like you need a new line, mate!"

"Hey, did you see the rack on her, Dude?"

There was more but thankfully, I blocked it out.

Having lost sight of the tasty tour leader, I moved into the shade of a nearby building and shuddered. My CSO (punishment for an offence which did not deserve punishment, but more on that later) was to help supervise this gang of juvenile offenders on a life-altering tour of the Outback. *As if a week in the country could actually change anybody's life*, I thought bitterly. One week in hell for me, and then I'm off back home just as fast as QANTAS can fly me.

I glanced at my reflection in the glass door that sheltered me from the heat. I hardly had the complexion for this trip, in spite of my solarium tan. My curly, light brown hair was cut short although it was three weeks since I'd been to the hairdresser and the shag was becoming careless. This morning I'd gel-spiked it off my forehead, which is way too low for my liking. My blue eyes are set wide to accommodate a humungous nose, which, my mum always assured me, added character to a face that would otherwise have been too pretty. That's what mothers are for. I wore tailored cargo shorts (yep, me as well, but mine were powder blue, not black, and belted around my waist, not my pelvis) and an expensive, well-cut white singlet with a Kathmandu label. My brand new (also blue) Akubra hung down my back on its leather thong, á la Nicole Kidman in *Australia - the Movie*. The wide felt brim would have protected my delicate complexion if I'd worn it on my head, but then I'd have "hat hair" to worry about. I watched the proceedings through Yves St. Laurent sunglasses. Fortunately, I had done my Top End shopping before I'd left Sydney and before Daddy had done his dirty work. I rummaged through my bag, pulled out a packet of Indian Beedies, and extracted a slim, brown cigarette. Mistake Number Two. I lounged against a wall and lit one up, hoping its aromatic smoke would cut through the diesel and dust, waiting for someone to tell me what to do. It didn't take long.

"Hey, you! No smoking on this trip!"

One of the boys-in-khaki was hollering at me from in front of the station. I looked up and saw that it was the slob who'd been smoking when I first arrived. Could this be the pot calling the kettle black? He was certainly bigger than my great-grandmother's copper (which I'd seen only in photographs—don't start thinking I have any idea how to operate contraptions like that!) and, I suspected, far more tarnished.

"Get your arse over here and sign in."

I deliberately finished my smoke, dropped it on the footpath, and ground out the end with one of my $500 walking boots. Once I was ready, I straightened up and ambled over. When my face was about six inches from the copper's (Get the pun? See, I'm witty as well) I looked at him, squinting, but had to withdraw a bit when I got a whiff of his breath.

"Was you talkin' to me?" I asked in my best Robert de Niro but the irony was lost on Darwin's finest. He sniffed, hitched at his trousers and tried to look down my shirt. He stunk of stale cigarette smoke, cheap aftershave, and whatever he'd been drinking last night.

"Yeah, I was talking to you. Who the bloody hell else would I of been talking to? From that flash outfit I'm guessing that you are Miss Louisa Smith, here to do your CSO. Am I right?"

I stepped back, trying to find fresh air, and nodded.

"OK, so I want for you to go inside the office here, fill out your papers, and then come outside and report to Officer George and find out where he wants your fancy little arse. Got it?"

"Well, Officer–Gary O'Brien," I said, checking out the name on his badge, "I've already filled out my papers. Perhaps you fine policemen could improve on your communication skills?" I turned on my heel to leave his presence but wasn't quick enough and he gave my fancy arse a smack as I left.

I turned back sharply, nearly committing Mistake Number Three. I am not in the habit of putting up with that kind of shit and I was about to remind him that sexual harassment laws extended to prisoner/guard relationships. I took one look at his face and realized that he didn't care. He'd probably been getting away with slapping defenceless arses for his entire career. He looked about seventy but I was pretty sure that wasn't accurate. I let it ride and moved quickly away. That giddy feeling of sudden panic surged through my body again and I thought that the faster I moved, the faster this torture would pass.

I spotted the hunky Aboriginal guy near the far side kerb and quickly decided, totally without the facts, that he was my ally. Clipboard in hand, he moved among the teens, their families, and friends, speaking softly and separating some of the juvies into their own little group. The orange-topped girl was tearfully handing the baby to another girl not much older than she was when I sashayed up to him with my best "come hither" smile. The pocket of his blue uniform said "*Delta Tours*" and his badge said "*Warren, Your Tour Guide.*" Thank God! He belonged to the bus. Relieved that at least somebody on this trip wasn't a policeman, I spoke to him. Mistake Number Four–my day was only beginning but the mistakes were mounting up quickly!

"Hi. I'm supposed to check in with an Officer George. Could you tell me where he is, please?"

"I'm Officer George," he said.

"*You?*" The air exploded from my poor body like I'd been king hit. I couldn't quite catch my breath for a moment. "You can't be. Your tag says you're Warren, the tour guide."

"I am Warren George, Aboriginal Liaison Officer. And you are?" He spoke ever so sternly. His eyes were a deep sea green and I longed to plunge right in.

"More disappointed than you'll ever know. I am Louisa Smith, Babysitter of Losers. What do I do now?" With my luck moving rapidly from bad to worse, a sudden horror thought hit me. What would happen when it reached "worst?"

"Miss Smith." Officer George put his hands on his hips, clipboard protruding, and pursed those luscious lips. He tapped his polished black shoe and, for just one second, he looked cute enough to hug. Then he opened his mouth and got bossy again. "We are here to set an example to these young people so, please, no labelling, OK? They get enough of that from their parents and teachers."

"Are you sure they *have* parents and teachers? I've taken Biology and I'd be willing to bet that that boy over there crawled out from under a rock." I pointed to a short lad who kept brushing greasy hair out of his face with dirty, scabbed fingers.

"Miss Smith, please!" He sounded flustered, and hugged that blasted clipboard tightly to his chest. He looked like he needed protection and I was beginning to feel the tiniest bit of sadistic pleasure. Using what was obviously meant to be an authoritative tone, he sounded more like a haughty old woman. "Miss Smith, in addition to trying to treat our charges with some respect, there will be no smoking, no drugs, no alcohol, and no swearing. OK?"

Exhausted by exasperation, I could only shake my head. No, it was not OK. I was desperate to get that message across to somebody. I couldn't take it any longer. How could he be so cute if he was a copper? I felt severely cheated and determined to set him straight.

"Jesus H. Christ! Hasn't anyone in this Northern Territory ever heard of the appellation 'Ms?'" I cried, almost literally. The burning behind my lids told me I was very close to tears. I blinked hard, stepped back, and removed my sunglasses so he could get the full benefit of my glare. "OK, Warren, maybe you should remember that I am here because of a court order. I broke the law, just like the kids, so don't include me in your 'we.' I will not drink alcohol or take drugs but I make no promises about my Beedies. I don't know what they class as swearing up here in the Top End so I reckon I'll say what I fucking well please."

A cheer went up behind me and the boy with the weed in his sock shouted, "Right on, Lady! Nothin' but crims and cops on this bus!"

I must admit, I do love an appreciative audience. I stepped over to the bus, mounted the steps, turned, and waved to my adoring fans. It was Warren's turn to glare at me, muttering something unintelligible. I hoped he wasn't swearing.

"Hey, I'm respecting them!" I said, and then shrugged, turned back around, and saw that the driver of this bus was the fat sexist pig who had accosted me earlier. His belly hung out over his shorts when he sat, the shirt having obviously given up the fight. Sweat dripped down his pasty face and he leered at me through the filthiest mouth I'd ever seen. The teeth that weren't yellow were broken and black, and his thick tongue had a mysterious grey coating. Each time I thought that things couldn't get any worse, they did. I did some serious swearing but kept it under my breath.

Stepping backward carefully, I exited the bus and fronted up once more to Officer George, who was now busily scribbling something on that damned clipboard.

"Are you serious?" I spoke quietly. "Is that Neanderthal really going with us?" Beads of perspiration formed on my forehead and upper lip. Smith women do not sweat in public. Reaching into my shoulder bag for my tissues and not finding them where they should be, I realized that this morning's chaotic thrusting and throwing around of luggage had left the bag's contents in a mess. My fingers searched franticly before the first bead of moisture dripped from the end of my nose. I finally found the soft packet of tissues but, while pulling them free, also disgorged my little can of Mace, causing it to fall at the tour guide's feet. I patted my face dry gratefully, admiring his form as he bent to pick up the Mace.

"And what are you doing with this?"

"Oh, thanks." I reached for it but he pulled it back.

"I don't think so," he said. "This is an illegal weapon."

"Oh, for fuck's sake!" This reaction was so unbelievable. "You, as an employee of the Northern Territory Police Department must surely understand that a defenceless female needs to have protection!"

I'm absolutely certain that I heard him mumble, "Defenceless female, my sweet Aunt Fanny!" as he turned to give my precious Mace to the young female copper with the whistle. At least I still had my hair spray. No way was this guy getting into my toiletry bag!

This was so absolutely going to be a week of torment. Would I even survive? Which government department defined 'cruel and unusual?' Hadn't the death penalty been outlawed in Australia years ago? Hanging had to be better than what I was about to endure. Shaking my head bitterly, I made my way to the back of the bus. If Warren wanted me to help him round up juvies and get them on the bus, well, that was his tough luck. I had my own problems to deal with.

I made an executive decision there and then that I would make up the rear-guard action until told otherwise. After all, our perfect Officer George was the tour guide. He was the one with the blue shirt and the badge and the, apparently, squeaky-clean record. He would undoubtedly want to sit up front with his microphone and be in charge, which I was only too happy to let him do. He'd have ten juvenile offenders and at least one recalcitrant woman to keep in line. I didn't fancy his chances. And I would do my best to enjoy tormenting him.

CHAPTER FOUR

As I MADE my way to the rear of the bus, I tried not to touch or even brush up against any of the grimy plastic seat backs or sticky metal railings along the way. I was surprised to see that there was another woman seated there already, reading a paperback and seemingly oblivious to all that was going on around her. She looked older than me, was a bit on the heavy side, and had a sweet face. She was Aboriginal as well and wore a bright, floral-patterned dress, not the telltale tan of the constabulary. She was in the three-person seat next the toilet that I'd been after so I claimed the two-person seat opposite and slightly in front. I threw my rucksack onto the seats across the aisle, marking my territory, and flopped down against the window.

"You can put your bag in the trailer back there," the woman said without looking up. I thought she must be one of those mothers with periscope vision. Damn! Just because she didn't dress like a copper, was she going to treat me like a crim?

"Not likely. I may need to leave in a hurry." I answered sullenly as I lifted my booted feet onto the upholstery and wrapped my arms around my knees. I was trying to look nonchalant.

She threw me a puzzled look instead of the disciplinary rebuff I'd been expecting and returned to her book. Did I dare feel relieved?

At least the bus was air conditioned and I was grateful for that. I couldn't wear a bra in this Darwin heat but, fortunately, I'd been endowed with firm, pert breasts that don't jiggle too much, so I could get away with it. My nipples hardened as the cool air from the vent blew across my chest and pressed against my ribbed singlet, but since it was good quality cotton it didn't scratch or irritate. With all the things I had to worry about, my mammaries were the least of my problems. I took no notice of them.

Sock-Boy, who had followed me onto the bus and who might have been developing a serious crush, obviously had noticed. He dropped down in front of me, slobbering over the back of the seat, thick bodily juices pooling on the floor. I'd never be able to put my feet down now! I tried a bit of periscope vision of my own—not that I was interested but, as they say, forewarned is forearmed. His lack of colour was accentuated by his dyed black hair, the numerous silver studs and rings on his face, and his black clothes.

Oh, great, a Goth, I thought and continued to ignore him, though I doubted that ignorance would be bliss in this case. I could not ignore the odour of teenage glands soaking into that heavy coat. I had a disturbing premonition of this loser dogging my footsteps for the next seven days. With a violent, involuntary shudder I pressed my face against my knees to suppress my tears.

Warren must have been pretty good at his job as a sheepdog because he'd apparently separated that mob outside, sorted those who were *assigned* to come from those who weren't, and all at once the bus was full of very loud children (surely only ten couldn't make that much racket?) fighting over thirty seats. Nobody wanted to sit anywhere unless someone else had claimed it first. I heard the wheeze of the hydraulic door close, saw the crowd on the street step back from the blue exhaust as the engine started, and heard tapping on the microphone as Warren prepared to give orders.

How the *hell* was I going to survive? I turned to the other woman in what would surely be a misguided hope.

"You're not an Aboriginal Liaison Officer as well, are you?" I asked timidly, afraid of her answer, but she looked up at me in shock and horror. I saw her eyes for the first time and they were beautifully sympathetic.

"Never you fear, sister. I'm Mary, camp cook, doing my CSO just like you. Mine's for unpaid warrants."

I hadn't meant to get into a conversation with the woman but curiosity got the better of me. "What the hell's an unpaid warrant?"

"You know...warrants...fines." The sympathy in her eyes turned into confusion. She looked like she thought I was really dumb and began speaking slowly. "It's when you do something they don't like and they give you a fine to pay. Then you don't pay the fine and they make you work it off in the community."

"Oh, really?" Now it was my turn to look confused. "So they give some people a choice?"

"How'd you get here? Drunk driving? Hell, you coulda sold them boots to pay the fine!" She shook her head and returned her book. She apparently didn't want to talk to outlaws in expensive footwear. Well, maybe I didn't want to talk to her, either!

"I wish!" I leaned across the aisle to my rucksack, opened it, and dragged out my own paperback. I was aware of a strangling sound behind me and surmised that my butt might be sending Sock-Boy into fits. His problem, not mine. I'm not a nurse.

I'd brought a few books, thinking I might take advantage of this enforced time out to catch up on my reading. No such luck. I'd only started the second paragraph when Warren turned up. His shoes had rubber soles so I hadn't heard him approach, but his white socks dazzled my eyes. I ignored him as long as I could, but he just stood there, holding a folder thick with dog-eared files. I finally gave up and looked at him.

"Can I help you, Officer George?" I asked sweetly.

"Work before pleasure," he barked as he thrust the folders into my face. "These are the reports on all our charges—and please note that I said *our* charges. Study them thoroughly. Learn names, ages, weaknesses, allergies, and what they're here for. If you are aware of what naughty things they like to do, you'll be better prepared to handle them."

"Yes, sir. You bet, sir. Anything you say, sir." I took the folder from him, fighting down the urge to ask him what naughty things he liked to do.

His blue drill shorts, directly in front of me, fit him like a glove. I had difficulty pulling my eyes away, but when I did and finally looked up at his face, I saw that his eyes were saying "hi" to my tits. His full lips were pursed in disapproval and I couldn't help wondering how they would feel warming my cold nipples. He noticed that I had noticed his focus, turned abruptly and walked away. I continued to watch.

"Careful there, Sister. Remember which side you're on." Mary had been watching me watching Warren.

"No harm in looking," I said lightly but what I was thinking was that there would be no secrets here. "Is—um—does Officer George have a significant other when he's at home?"

"Never you mind what Officer George has at home."

"He looks like the sort who'd wear a wedding ring if he were married."

Mary chuckled. "You got that right. Now, if you've got work to do, I've got a book to read."

She turned back to her well-worn paperback and I pulled out a file to peruse, not that it would make any difference. I was so not going to be "handling" any teenagers.

We left Darwin, left the salt smell of the sea, the sight of buildings and people, left any semblance of civilization. OK, Darwin definitely had its drawbacks but I realized, as the last street sign disappeared from the back window, that if you looked hard enough, you could see that it was trying. Not so, this Outback. The highway was paved but the isolation was so stark the track might as well have been dirt. The only traffic was the occasional road train driven by Bradley John Murdoch look-alikes or caravans towed by grey nomads, seeing Australia before they die. *Why would anyone* choose *to be on this road, for God's sake?* It also occurred to me that I could very possibly die while being forced to see Australia. I would rather have rented the DVD of the movie...and watched it again with Suzanne and Claudia while drooling over Hugh Jackman...with a bottle or three of nicely chilled chardonnay. That cute little Brandon kid hadn't looked like a juvenile offender.

"Hey, look! Camels!" a juvie shouted and all the others took up the cry, bringing me abruptly out of my dreamtime. Camels in the desert—this was a thrill? I shivered at the emptiness, longing for the towering buildings, the throngs of people and the gridlocks of traffic I'd grown up with. From Sydney, you could drive north to Newcastle or south to Wollongong without any let up in traffic, but here, drive even ten kilometres out of town and you were in the Never-Never. The scenery flew by with tedious monotony. Red dirt, red rocks, brown scrub, and a sky so brilliantly blue that it could blind you if you looked at it too long.

"I never get tired of coming out here," Mary said and I turned to her in amazement. She was staring out the window as well, but looking wrapt, not bored. "So many colours, so much life."

The poor thing was obviously out of her mind. Those Northern Territory police had a lot to answer for, arresting a mad woman. I returned to my work at hand but couldn't concentrate on Warren's dossiers. I was feeling so homesick. Would I see my beloved city again before I died? I even missed Dalby whom I had been dating for the last two years and would probably marry.

I HAD MET DALBY at the University of Sydney while doing my undergraduate degree. He'd been doing his PhD in the same department, lecturing us undergrads and I'd been overwhelmed by his knowledge of engineering. He was a handsome academic with floppy hair, strong jaw, and weak eyes—sincere, brown, and magnified behind his horn-rimmed glasses—a tweed jacket with frayed cuffs and worn blue jeans. All the girls in class were hot for him and I couldn't believe my luck when he asked me to stay back after class one day. I was having trouble with that pesky quantum theory and he suggested we get together for some private tutoring sessions. I was ever so grateful, of course, and dropped the elderly Arts Professor like a hot electrode.

It was so flattering that he took a personal interest in little old me. He was twenty-seven, so mature compared to my tender twenty-one. Our study sessions were fun, we laughed at the same people and liked the same movies, and one day he suggested we meet in the evening for further tutelage. Our first night session was over a bottle (or two) of wine. He drank rather a lot so I walked him back to his flat. When we arrived his arms were full of books and his feet were a little unsteady.

"My keys are in my left pocket," he said. "Can you get them for me, please?"

I reached into his left pocket but it turned out the keys weren't in there after all. That pocket was ripped and my hand slipped right through to his flesh. He wasn't wearing underwear so the flesh I felt was a furry testicle. I didn't pull my hand out straight away but moved it around until I found a penis as well.

"Oh, dear, wrong pocket," Dalby said and didn't move.

The rip was quite wide so I fit my whole hand through and wrapped it around the penis to warm it, this being a cold night and all. It got warm quickly and rather large. Dalby leaned forward, kissed me gently, and said, "Let's get those keys and step inside." I found the keys in his right pocket, nestled among the condoms.

Once inside, he dropped the books, took me in his arms and kissed me tenderly. His hands slid down my back and up my tartan skirt where they found my thong. While his hands were busy ensuring that I would be well lubricated I was peeling off his jacket, unbuttoned his plaid shirt and unzipped his jeans. We didn't make it to the bedroom that first time. I sat on the sofa and he knelt in front of me, rolled on the condom while I licked my lips, and then entered me, sliding in easily, what with all that lubrication. He held my hips and I gripped his shoulders as we pumped our pelvises, grinning into each others' eyes. He helped me come with one of his thumbs and, while I was still throbbing, he plunged in deep and came as well.

"Thank you, sir," I said when I could speak. "I've never had the nature and behaviour of energy and matter explained quite that clearly."

He pulled out carefully and smiled. "You can bring all your questions to me, Ms Smith. I could explain to you forever." Then he left me while he disposed of the condom. He was gone quite awhile, and when he finally returned he was wearing a towel wrapped around his hips. He'd obviously washed himself but gave me a damp cloth. I was a bit nonplussed that I wasn't good enough to share his shower but, then, professors are supposed to be absent-minded and eccentric. Even so...

"What's that for?" I asked.

"To wipe yourself off. Don't want to stain the furniture."

The furniture? If he'd paid more than $25 at Vinnie's for that sofa, he'd been robbed. I didn't see the bedroom furniture that night because he had to get up early. I forgave him a lot of questionable behaviour under the heading of "eccentricity."

Those first heady months of our (almost) illicit relationship were brilliant. I got a real thrill out of our "sessions" and an even bigger thrill from the jealousy all the other girls in class exhibited. He wasn't fantastic in the sack but he wasn't the worst I'd had, either, and he could be very considerate which, combined with excitement of doing it with my lecturer, was probably more than many girls get in a lifetime, and I learned to appreciate that. Like, the first time he asked, "Is it all right if I come now?" I nearly laughed out loud but soon realized that it beat the hell out of those morons who either think women don't need to have orgasms, or worse, think we have them just by looking at their naked bodies. I don't know when I decided that this attraction was love, but after eighteen months our relationship was beginning to stale. Dalby assured me that it was only because it was time for us to get married and move in together.

"We've done everything we can do as singles," was his argument. "Now it's time to start married life."

I remember wondering if married people were allowed to experiment sexually. He'd made it clear that singles weren't. Nevertheless, some perverse, unformed doubt had kept me from setting a date just yet.

"Let me finish my degree, then we'll talk about it," I would say and drive back home to my parents' house. He didn't have a car and hated the long commute from the North Shore on public transport. I didn't think it odd that I'd never wanted to move in with him. He was still on a student lecturer's salary and his flat in Redfern was too dingy to be what I considered liveable. Mr and Mrs Smith had more money than they could count and I occupied my own suite of rooms. I had cooks, cleaners, and cars at my disposal and, to be honest, I'd never really understood women who could love a man more than their creature comforts. I don't know where Mr Maslow did his research, but my own hierarchy of needs began with luxury. Daddy had promised us a place in Glebe as a wedding present– where the wealthy rub shoulders with the intellectual.

Then, a few months ago, I'd started hanging with these

people I'd ended up coming to Darwin with. Dalby had totally disapproved.

"It's time to wake up to yourself, Louisa. They're not our sort," he'd say whenever I'd blow off coffee with him to go to one of their meetings. "They're from UTS!"

Granted, students from the University of Technology in Sydney tend to be rather pedestrian, but it's still a good school. Maybe they weren't "our sort" but I was looking for a change and these people were certainly different, as were their philosophies. They held meetings on a rickety timber porch behind a Turkish restaurant in Glebe where we drank gallons of Turkish coffee, listened to radicals preaching sedition and change, and made plans. After the meetings we'd indulge in baklava and port and I inevitably left these get-togethers feeling more satisfied than after a whole night of sex with Dalby.

I attended every meeting but, sometimes, I wondered if he was right.

CHAPTER FIVE

MAYBE THE SAD TRUTH was that now, in this bus full of losers, I was finally waking up to myself. There was so much to think about. I stared out the window at the miles of red dirt, dry scrub, and pitiful trees. Flowers were small, scruffy, and either yellow or purple. How could anybody love a desert?

Inside the bus the noise level had dropped a few decibels but it was still bloody boisterous as the juvies paired off. There were four girls and six boys between the ages of fourteen and seventeen and every colour from Sock-Boy's ghostly white to a lad whose skin was a velvety black. There was a virtual United Nations of budding criminals here—did that make Darwin feel proud? I could see the tourism posters now: "*Come to Darwin–Our Muggers Do Not Discriminate!*" In between bouts of self pity, I'd shuffled through the profiles and had read enough to know that most of these kids were only guilty of such heinous crimes as smoking marijuana and vagrancy. For this, they'd been arrested and punished? Stop the world–I want to get off!

Despite my determination to ignore everything connected with children and Outback justice, it did get me thinking. How could a fifteen-year-old girl be a vagrant? Wouldn't her parents have been worried about her? How many times, when I was younger, had I prayed for my parents to ease up their vigilance? They used to stick so close that I'd suspected a microchip had been implanted in the base of my skull while I was sleeping. Vagrant? Give me a break! I glanced surreptitiously at the hardened criminals surrounding me.

Girls were sitting with girls today, undoubtedly talking about boys, and boys were sitting with boys, undoubtedly talking about sports, but I was sure that more than a couple would find romance before the week was up. That wasn't the purpose of the trip, but kids will be kids, right? Sock-Boy still sat alone, his face inches from mine. I pulled back a bit, afraid I might catch something and even more afraid to think what that something might be.

His nose was red and swollen around the silver stud poking through his left nostril. His acne had carved craters in his cheeks and his right eyebrow was inflamed around its ring as well. A constant sniff and rattle in the throat added to the general impression of poor health. Whatever he had, I remained very wary as the puddle of dribble forming on the floor near my feet continued to spread and the spray from his cough sprinkled my sunnies. I was pretty sure that the only place I would be safe from him was in the toilet, but nothing– not even Sock-Boy–could get me inside that box of disease. I shivered, pulled my feet onto the seat, and huddled closer into my corner.

One of the boys up front had an iPod and a couple of the girls had portable CD players and were sharing earpieces with their partners. The two youngest lads sat together and, from what I could see, it didn't look like they were getting along at all. Warren's problem, not mine. That was going to be my mantra.

He was making his way slowly down the aisle, looking into brightly coloured plastic backpacks, checking that the required headgear and drinks bottle were present and that the contraband drugs and alcohol were not, interrupting squabbles, and generally being an interfering busybody. At last he came to Sock-Boy and stopped. Sock-Boy reluctantly removed his wet chin from the back of the seat and turned to Warren, his mouth hanging open because his nostrils were plugged with green snot.

"Hey, don't look at me, Boss," he protested with a nasal whine. "I wasn't doing nothing."

"Not yet, Jason. Take off your shoes and empty your socks."

Sock-Boy, aka Jason, turned back to me angrily. "You friggin' snitch! You said you was one of the crims. Whatcha tell him for?"

"As if." I didn't even look up from my reading but watched clandestinely from the corner of my eye. Our leader was trying to look stern but mostly he just looked exasperated. I wanted to take him in my arms and tell him that it would be all right. I wanted to stroke his brow, stroke his back, stroke his...*Stop that right now, Louisa!*

"Jason, you hide dope in your feet every time you get dressed in the morning." Warren sighed. "I didn't need an informant to tell me you were just as stupid today. Now give it to me and empty out your pockets as well."

Grudgingly, Jason unlaced and removed his black, high top boots and synthetic uppers and lowers. The stench made my nose drip, and when he peeled grey socks from grey feet, I gagged. As he handed Warren a baggy containing a green leafy substance, I was breaking my fingernails trying to get the window open. The outside air might be hot and dusty, but at least it was fresh.

When he was finished with Jason, Warren moved on to my seat and stared at me until I finally pulled my head in. Without thinking, I moved over to make room for him to sit beside me but he remained standing.

You might say "we must" and "our duty", I thought, *but you're the guy in charge and there's no way you're gonna let me forget that. OK, mate, "we" will both find out how well I take orders.* Aloud I said, "Can I help you, Officer George?"

"I want to check your backpack." He leaned over to pick it up.

"You what!" I spluttered and grabbed for it, but he got it first, turned his back to me, opened the zipper, and began rummaging through. He left my Beedies alone (we'd had *that* conversation) but confiscated my cell phone.

"I believed you were told that these are not allowed?"

"Sorry, sir, guess I forgot."

That must have been the straw that broke his patience. Leaning forward with barely concealed ire, he shook my phone in my face and said through gritted teeth, "Look, I don't want a prima donna like you on this trip anymore than you want to be here, but this is what we both got saddled with so I want to set you straight about your responsibilities." Not "our" responsibilities anymore. "These are kids that need looking after, whether they think so or not. That is your job, *if* you want to expunge whatever offence got you here. I don't care what you think of the police, but I do care about these kids, and if anything happens to any of them through your bad attitude, you will have me, personally, on your arse forever. I can't ship you out so I suggest you shape up—now!"

He turned on his heel and walked up the aisle before I could think of a suitable comeback. I watched him walk, so clean and crisp in his freshly ironed uniform and couldn't help noticing yet again that he had an absolutely magnificent butt. Up my arse forever, eh? He should be so lucky.

Jason watched me watching Warren's butt and grinned, nervously picking at one of his larger pimples. Mary shook her head but didn't say anything this time.

I leaned down and patted my sock with a sly grin of my own. Jason had given me the idea. My iPhone was tucked in there, out of sight. Of course, I'd been told that phones, computers, etc., were not allowed on this trip, which was why I'd left my prepaid phone in my bag where he could find it. I doubted old Warren had even heard of Blackberries. I couldn't wait until we stopped somewhere and I could be alone to contact my friends in the real world. Oh, Suzanne—oh, Claudia—am I going to be forced to admit that Dalby was right?

We drove for hours, the drone of the highway overriding the hum of the air conditioner. We passed more camels, much to the excitement of the young boys in front. We spotted herds of brumbies and kangaroos (I guess they come in herds as well. I never actually thought about it) and, once, saw a dingo chewing on something that was small and alive. There was very little traffic, fortunately, because meeting a road train—big trucks hauling four or five carriages—was nerve-wracking, to say the least.

"You know, if one of them things is doing eighty klicks an hour, it'll take a whole kilometre to stop." Jason informed me. I grunted and stored the knowledge with other facts I never wanted to know.

We'd see an occasional pick-up truck, some caravans, and a few battered cars. These were usually driven by Aboriginal people and we passed more than one that had broken down on the side of the road, its passengers huddled in its shade until help came.

The first time we encountered a stranded group Warren

asked Gazza to pull over and help. ("Gazza"? I didn't think I'd be able to call him that!)

"Not likely," was the charming response.

"We can at least give them some water. We have plenty."

"They knew that old heap wouldn't make it before they started out. Then, when it breaks down, they act all victimized. They're just looking for a hand-out and a free ride. Not my responsibility. Let them pay for the bush bus."

"Oh, please, Mr Gazza," one of the girls pleaded. "They look really thirsty."

In reply, he revved the engine, spraying road grit over the wayfarers and sped past. Warren pulled a cell phone from his shirt pocket (rank obviously had its own privileges here!) and punched in a number. Not that I cared, really, but a little part of me hoped that he was contacting somebody to come help those poor people.

"Bush bus?" I asked Mary.

"Greyhound don't service the Communities." She looked surprised that I thought it would. "Only charter companies send buses around a couple times a week to bring people into Darwin."

We drove through a small town called Batchelor (I think you'd find plenty of them around here. What woman in her right mind would agree to live in a place like this?) but didn't stop. We finally pulled over for morning tea at Litchfield National Park, a place with waterfalls, termite mounds, and very tall grass—where *anything* could be lurking. The kids disembarked slowly, as though they were reluctant to leave the security of our vehicle.

"Are you sure it's safe out here, Boss?" a brown girl with long, dark hair asked. "Ain't nature dangerous sometimes? I seen that movie *Wolf Creek*."

"You've probably seen too many movies, Brooke," Warren answered. "That was fiction."

"What about dingoes?" a nervous boy with black hair and big teeth asked. "They ain't fiction."

"A dingo ain't gonna eat you, Dickhead, they're too smart," one of the black boys said.

Warren wanted me to learn their names but there were just

too many, and all teenagers look alike to me. Honestly, I was just too overwhelmed to care at the moment. Maybe by tomorrow, if I was still alive because, actually, the same questions had occurred to me. Taking tiny, cautious steps, I was glad of my boots and stayed close behind Mary. Warren dismissed their fears and took his charges on a short tour of termite mounds while Mary boiled the kettle and made tea. I decided the area immediately around the picnic tables was safe and unpacked boxes of cream biscuits. The foul driver sat, sweating more than ever, on one of the concrete benches, smoking and taking playful swipes at me each time I passed by.

I could ignore him for now but I dreaded the effort it would take to avoid him for a whole week. How many more hours of CSO would I get for kneeing a copper in the groin? Would they let me pay the fine this time? Should I speak to Warren about it? I couldn't imagine that Warren would take my side. They were probably best mates. I looked over at his little group.

A light-brown skinhead in jackboots whose name might have been something like "Spider" but I wasn't sure, was kicking a termite mound. Warren laughed and said something, putting his arm around the boy's shoulder as he pulled him away. Warren had a lovely laugh, more like an infectious little giggle. He'd probably giggle just like that if I asked him keep The Pig away from me.

"At least having you here keeps that Gazza off me," Mary muttered behind me. "He usually works in the office and us women dread him being on the desk whenever we have to go sign in."

"Why doesn't somebody do something about it? Put in a written complaint?" Surely even the Northern Territory would have laws about sexual harassment, you'd think.

"Oh, sure. Us Indigenous women will just ring up all our solicitors and get them to file a written complaint against a police officer who's related to the commissioner. Now *that's* a beaut plan. Wonder why none of us ever thought of it? You city girls!"

She shook her head and went over to a gas barbecue to heat the kettle. I bit into a nauseatingly sweet biscuit and longed for another city girl–or boy–to talk to. Warren and his crew returned from their brief explorations and ten youngsters finished off the family pack of biscuits in about fifteen seconds flat. I was flabbergasted.

"My God! I've never seen anything like it."

"Wasn't you ever young?" Mary asked as she spooned an incredible amount of sugar into each cup of tea.

"I don't think I was ever that young." Actually, and more to the point, I don't think I ever had to help myself to food. The cooks or waiters always served up my portions and if I wanted seconds I simply asked for more.

She looked at me in a funny sort of way. "Make yourself useful. Put the milk in these cups," was all she said as she handed me a large tin of powdered milk and a clean spoon.

"Yo, Miss, you totally should of come with us," one of the boys said to me. "Them termites was deadly, yo." His thumbs jutted upwards and I gave a weak smile. American MTV reaches the Australian Outback.

CHAPTER SIX

SHORTLY AFTER we'd hit the road again, the inside of the bus turned into a zoo. Those kids sang, screeched, scuffled, and fought. Two boys–the skinhead and the dreadlocked–were locked in mortal combat in the aisle with the girls urging them on when Warren finally lost his patience. He stood up, grabbed each boy by a shoulder and hurled them into their respective seats.

"Enough!" he shouted.

"Aw, Mr Warren, it was just getting good," complained one of the girls, the chubby one who fought a losing battle with her tube top–hang on–hadn't Warren called her Brooke earlier? "I reckon Timbo was winning, eh?"

"No one wins in a fist fight, Brooke. Now, sit down and be quiet for five minutes, all of you."

Yes! "Brooke." I was right! Would it take me ten days to learn ten names? Warren marched back to my seat, where I was, apparently, studiously perusing file number six, not even trying to suppress my grin. His rubber-soled shoes weren't silent this time.

"So, you think it's funny, do you? This is all a game to you, is it?" He stood above me glaring, fists on hips. I looked up, my smile widening. He was so cute when he pushed his lower lip out like that. It would feel so soft on my...

Pay attention, Louisa!

"So far, yeah. I'm just doing like you told me, Boss, learning about our charges. I'm guessing that...um..." I glanced down at the folders. "Laurel, or maybe young Andreas, or maybe both, got some of their speed on board and that's why everyone's so...um...energetic."

"No," he said, arms dropping in a gesture of defeat. "It was even more devious, eh, Mary?" He turned to the cook who was trying her best to look uninvolved. "Cream biscuits *and* sugary tea? What on earth were you thinking?"

"Gee, I dunno, Boss. I was just trying to do my job. I ain't no dietician, you know."

"Don't go busting my chops, Mary. You forget how long I've known you. Anyway, it'll be flavoured milk and savoury biscuits or fruit for all future smokos, OK? I ordered heaps of fruit and that long life, flavoured milk."

"Yes, Boss, but *somebody* packed plenty of them cream bikkies, eh."

"I can guess who that was." Warren looked at the driver who was eating something unidentifiable as he steered with one hand. "And don't call me 'Boss,' not either of you." He returned slowly to his seat, gently clipping a few ears on his way. I looked at Mary. Gee, maybe we *could* be pals.

"Am I right in thinking that there's a little bit of evil in you?" I asked with a little grin.

"Not evil, more like cunning." Mary returned my grin. "Warren's a nice kid but we can't let him get above himself."

*I'd like to get him above me...*The thought flitted unbidden through my mind. It was hopeless, of course, since everybody would be sharing a tent with somebody else. I was reasonably certain that my buddy wouldn't be Officer George. Daydreams are lovely until reality breaks in and it was fairly obvious that Officer George had no time at all for Louisa Smith.

Late in the afternoon we arrived at a campground near Katherine Gorge. The crowd had settled by then and many were napping, but when the bus came to a stop, a cheer rose up that nearly took the roof off. Suddenly, everyone was awake and bustin' a move. This time those juvies couldn't get out fast enough. Their collective fear of nature had dissipated. I remained seated until the coast was clear. When I finally stepped from the bus I got my first inclination that nature could, in fact, be beautiful–under the right circumstances, of course.

We'd be spending the night here but there wasn't a single holiday cabin in sight. Where were we going to sleep?

"Tents," was Warren's short reply. From that I surmised that it was we who would have to go to work setting up camp. The sight of concrete toilet blocks relieved me a little. I knew about camping. My dad and brother did it once and I'd seen the photos.

Before we got started, though, Officer George allowed us to have a look around while he and Jason emptied provisions from the trailer. Steep, lacy waterfalls carved niches through ancient rock walls whose brilliant colours reflected deeply into the still waters. Two of the girls attached themselves to me (why, I don't know) and we walked past caves full of ancient Aboriginal paintings, including tiny handprints left by the children who had once been at home in the caves. I'd never seen anything like it. Oh, I'd admired plenty of indigenous art at the Art Museum of New South Wales, but nothing there had been a patch on these thousand-year-old signatures.

"Wow, this is so amazing! Don't you wonder what those children must have been like?" I looked around at the scruffy little outlaws who were with me and decided to experiment with my new "guardian" role. "I'm betting none of those kids ran away from home or got so stoned they couldn't walk."

"Poor buggers." Sara (they'd told me their names) nudged Laurel. "Didn't know what they was missing, eh?" Both girls laughed so hard that Warren looked over at us and scowled.

"What's your problem now?" I called to him. "Can't we even enjoy ourselves? Jesus, I can't win!" I was so pissed off. The girls looked at me, and then looked at each other, and giggled again.

"He is so up himself," said Sara.

"Yeah, but he's so hot!" added Laurel.

"He is a bit, but you like him, Miss, eh? Do you fancy the boss?"

"Not likely! Now, behave, you two, and go over to help Mr Warren. You can look around more after the work is finished." In short, I wasn't allowed to be their ally, I refused to be their mother, and I didn't know how to be their manager. So what was I? Guardian *ad litem*? Shit, I needed protecting more than they did. Fed up with nature and with trying to make sense of anything, I stalked over to where the bus was parked. The girls ran off to join Jason and Timbo (I recognised him from the fight) in their attempt to scale a boulder. My word obviously carried a lot of weight around here...not!

I sulked for a minute, and then wandered off alone and

soon, despite my determination to remain angry and unmoved by my surroundings, I found myself softening in the stillness of the country. Warren's annoying criticisms were soon forgotten as I watched the leaves change from bright green to dark green in the changing light. The reflections of trees on the water turned to shadows as the day drew to a close. I was stunned by this majesty of the earth and, for a brief moment, grateful to be its witness. But then Gazza appeared and had me cornered in a rocky crevasse. His breath stank of alcohol and vomit.

"What 'cha thinking, girlie? You like this Abo shit?"

My fury returned with a vengeance and I reacted swiftly but, at the last minute, considered that discretion may be the better part of valour here so I checked my knee on its way to his balls. Not a single other person was in sight and Gazza was twenty stone if he was an ounce.

"I think these paintings are wonderful," I said sweetly. "Let's go find some more."

"Hell, I got tattoos prettier than this," he grunted into my ear. "You wanna see them?" He pressed me against the rock with his enormous belly. If his cock was hard it would remain his secret, buried under that apron of flesh.

"Maybe later. Say, where is everybody?" Anxiety rose like bile in my throat and I wanted nothing more than to be with the crowd from which I'd been escaping. Man, did I need protection now!

"Aw, we don't need to worry about them. This here's their country, didn't 'cha know? It's just you and me, baby, the only whities who ain't baby toerags, and we're gonna get on just fine. How's about a little kiss?" He closed his eyes, puckered up, and leaned forward.

To hell with discretion! Even ladies learn self-defence in Sydney. My anxiety converted rapidly to anger. Could I get away with just paying a hefty fine for injuring a policeman where the sun doesn't shine? When the drunken Casanova moved an arm to scratch his balls, I managed to duck under and break free. The sudden movement knocked him off balance but he grabbed my singlet as I ran past, nearly pulling the sleeve off my arm so when I came dashing around a boulder, I was adjusting my clothing. I looked up to see Warren watching me. He glanced over my shoulder and I turned to see Gazza coming up behind me, buttoning his shirt and grinning broadly. Warren looked back at me, shaking his head with a look of disgust on his face.

That brought me up short. Oh, surely he couldn't be thinking that...me and Gazza? Oh, sick! For an instant I wanted to set him straight but common sense saved me at the last minute. It was more than I could bear. How dare he judge me! How dare he assume that I had been party to what amounted to sexual assault! Bloody men! From what I'd observed so far, Jason was the best of this godforsaken lot. Next Monday couldn't come quickly enough for me. I'd be on the first plane home so fast they wouldn't see me for the dust. But how the hell was I expected to survive until then? Was even Mary willing to throw me to these wolves? Why, oh, why hadn't the judge let me pay a fine?

"It's getting late. You're needed at the campsite, if you can pull yourself away." Warren called, and then turned back to the tent he was pegging. I threw a mini tantrum by kicking a rock so hard that even my flash boots didn't stop my toe from bruising.

By the time I'd limped over to our campsite, he and some of the boys already had most of the tents up. I decided to join Mary, who was building a fire. She placed some leaves and a few twigs within a ring of stones, struck a match, and a fire was roaring away inside a few minutes. I thought of what we went through at home to get a fire going in our ornamental fireplace–fire bricks, gas lighters, treated wood, etc.–and I was impressed. It was pretty obvious that she didn't need my help.

"Why aren't you using the gas cooker tonight?"

"Search me. This is the boss's idea. I guess the he wants me to get back to my roots and cook over an open flame. The kids'll like it because they're a right mob of pyromaniacs. We'll all likely wake up roasted in our tents."

"Louisa!" The boss was calling me. "Mary can manage by herself. We need some assistance here."

"Oh, shit," I muttered to Mary. "I don't know jack about tents. The first time I ever touched a tent was when I was in the Kathmandu shop last month buying my boots."

"This'll be good," the other woman chuckled. "You go on over. I'll be watching."

Totally without enthusiasm, I joined Laurel and Brooke who were wrestling with long, skinny poles that whipped around like antennae. Laurel had welts on her bare arms and Brooke had only just missed being blinded by one of these weapons. I grabbed an errant end and called to Warren.

"Do these things come with directions or are we supposed to have some innate knowledge from the Dreaming?"

Laughing in spite of himself, our tour guide came over and demonstrated how the antennae slipped through slits in the tarpaulins, how they bent, got pegged down and–*voila!*–a two-man tent was born. Brooke and Laurel whooped for joy and dragged their backpacks inside. I was given another tent, which Mary and I would share, and eventually got it raised and secured by myself. I couldn't help it. I thought I was quite clever and was even proud of the various bruises now decorating my arms and legs. I had ensured that our tent was close to the bus. God only knew when I might need to escape from out here.

By then it was time to help Mary with the dinner. I'm a fairly accomplished chef when I want to be and looked forward to exhibiting my prowess to this motley crew. Warren dragged a heavy metal plate from the trailer and placed it on the ring of rocks that enclosed the fire. Mary added a couple more leaves and had a flame big enough to cook the meat, which turned out to be several dozen sausages. Well, at least I could make a nice salad.

"The veggies are in the cold box and you'll find what else you need in that container marked 'condiments.'" Mary told me.

I eagerly went to see what I could find. Lettuce, tomatoes, and apples. Not a good start. I sliced and diced and flowered, and then opened the condiment container, looking for fresh herbs. A little basil, coriander, and Vietnamese mint would do wonders. What I found were enormous, white, plastic salt and pepper shakers–economy size–a four-litre cellophane package containing orange, white, and green bits of vegetation, and a two-litre jar of something marked "coleslaw dressing." Every bit of food we had was labelled in white with heavy black lettering. I'd never seen anything like it and wondered if it was Government Issue. I carried them back to my vegetables. Mary was there with a cleaver, chopping madly at my lovely salad, and then throwing it all together into a large basin.

"Here, Lou, give me that," she said and ripped open the bag of anonymous vegetable bits, poured salt, pepper, and gallons of coleslaw dressing over everything and mixed it well. "This Home Brand dressing makes it all taste pretty good, even to teenagers," she said as she stirred. "And, by the way, apples, lettuce, and tomatoes are for lunches, not salads."

I was devastated. Useless yet again. I moved away and lit up a Beedie.

"You're lucky, Lou," Mary called. "My smokes are the only thing I miss out here."

I gave a weak smile and held out the pack to offer her one but she was too busy with dinner.

Dinner! Now that was a worry. What would I be able to eat this week? I'd heard of Home Brand but I'd never met anyone who actually *bought* generic or, God forbid—*ate* it! Fried sausages and Home Brand vegetable slop were not my idea of nutritious or even edible meals. Would starvation would kill me before the Outback got its chance. I filled some jugs with yellow (Lemon? Pineapple? Who knew?) cordial and water from what looked like a garden tap, if there'd been a garden. At least nobody yelled at me.

It turned out that, despite her complaining, Mary was a very accomplished camp cook and served us a damper she'd made from the Home Brand flour and powdered milk and baked on the open flames. It melted in your mouth. Even in my mouth and, in the end, I ate a sausage as well. I must have been really hungry because it tasted fine.

Gazza never lifted a finger to help in the preparations but managed to eat nearly half the food we'd prepared. Once he finished, he grunted and, thankfully, disappeared. The juvies complained about the amount of salad they were expected to consume but finished everything anyway. Watching them eat with such incredible gusto, I was worried for the plates and hoped nobody would break a tooth on the tin.

"Top tucker, Mary," they said by way of thanks.

I smiled and thought of my little sisters, both of them still in high school. They liked sushi bars and fresh juice bars and, in short, any meals that were low in fat and high in price. On the rare occasions when our cook used the $2,000 barbecue on our patio at home to prepare the meals, she grilled thick lamb loin chops and tossed a gourmet salad with extra virgin olive oil and balsamic vinegar. Although my sisters were nice kids and no doubt grateful, I couldn't remember the last time I'd heard them thank anyone for the meal. I couldn't remember the last time I had either, for that matter. At least, I consoled myself, our cooks were paid extremely well.

CHAPTER SEVEN

WE HAD TRIED to stay under cover for most of the day but, despite our caution, the white kids who'd been wearing muscle shirts and tube tops to show off their skinny, undernourished bodies now had sunburned shoulders. My solarium tan must have given me some protection (not to mention my compulsive avoidance of the sun) because I had escaped the burning. Watching the red shoulders glow in the firelight, I suspected it would be impossible to avoid third-degree burns this week considering their wardrobes, and then Warren presented the solution.

Before dessert (the rest of the cream biscuits), he'd ducked into his tent and had returned with a large plastic bag, which he opened like it was a big ceremony. He pulled out a bright, fluoro orange T-shirt with the words "Darwin Juveniles Reaching Out Congress." The logo was two hands, one black and one white, clasped in friendship and the acronym, of course, was "DJ ROC." I'd seen the logo, or something similar, done by Benetton but somehow this looked better. Must have been the flickering shadows of the campfire.

"OK, you people, these T-shirts will be our uniforms for this trip. They will not only protect bare shoulders and backs from the sun, but it'll be hard to lose you when you're wearing this colour! There's one for each of you."

He began tossing T-shirts to the juveniles who held them out to admire, critique, check the seams, etc. Maybe they weren't accustomed to receiving gifts because there was a lot of mumbling and muttering and what sounded like decision making, as in, "Do I really want this or not?"

Warren watched anxiously as if their reaction was very important to him for some reason. Jason the Lad finally broke the ice when he removed his coat and the sweaty garment he'd had on beneath it, pulled his new T-shirt over his head and strutted around the circle, chest puffed out and thumbs turned up.

"Yo, look at me, I'm DJ ROC," he repeated over and over.

Nobody wanted to be outdone by a dweeb so within a minute all T-shirts were on and each kid reckoned he/she looked best. It reminded me of *Little Black Sambo*, the story my mother used to read to me with the tigers chasing one another in a circle, each crying, "Now *I'm* the grandest tiger in the jungle!" I imagined the kids were going to turn into butter— or *ghee*, as it is called in India.

Mary, beside me, looked astonished at first, and then her face split into the widest grin I'd ever seen.

"That boy," she said, looking at Warren. "Will you look at what that boy gone and done? I reckon where he got the money?"

I reckoned he got the money from the NT government and thought no more about it. After all, this was his job, wasn't it?

It was well past dark before the juvies were through showing off, but the fire still burned and everyone was hanging around so Warren tried to interest us all in singing campfire songs. Unfortunately, he was the only one who knew any.

"Come on, Miss Smith," he teased. "Surely you remember some from when you were a kid. I thought all city kids went into the Guides?"

Not I! While other kids at school had been off Girl Guiding, I had been doing ballet, drama, music, and trying to blow things up with my chemistry set. Even then I had considered nature to be a danger best avoided or destroyed.

Warren finally decided it was bedtime when DJ Jason began his rendition of "Hill Top Hoods."

"When you're hangin' at the back of the bar, like you're bangin' in the back of your car..." he croaked, hammering a ladle on the coffee tin while several of the others played manic air guitars.

"That's it, boys and girls!" Warren laughed. "Lights out. Andreas, put that stick back in the fire. We'll be up with the sun come morning!" The boy with the burning log reluctantly threw it back while the others set up a chorus of supplication.

"Aw, come on, Mr Warren, just a bit longer. Tell him just a bit longer, Miss."

It was oddly gratifying to be chosen as their advocate so, of course, I intervened on their behalf.

"It's the first night, Boss," I pleaded. "Surely we can sit out here a bit longer."

"Maybe just a bit—and don't call me Boss," he conceded, but then Jason picked up a large burning ember and started waving it around to scare the girls. Sparks flew, one landed on the blanket where Brooke and Sara sat and Mr Warren ordered us all to bed—NOW! I tossed the last of my tea onto the singed cloth. Mary had been right about the pyromaniacs.

There were a few more complaints but the youngsters crawled into their tents and were fast asleep before the fire was extinguished. Gazza had been seen earlier, stumbling into the tent he shared with Warren and, soon, the only sounds around the camp were his blubbering snores.

Mary crawled into our tent while I was in the shower block cleaning my teeth and was softly snoring before I got my sleeping bag rolled out. Everyone else had been provided with a sleeping bag but I'd thought it was safer to supply my own. God only knew, and I didn't want to, who or what had occurred in those provided by NT Correctional Services, Inc.

Mine had been purchased at Paddy Pallin along with my rucksack and was filled with down, guaranteed to be warm in winter and cool in summer. Considering what I'd paid for it, I fully expected to be comfortable. It had been such a big day with such an early start that I was sure I'd be unconscious as soon as my head hit the pillow but something else happened instead. It was like the secrets of this Outback crept in through the tent flap and seeped into my soul and I found myself wide awake with wonder. I lay still for awhile, willing sleep to come but it wouldn't. The sleeping bag wasn't comforting me at all so I got dressed and crept out of the tent to see what I could see.

Sitting on a stone at the edge of the camp, I watched the quarter moon climb through more stars than I had ever imagined. I wished Claudia and Suzanne, and even Dalby, could be watching it with me. I'd bet that they didn't even know a sky could look like this. In a sudden rush of homesickness, I hurried back to the tent and retrieved my iPhone from my boot. I needed to SMS an SOS to somebody—anybody!

Returning to my rock, I flipped it open, turned it on and...

Waited for a signal that never came.

I watched the words SEARCHING FOR NETWORK flit back and forth across the screen for five minutes before I gave up and snapped it shut. Outback Australia! I might as well have been on Mars. I tried to find the red planet in the black sky.

The night lay still against my skin, caressing me with an unfamiliar peace and the air smelled...I don't know...*clean.* All thoughts of old friends and new enemies soon left my mind. I heard a curlew call, and then another and another, but I didn't know what was making those haunting sounds and wondered if I should be frightened. As I sat quietly, I heard a door close behind me and turned to see Warren leaving the men's shower block. He had not seen me.

He walked slowly, looking at the sky, wearing only a red sarong tied around his waist. His damp hair curled loosely around his ears and neck. The pale moonlight painted his muscular chest in dark relief and his legs were lithe and supple, the muscles rippling as he walked. He carried a towel and shaving kit and passed close by my stone. I made no sound, didn't even breathe, but he paused, as if suddenly aware of my presence. He turned slowly to face me, eyebrows raised, surprised it was me.

"Miss Smith? You're outside alone?"

"Guilty as charged." I shrugged. "Couldn't sleep. What's making that noise?"

"Curlews. The old people say their call is lost souls calling to each other."

"That's what it sounds like. Are they dangerous?"

"Of course not, they're just birds."

"An emu's just a bird but I wouldn't want to get up close and personal with one." I smiled. It was nice talking to him without rules and kids surrounding us. "Do you take these trips often?"

"This is..." He started to say, but then his eyes dropped to my singlet where those naughty nipples strained against the cloth. He looked up at the stars and frowned. "It'll be another long day tomorrow," he said harshly. "You should get back to your tent now."

His rudeness was uncalled for and my anger rose again,

spoiling the night. Then I became aware of another rising. He was standing very close, and his scarcely clothed body was inches from my face–which was level with his groin. His sarong began to dance and gape and I couldn't take my eyes away. I was mesmerized. He crossed his hands, strategically using the towel and shaving kit to hide his interest and turned away, frowning.

"Go to bed," he commanded and rushed away to his own tent.

"So, he's human after all." I grinned and returned to my tent. With Warren, not curlews, on my mind, I curled into my sleeping bag, hand between my legs, fingers wriggling. Funny how I hadn't wanted to knee that copper in the groin. He was still a bastard, though.

I thought of the bastard's red sarong, how it had danced. When I imagined the one-eyed puppet beneath that was pulling the strings, I climaxed with a sudden spurt. I gasped my surprise and Mary rolled over. I lay absolutely still, holding my breath until her snoring resumed. Wouldn't do to wake her up at a time like this.

Just before falling asleep I remembered Dalby, the guy I was actually engaged to. In my mind, I reassured him that I wasn't being unfaithful and also reminded him that he was partially responsible for me being so damned horny.

IN THE WEEKS leading up to my departure for the NT—of which he totally disapproved—Dalby had found one excuse after another for not spending the night together. He blamed work, but I recognise the withdrawal of favours when I see it. And they accuse women of pussy-whipping.

I had believed his excuses at first and, to be honest, I hadn't missed the sex that much. Our love life had become so very predictable and very close to boring. For one thing, it only happened when we were in bed at night and I didn't sleep at his place more than two or three times a week. Foreplay was his hand on my shoulder. I was only allowed to initiate sex if I wanted to go down on him and *that* was a thrill I'd pretty much outgrown. Nevertheless, sex was a habit I didn't want to break so after a few weeks of this denial I was becoming unbalanced. If it hadn't been for my vibrator, I'd have been climbing the walls.

I DIDN'T WANT the vibrator when I thought about Warren, though. It was *him* I wanted inside me! Oops! My fingers were frolicking again.

After my busy day and even busier night, I slept like a baby...until Brooke was sent into the tent to shake me awake.

"You better come on, Miss. Breakfast's almost cooked and Mr Warren ain't too happy about you having a sleep-in."

My eyes were glued shut and I pulled the pillow over my head. "What time is it? Is the sun even up?"

"Welcome to Outback Tours, Miss," Brooke laughed and backed out of the tent.

Rubbing my eyes open, I crawled out of my expensive sleeping bag drenched in sweat (Cool in summer, my arse!), picked up my toiletries case, wrapped a brightly flowered sarong around my slim, naked body, and headed off for a nice cool shower. Certain parts of my body required special attention. While trying to crawl out through the ridiculously small tent opening, my knee got caught and dragged the sarong right off, exposing that slim, naked body to the entire crew, who were gathered near the bus, listening to our fearless leader.

Oh, shit! I ducked back inside as quickly as I could, treating them to the sight of my now-bare arse. I groaned to the sounds of Jason choking, others laughing, and Gazza barking like a wounded seal. I could just imagine what Warren's reaction would be—another ten demerit points off my CSO! At this rate it would take me ten years to finish it.

I pulled on a T-shirt and boxer shorts, the nightclothes I'd meant to put on before going to bed if my mind hadn't been on other things. *Oh, no, Lou, don't you start thinking about those other things*, I had to admonish myself severely as an itching in my nether regions made me want to reach down and relieve it. Soberly, head down, I walked to the shower in a manner as contrite as I could muster. When I soaped myself under the spray, however, my body got the better of me and I couldn't help caressing my clitoris, trying not to drown as I gasped and came again.

The twitching stopped, my breathing slowed, and I leaned against the shower wall, feeling a sober regret. *Cut this out now, girl. There is no future in it. He's an arsehole and you are here to look after idiot teenagers, not to act like one yourself!* With this lecture ringing through my mind, I finished washing, dressed, and joined the others.

The kids had already left the breakfast table and were running off in all directions.

"Nothing left but cold toast and coffee," Mary said.

"Which you can eat while washing the dishes. We've got no time for slackers here," Warren said as he rose from the table. Obviously he didn't want to be seen sitting next to any slackers. Was it my imagination or had his rudeness been turned up a notch? And was it my imagination or was I feeling a little bit hurt and disappointed? Now, that was something to be worried about.

I accepted a mug of coffee from Mary, took a large swallow, and gagged. Damper and fresh meat cooked in the open might be fine, but the drovers could keep their campfire coffee!

"Don't be too proud to drink it, girl," said Mary as she ladled sugar into the tin cup. "You'll be wanting that caffeine before the sun gets much higher. Try dipping your toast in it, might help."

God help me, I did it. Soggy toast smeared with congealed margarine dunked into coffee the consistency of molasses. And then I ate it. Without gagging. If Claudia and Suzanne could see me now, I'd be banned from Starbucks for the rest of my natural life.

CHAPTER EIGHT

I SHOULD HAVE BEEN waking up to a Sydney sunrise coming through the pale green damask curtains that hung over the casement windows in my bedroom at home instead of the harsh green nylon of a tent. I should have been hearing the soft *shooshing* sounds of waves lapping the beach below my window instead of the coughing and hacking of emphysemic campers. After a private shower in my *en suite* of grey marble with golden taps, I should have been following the smell of freshly brewed coffee down to my mother's rose granite kitchen, where she would be pouring a cup just for me instead of sitting at a dirty, concrete picnic table surrounded by noisy teens. I should be sitting quietly with my mother in wrought iron garden furniture, surrounded by creeping ivy and sweet-scented jasmine. And, instead of tin, my cup should be of bone china.

"Oh, Mary, who am I and how did I get here?" I moaned and Mary chuckled, pouring hot water into the wash pan.

"Get scrubbing, girl. The big boss is packing up."

When the dishes were washed, dried, and stowed away and the children rounded up, I was still chewing the coffee grit that coated my teeth and gums. That would be for later, when I needed another caffeine hit. I tried my best to cheer up. The sudden memory of the boss in his red sarong did the trick and I bounced up the steps and boarded the bus, avoiding Gazza's filthy smirk and Warren's disapproving glare. At least The Pig was easy to figure out. Our tour leader was a mystery, and I had to convince myself that I did not want to unravel him—oops, I meant unravel *it*—the mystery, that is.

This morning we were going to drive to Nitmiluk Gorge, a place I'd never heard of and couldn't pronounce, for a two-hour boat cruise. The drive was only a short one but I couldn't keep my eyes open. There's nothing to look at even if I had, and that caffeine hit only served to give me nightmares. I dreamt of riding through the bush in the back of a Ute, trying my hardest to shoot a wild boar's butt full of buckshot, but each time I pulled the trigger the Ute hit a bump and the shot would go wide. Where did that come from? What did I know about pig shooting? Not a lot, judging by my lack of skill in the dream, and it was very disturbing to consider that, because I was living with the great unwashed, I was becoming one in my dreams!

When the bus jerked to a stop, my nodding head flung back so abruptly that I nearly got whiplash. Trying to recover from the pain in my neck and the pain of that dream, I sat very still. The juvies, on the other hand, poured off the bus like they'd been imprisoned for years and whooped around like mad things until Warren came and dragged me out into the fray. I looked around, trying to take it all in.

The parking area was paved but, from its edges, numerous dusty walking tracks led off into the trees and bushes. There was a small barbecue area adjacent, with the obligatory toilet block, gas barbecues and concrete tables and benches. About a half dozen vehicles were parked and three or four anonymous adults were frying up onions and meat. I couldn't smell anything else over the onions but I could hear water running in the distance. It must be the famous gorge.

Mary and Gazza chose to stay with the vehicle while the rest of us went off on our adventure.

"Spending the morning with Officer Pig wouldn't be my first choice," she whispered, "but somebody's gotta protect the food supplies or we'll be mighty hungry tonight. Besides, I prefer to appreciate the bush from a reclining position."

That sounded like a sensible philosophy to me but Warren must have disagreed because he was nudging me.

"We have a boat to catch, Miss Smith!" Like that was important to me. I took a deep breath and feigned enthusiasm.

"Hear, hear, boys and girls!" I tried to restore order but my feeble calls fell on deaf ears. I followed Warren and the others down the trail marked "To the jetty," but the long hike down there didn't do anything to reduce the excess energy they wore like auras. Note to self: cut back on bush coffee for the youngsters. Was this more of Mary's cunning? Was she trying to keep me in my place as well?

So we went in search of a gorge, following a narrow, red-dirt trail through dense scrub and occasional trees. Birds were calling but not the curlews I'd heard last night. I surmised that they must be nocturnal and congratulated myself on having actually learned something. We finally arrived at the water's edge amid much screeching and horsing around. One boy grabbed a handful of blue berries and tried to force them into another boy's mouth.

"Go on, it's only bush plums, I swear. I seen it on *Bush Tucker Man*."

I knocked the berries out of his hand and shook my head.

"Aw, what would she know? She's from Sydney," the first boy said and the other answered, "At least *she* ain't trying to poison me."

Two of the girls ducked behind one of the few trees for some skulduggery but their bright, new T-shirts were easy to spot. I followed them.

"Gee, Miss, we were only going to have a squat," they protested innocently but, when I offered to stand guard, they decided they didn't have to pee after all.

I saw the sightseeing boat for the first time and let out my own small screech. That boat was a worry. It was tied up to a small wooden pier under the shade of some trees that were— I'm guessing here—probably eucalypts. The boat was flat with bench seats lining either side with a flat, black roof and no railings—not any sort of bar or cabin, either. Great! It was not my habit to expose myself to elements such as waterways or to even board a boat that would be leaving the dockside unless I was accompanied by a bucket of ice chilling a bottle of champagne. I thought of Daddy's yacht and how even the lifeboats looked safer and considerably more comfortable than this thing we'd be riding in. The only other human being in sight was an authoritative-looking fellow wearing the ubiquitous khaki with Wildlife Warrior-type badges sewed onto his shirtsleeves.

Now we were here, I thought things would calm down but had no such luck. Jason ran whooping out onto the pier and managed to fall backward into the water, black tailcoat floating around him. Several of the others (maybe I should try to learn their names) fell to the ground in hysterics as he flailed around in the shallows. One boy shouted, "Watch a croc don't eat you!" and another, who looked very young, called back, "Eating Jason would kill the poor croc! Mr Warren, Jason's trying to endanger the wildlife!"

That remark caused such hilarity amongst the kids that even the ranger with the badges began to look annoyed. How demented, or maybe vindictive, was the judge who had sent these numchucks into the wilderness? It had to be the same one who sentenced me and I was beginning to realize why he had been banished to Darwin. He was obviously unsuited for the solemn courts of civilisation.

"Miss Smith!" Warren had come up behind me and his bark in my ear scared the bejesus out of me. I jumped a mile.

"What!" I shrieked, whirling around and losing my balance with the shock. He grabbed my arm so I didn't fall and shook me like my dad used to do when I was really naughty.

"Do something about this behaviour and get these youngsters on board immediately!"

"So now it's my fault when teenagers act like arseholes?" I was so angry I could feel my eyes burn hot from the flashes. How dare he treat me like a child? Especially when I had it on good authority (the red sarong) that he didn't think of me as a child.

"This trip is *not* a holiday for you. I saw you sleeping on the bus. Kindly do your job or you'll find yourself in Berrimah when we get back!"

He dropped my arm and leaned down to pull Jason out of the water...calf, thigh, and buttock muscles tensing as he steadied his stance against falling in as well. I hadn't meant to be distracted but I couldn't help wondering how he kept his creases sharp while living in a tent. His back was so straight his shirt didn't even wrinkle and his butt...it would fit perfectly in my two hands...

"Christ, Louisa, get a grip!" I whispered savagely to myself. "I don't even know what Berrimah is, but you can bet that I'd rather be there than stuck here with you!" I shouted at him.

"Berrimah's the prison, Miss," an awestruck whisper informed me.

"Prison, eh?" I was still yelling. "I wish that stupid judge *had* stuck me there!" I turned to the youngsters and said, "All right all of you, enough horseplay."

Jason flapped wetly up the bank and stood in front of me, dripping and grinning like an imbecile. I scowled at him. "Jason, get that damn coat off and hang it on a tree. You'll catch your death of cold in that." Looking around, I spotted Warren's rucksack lying on the ground with the corner of a towel sticking out. I helped myself and tossed the towel to Jason. "Dry yourself off. And the rest of you, on the boat now— please."

Warren turned around just then, opened his mouth to speak, and then closed it again. I must have looked really fierce. Shouldering a large string bag filled with water bottles and apples for a healthy but boring smoko, I herded those kids before me and onto the jetty.

"It's OK, Miss. I'll dry off in the sun quick enough." Jason threw Warren the towel, got on board, and the rest followed him, casting furtive glances at the mad woman who would rather be in jail than about to embark on a river cruise. Not wanting to leave that precious coat behind unguarded, Jason draped it over the back of one of the seats. The three adults followed, found seats, and the ranger started the motor. Warren, no surprises here, sat at the front of the boat and I found a seat alone where I could nurse my wounds in private.

CHAPTER NINE

THE RANGER DIDN'T SAY MUCH, and I doubted whether he'd been informed of his cargo ahead of time. Probably not. Who in his right mind would have agreed to this? A microphone lay on the seat beside him so I assumed we'd be getting a commentary later. I smiled at him sympathetically and he smiled back.

That was a bit of all right. He looked to be in his early forties, a rugged man of the land, and his khaki cords were much more attractive than blue drill. He looked like he needed company. *Great thighs*, I thought as I moved to the back of the boat. When I got close I could see that the name on his badge was "King." Just "King." First or last? Who cared, it was a fine name and I could be his subject for awhile. We couldn't really talk over the noise of the outboard but we could smile at each other and sit close. He had a lovely scent of eucalyptus and pine and cigarettes. A plastic packet of loose-leaf tobacco peaked out from his shirt pocket and the fingernails on his left hand were stained yellow. I could imagine him at his job each day, one hand steering the boat as the other deftly rolled smokes. His tan face creased as he squinted into the sunlit water, scouting for danger, King of all he surveyed.

Of course, smoking, other than the occasional Beedie, is a disgusting habit but, sometimes, what I like best about men are their disgusting habits. I like men, have I mentioned that? I like their scent and the way they feel against my skin and their work clothes as I imagine all those tough, manly things they do to keep me safe and warm. I love being around them until they end up trying to have really bad sex with me, but even that doesn't discourage me because sometimes I find one who realizes that good sex is when *both* participants are happy and satisfied. Then those awful sessions are almost worth it because I really love having a really good root. Not that I've had that many great roots since becoming engaged to Dalby...but I have a good memory and I live in hope.

Maybe—and this probably isn't a topic that requires sorting while I'm struggling just to stay alive in Wild Australia—but, maybe, we shouldn't get married.

The deep blue water was still, the ride gentle, and the soft breeze cooled what promised to be another bloody hot day. This was the Northern Territory, what else could one expect? Warren was in the front with most of the kids, pointing out sights and looking for crocodiles. Two of the boys sat in the back speaking quietly to one another. I glanced over at them and wondered what their names were. Not that not knowing their names was a problem. I wasn't here to bond with the juvies, I was just here to do my time and be set free.

I decided to relax and to enjoy the experience, settling into my ranger while watching multi-coloured rock faces rise high above the water's edge. The green trees and bushes below skirted the cliffs like a tutu. It wasn't long before the peace overcame me and I started to nod off. The ranger rested my head on his shoulder, placing one arm around my waist as he steered with the other and I was soon fast asleep again, this time without dreams.

Loud thumping from overhead, a scream, and Warren's angry shout woke me with a start. Warren was shaking me viciously. Ranger King had removed his arm from my midriff and cut the motor to idle. He was shouting as well, accusing Warren of who knows what. I was still too groggy to have any idea of what was going on.

Warren pointed to the seats where the two boys had been sitting, which were now empty. The thumping from above continued and I stood, beginning to understand. Those boys must be on the roof making all that noise. *How had they got up there?* I marvelled and was just about to ask my cranky boss when a body hurtled past my eyes and landed in the river with a mighty splash.

"Who was that?" cried Warren, still shaking me.

"I don't know!" I shouted through rattling teeth. "I don't know their names! I was asleep!"

The ranger, the only one who'd stopped shouting, grabbed a life ring and tossed it into the water. Warren hurried up the small iron ladder that led to the corrugated iron roof and I leaned over the side of the boat, waiting for whoever it was to surface. The boat's edge tipped perilously close to water as all the other kids rushed to the side for a look.

"Keep your hands in the boat," the ranger warned. "There are crocs in there."

"Oh my God!" I sobbed, suddenly worried sick for a boy I didn't even know. I looked around frantically for a life jacket, finally spotting them strapped to the ceiling, firmly out of reach of a drowning man. I turned anxiously back to the brown water. "Oh, why doesn't he come up? Did you see them go up there?" I asked King but he was busy manoeuvring the life ring to answer.

The lad came up just then, spluttering, coughing, grabbing for the life ring. Within seconds that seemed like hours, the ranger had pulled him into the boat just as a large crocodile jumped out of the water right behind him, jaws snapping, teeth missing the boy's sneaker by millimetres. I fell back against the seats and we all screamed. But soon the kids jumped up and down and cheered. The boat jerked convulsively, about to sink, with all life jackets still firmly attached to the roof. The boy, forty kilos ringing wet, with pink skin and red curls plastered to his skull, lay on the deck panting, shaking, and looking like a drowned rat.

I ran to him, grabbed him up, wrapped my arms around him, and held him close, still sobbing, his dripping board shorts and T-shirt soaking me. Warren reappeared, with a small plastic packet in his hand and ushering the other boy in front of him, none too gently. He pushed me away from the boy I held.

"He's not dead, no thanks to you. I'll deal with you later," Warren growled and then turned to the boys. "Now, Andreas, Corey, do you want to explain this?" He opened his hand, revealing a sandwich bag containing five blue tablets.

"It's his!" the drowned boy accused.

"Bloody snitch. You know how far that'll get you." They both looked like babies! The dry one, Andreas, looked Indigenous, with big dark eyes that probably got him into more trouble than they got him out of. He turned these on Warren to justify himself. "He ain't so innocent. He was trying to get them off me so he could take the lot. That's the reason how come he ended up in the water."

"So you threw him off the boat?" Warren didn't sound impressed.

"Naw, Boss, he *slipped*," Andreas said menacingly, stepping up to the other.

Warren grabbed his T-shirt and pulled him back.

"That'll do, Andreas. There will be no bullying on my watch. No drugs, either, got it?" He slipped the baggie into his pocket. "Now get up front, both of you. Eat an apple and enjoy the wonders of nature."

The boys did as they were told, nudging each other with their shoulders as they went, a power play without fists. Warren looked down at me, still seated on the boat's floorboards, damp and shaking.

"And what, pray tell, do you have to say for yourself? Under your watch they were dealing with dangerous drugs, fighting, and Corey was very nearly killed."

"Corey—is that his name?" My mind was a blur, I couldn't concentrate. This place was really dangerous. How could it be OK to bring street kids here? How was I expected to protect them from nature when I hadn't even known it existed? In my experience, things from nature were what you bought at the Body Shop or the Tree of Life.

"You don't even know his name?" Warren's fists clenched at his sides and I thought he'd hit me. It was probably what I deserved. That poor boy! Warren took a step closer. "I bet you know *his* name." He pointed at the ranger who immediately held up his hands.

"Hey, don't get me involved," he said and returned to his seat by the outboard. "I'm the one who saved the kid, remember?"

I retreated, creeping backward until I came up against the side of a metal bench.

Instead, Warren shook his finger in my face and said, through clenched teeth. "Don't think, for the briefest moment, that your CSO is being served. The judge will read my report and you'll be doing time in Berrimah Prison before you can even blink!"

He dropped his hand, slapped his thigh in frustration instead of my face, and rejoined the juvies. I clawed my way up into the seat and was still shivering when the cruise ended an hour later. Ranger King never did give us a wild river talk. The walk back in the sunshine dried everyone's clothes but I could not stop my teeth from chattering.

"See any crocs?" Mary asked me when we returned and sat down to a lunch of freshly cut sandwiches and fruit.

The vision of Corey being snatched from the jaws of the hungry reptile flashed through my mind again. "I'll be seeing them in my dreams for the rest of my life. Oh, Mary, that fool judge should have just fined me! Sending me out here has endangered not only my life but also the lives of each and every one of those kids!"

"Now, Lou, I'm sure you're exaggerating," she chuckled but she hadn't heard the story yet.

"Warren's so good with the kids." I sighed. "Does he have any himself?"

"Not yet."

What did that mean? Did he have a wife or girlfriend and it was just a matter of time? I tried to ask Mary, but she was being dragged away by two of the girls. I didn't really care, anyway.

Once lunch was over (I could only force half a tomato-and-cheese on white bread sandwich down my trembling throat) and the kids were running it off, Warren approached me. I was stacking plates and cups to take to Mary for the washing up, the tin rattling in my still-shaking hands. He gripped my arm and nearly dragged me to a place where two spindly gum trees grew together and almost created some shade.

"What was that business with you and the ranger?" he asked. He still had me tight by the arm, and his head was lowered so he could speak softly and not be overheard. His voice was grim. "You're not on some dating show. You weren't sent out here to find a mate so I suggest you quit trying. You were sent on this trip to find some backbone, to show some responsibility, to repay a debt you owe to society."

"A debt I owe..." I spluttered, hardly able to get the words out.

He gave me a shake, and then dropped his hand to his side where he held his arm stiffly, clenching and unclenching his fist. Then he shook his head as though thinking better of an idea and stuck both fists in his pockets. I was pretty sure I knew what he'd been thinking and didn't want him to change his mind and hit me so I stepped well back before I let fly.

"For your information, Mr Warren Fucking George, your stupid judge had no idea what he was doing sending me out here. I couldn't help falling asleep because that's what nature does to me! As for Ranger King..." I calmed down a little and smirked. "He was just being nice and showing an interest in a tourist. That's his job, you know."

Until that moment, I had not realized that a black man could turn red. His cheeks looked like chocolate-covered cherries, every muscle in his body hardened, and veins popped out on his forehead and pulsated in his neck. His fists came out of his pockets and I thought, for one moment, that he would literally explode. He didn't, of course, but turned quickly and strode back to the bus, shouting angrily for everyone to get on board.

The kids didn't know what was happening but they knew, by the sound of his voice and the look on his face, that it was in their best interest to obey the boss so we were ready to go in record time. Gazza turned the bus back toward Katherine, heading for the Victoria Highway and Western Australia. The change in direction didn't change the scenery or the weather. The midday heat was as visible as the anger radiating off one seriously hot tour guide.

CHAPTER TEN

INSIDE THE BUS IT WAS QUIET; like everyone knew the events of the morning required silent reflection. Steam still oozed from Warren's ears so nobody was game to talk to him.

We travelled west instead of east, avoiding the Kakadu because, for the last few weeks, Greenies protesting against uranium mining had been active in that area. The media had been full of stories about those pesky environmentalists and how they were boycotting, demonstrating, and generally making nuisances of themselves. Newspapers published stories designed to whip up animosity with the natives, accusing the interlopers of robbing the NT citizens of job opportunities. Television crews chased around looking for confrontations and, hopefully, a few brawls. No injuries had been reported (or filmed) but there had been some property damage and arrests and the judicial system concluded that the juveniles in its custody would be safer away from the trouble.

"Safer than what?" I couldn't help thinking as I hunkered down in my seat and pulled out the files to read them properly this time. From what little I'd seen so far, I thought that the juveniles would have quite enjoyed the demonstrations. Hell, they could have given those interlopers more than a few pointers! I opened the first folder.

I knew Jason, of course, the white Goth busted for marijuana possession. I was beginning to think that everyone in the whole Top End knew Jason. What was strange was that they all looked out for him like everyone wanted to make sure he got a fair deal. I couldn't figure that one out because, to me, he was just a painful adolescent who got himself in trouble every time he opened his mouth. No age was entered next to his name but this trip was for the under agers so he couldn't be more than sixteen, although he looked about twenty and acted about twelve. I heard his voice and looked up.

He was no longer hanging over the seat in front of me but he had draped his damp coat over it so I could still smell him. He was now trying to get the microphone from Warren so he could lead the group in singing "The Wheels of the Bus Go Round and Round." Fortunately, he wasn't having much luck. The boss didn't look like he was in the mood for singing.

"Do you know Goth Boy?" I asked Mary. "What's his story?"

Mary looked up from her book and smiled at Jason's antics. "He's a good kid, really, wouldn't hurt a fly. He just can't help himself and keeps getting into trouble."

"What about his family? Can't they do anything?"

"He was raised by his mum, lived in any number of caravan parks and housing estates with her and all of her boyfriends. His poor mum was schizophrenic and not much good at looking after herself, never mind her son, and kept looking for help in all the wrong places. Every time Family Services moved in, but, and put the boy in foster care, why, he'd run away back to his mum. 'I gotta look after her,' he'd always tell them."

"So, where is she now?"

"She passed away a few years ago and he's been on his own since."

"Doesn't anyone look after him?"

"That's one of his problems–he'll go home with anybody who has a kind word to say to him and finds out too late their motives may not be pure."

So, Darwin has a few Fagins, I thought. And why not? The real Fagin ended up in Sydney and a place like Darwin would probably suit his descendants.

"Our community does what we can," Mary continued. "Everybody likes Jason."

"But he's not Aboriginal, is he?"

"What the bloody hell difference does that make?" Mary snorted and went back to reading her book.

I didn't know. *I'm* not the one who studied sociology; that was Claudia. Here I was, trying to be PC and culturally sensitive and all that and I still couldn't get it right. I didn't want to alienate Mary, the closest thing I had to a friend on this bus.

"I'm sorry," I said. "I didn't mean to offend you."

"No worries, sister. Now go back to your studies. I'm

enjoying my romance here in the air con." She smiled and I was pretty sure I'd been forgiven.

Then there was Troy, the skinhead, aka Spider, sixteen years old, light brown in colour, classed "Aboriginal" under race, here for ABH. "Actual Bodily Harm?" I said to myself. What had he done and to whom? At sixteen more than one of my friends were getting into schoolyard scrapes and, yeah, sometimes punches had been thrown and landed, but they'd never been arrested for it! What kind of schools did Darwin have? I glanced over at his nobbly brown head, recently shaved. He was deep in conversation with Jason who had given up in the fight for the microphone. This was undoubtedly an unwise choice for a friendship, but an arrestable offence? Puh-lease!

"Mary?" I hated to interrupt her but I had to know. "What about Spider?"

She sighed and closed her book, finger stuck in place. "Am I going to get no peace?" she asked but she didn't sound mad so I persisted.

"Whom did he hit?"

"I'm not real clear about that, but I do know the boy's got a temper. Probably developed it watching his old man thrash his mother. All the men in his family are like that, but–violent drunks."

"Spider's only sixteen. He wouldn't have been drunk when he did this, would he?"

"Oh, Lou...," was all she said.

"Oh, yeah." I remembered my high school again. The thing is, when you're sixteen you don't feel nearly as young and stupid by the time you're twenty-three. ABH seemed like a biggie to throw at a kid nonetheless. Would he have been sent to prison if he were seventeen? I'm an engineer, not a solicitor.

I opened the next file.

It was about Melanie, fifteen years old, arrested for shop-lifting and this was not the first time. She liked DVDs but apparently needed practise in removing those pesky attachments that screamed "I'm being stolen!" as you carried them out of the shop. She was white and she was the one I kept confusing with Laurel, the other Caucasian female. Why didn't anyone think of attaching photos to these files? I guessed Melanie was probably the one with glasses, from watching all those DVDs. She was heavily made up and her long, scraggly, orange hair seriously needed a washing. She was quite fair and that thick make-up probably saved her from a severely sun-burned face.

If I was right, that meant Laurel was the one with long blond hair cut in a shoulder-length bob to look like Britney Spears—which she didn't. Too skinny, for one thing. She was sixteen and also acted like she was twelve and, according to her file, liked to smoke dope and drop speed.

I could understand the dope because there's nothing like it for chilling, but speed? Why not just down a few double espressos from Starbucks? I doubted that blond was her natural colour. Her pale skin was turning alarmingly red and I vowed to provide her with sun protection once we stopped and I found out where it was kept.

Then came Sara, fifteen, who was really black and really beautiful. Her file listed vagrancy as her crime. I was damned if I could understand how a kid could be a vagrant. Wasn't hanging around the shopping malls all day just part of growing up? Skipping school was called "truancy" and surely they hadn't made that a criminal offence. They just called your parents to come pick you up, you copped what was coming to you, and went back to school the next day. Mary was looking very peaceful over there but I couldn't stop myself. I just had to know.

"Mary, how can a fifteen-year-old be a vagrant?"

Again with the sigh, deeper this time, and the finger in the book. She gave me a long-suffering look. Mary had so many looks and I expected I was destined to receive them all.

"Who we talking about, girl?"

"Sara. It says she was arrested for vagrancy but she's only fifteen. Wouldn't it be loitering or truancy at her age?"

"Depends on where she was and what time of day. Knowing Sara, the charge was probably reduced from soliciting. Can I read my book now?"

My jaw dropped. Soliciting! Holy cow! Maybe I didn't want to know anymore about her story. I have a delicate soul. I think

I might have mentioned that I was not cut out for this job.

Timbo, sixteen, Aboriginal, was the 6-foot tall beanpole with dreadlocks who joked about everything and, according to his file, was a vagrant as well. If his real crime had been soliciting, then I definitely didn't want to know about it. I slapped his file shut and went on to the next.

Caleb, only fourteen, had "Indian" listed as his nationality. "Incorrigible" was how the judge described him. He would take anything from a shelf, and this latest crime was stealing a packet of crisps. Unbelievable! I didn't bother Mary with this one, either. I shook my head, despairing at this thing they called "the system." It was quite effective at dealing out systematic punishment but I had to wonder how effective it was in stamping out crime. I'm an engineer, though, as I've mentioned more than once, not a sociologist or a solicitor or even a student of human nature, for that matter. Maybe I should keep my ill-informed thoughts to myself. In my experience, people had always done exactly what I had expected them to and it had never occurred to me that there was anything to understand. Had I been wrong?

Fifteen-year-old Brooke had been picked up for public drunkenness, and fourteen-year-old Andreas liked his marijuana and speed. Brooke was Filipina and Andreas was another Aboriginal boy. Booze and drugs. My mind went back to my high school dances, to the spiked punch, the smuggled hip flasks, the bongs in the bathrooms, and the chaperons who turned their heads. Why weren't these particular kids allowed to be—well, to be kids? Somebody else might have suggested racism, but they all looked alike to me—equal members of that frightening species known as teenagers. I couldn't cope with my own little sisters. How was I supposed to deal with this gathering? If I couldn't understand their crimes, how could I be expected to understand them?

The last file belonged to Corey, the sixteen-year-old boy who'd nearly become a croc's dinner while drowning. Even I, who had little time for underage idiots, considered that a harsh punishment for smoking a bit of weed. Mind you, the episode hadn't done me any good, either. I was seriously wishing for a bit of that weed right now. I sat, drowning in the guilt of not being a proper mother to a boy who was only seven years my junior. The responsibility frightened me more than any wildlife and I briefly considered that I might have preferred a week or two in this so-called Berrimah. How many romance and crime novels could I have enjoyed during a week in prison? I looked at Mary with her novel and thought about the paperback waiting for me in my bag but knew I wouldn't be able to concentrate on any light reading.

Returning the ten files to a large manila folder, I set it on my lap, stroking its smooth surface as I sat, deep in thought. I tried to remember my own adolescent feelings but I wasn't old enough to have developed a proper perspective. I inexplicably missed my irritating little sisters who were the same age as these juvies.

I sighed and reopened the damned folder.

CHAPTER ELEVEN

WE WERE TO SPEND THE NIGHT at some place called the Gregory National Park and it was a bloody long drive–made longer by the unchanging landscape. Willy-willies danced across the scrub like miniature whirlwinds, dust storms obscured far off ranges, and even inside the closed-up bus the dust got up my nostrils. Somebody farted last night's fried onions and started a chain reaction, which the children thought was more fun than a movie but it was impossible to open a window amidst all that swirling sand. Death by gas or suffocation–what a choice! Warren pulled out a neatly pressed handkerchief to protect his nose and mouth and I think he was covering a smile as well. At least the kids remained seated as they released their toxic spray. I read and reread files, memorizing information which might be helpful over the next few days just in case I actually survived. Anticipating, of course, that I would forget it all just as quickly once the CSO was over. By the time we arrived at Gregory, I was pretty confident that I knew each of my charges by sight but I was nowhere near to knowing what made any of them tick. Well, first things first.

"I'm here to serve," I announced as I alighted from the bus. We chose a shady spot lined with tall pine trees to set up the tents. The ground was covered by tall, green ferns, which might have been lovely somewhere else, but here they obscured the ground, hiding whatever lived below. I erected my tent close to a well-trodden and clearly visible path.

With my boots tightly laced, I insisted on helping the girls set up their tents as well, despite their protests that they could do it better and faster without my interference. While fending off the attentions of Jason and Gazza, I got my own tent up in under thirty minutes which filled me with tremendous pride. Since Mary was fixing the dinner, I had to do the job all by myself, and those aluminium poles were deadly weapons (I got Gazza across the gob and he disappeared–*yes*!).

Nylon is a material I've never had much to do with. I didn't even know whether or not it had a bias. It was difficult to fold and didn't unfold so much as it fell open in a confusing heap. And then, once the poles were threaded correctly and the nylon was bent into a tent shape, I had to peg the corners into the ground. I'm not what you would call a hammering woman at the best of times, and this ground was impossible. Either it was sand which rejected pegs forthwith or it was solid rock. I overcame each obstacle as it presented itself and eventually erected a wrinkle-free, portable bedroom. I looked around for approval but nobody congratulated me. I only saw Warren watching with thinly veiled distaste. That hurt me more than I wanted to admit, but I wasn't going to let him know so I poked my tongue at him and walked over to Mary, who was showing Andreas and Corey how to find good wood for the fire.

"I saw that," she said. "Very mature, eh."

"I can't help it if that's how I feel. Sorry, I interrupted."

"But the bigger the log the bigger the fire, right?" Andreas asked her.

"Right, but we just want to cook dinner, not burn down the campsite," Mary answered.

I ran a hand gently down Corey's back. "Shirt's nice and dry now."

"Yeah, Miss, but it stinks a bit."

When we got back to camp the kids had scattered like beads of mercury dropped from a great height but I wasn't worried. What kind of trouble could they get into around here? There wasn't a shop to rob within a hundred kilometres! I lit a Beedie and perched on the nearest picnic table to chat to Mary.

Suddenly Warren was there, once again gripping my arm and dragging me away. I would have to start photographing those bruises, but the electric shocks that created havoc with my heart each time he touched me could not be recorded on film.

"How many times must I tell you—don't let these kids to go off alone. It's up to you to protect them from snakes and scorpions."

"Snakes?" I choked on the smoke. "What the hell do I know about snakes!"

I couldn't believe this jerk. How was somebody who grew up on Sydney's North Shore, who couldn't even look at a snake in a zoo without fainting, be expected to protect others from these scaly creatures? And scorpions? Nobody told me there were scorpions out here! Scorpions are found only on zodiac jewellery and mummy's tombs, right? I remembered my dad saying that a good offence was the best form of defence, or was it the other way around? Anyway, I attacked. I didn't try to pull my arm away, though.

"Face it, Mr Tour Leader, you don't want them going off by themselves because you're afraid they might have a smoke and might, just accidentally, have a little fun."

Corey sniggered into his hand, and then ran off with Andreas in search of wood for the cook.

Warren let go and stepped back, tilting his head, scrutinising me. "Like on the boat? Were they just having a little bit of fun? Believe what you want, woman, but look after your charges!"

A cold chill shook me as I remembered and I rubbed my arm where he'd been holding it. I suddenly needed his warmth, but when I moved close to him he knocked the cigarette out of my hand, ground it into the dirt with his boot, and then pointed behind me.

"Watch them *all the time!*"

I looked around just in time to see a barefoot Jason disappear behind an enormous boab with Melanie and Laurel. Looked like snake fodder to me. I bit my lip and followed, catching up with them just as they were lighting up a small joint. I guessed that they might be just as stressed as I was, what with nearly losing a friend and all, so I allowed each to have a toke before I interrupted and took it away, burying it in the loose dirt.

"You can't be smoking this shit here," I said, trying to sound authoritarian. "Jason, put on your shoes before you step on something deadly, and not one of you is wearing a hat. Get back to the camp now and get ready for dinner. You three can do the washing up tonight and thank me later for not reporting this to Officer George."

Oh, my God. Did I sound like a copper or a mother or what? Once the kids were gone, I dug up that sorry excuse for a joint and stuck it in my own sock. It made me feel a little bit like an outlaw again, but when I wandered back to our group to see the kids in their own little huddles, I just felt like an outsider.

From the shelter of my lonely tent I looked around the camp ground, my world for the moment. It wasn't very full since November, especially late November, is hardly the shoulder season in the NT. If the wildlife doesn't get you, the heat will. The few campers there were primarily the Grey Nomad types, people trying to avoid crowds of unruly teenagers. I probably should have been sympathetic to their bad luck, i.e., arriving at the National Parks the same time we did, but mostly, I was envious of their TVs, satellite phones, adult company and, yes, their friendships. I was very alone in our group of fourteen. Every time I approached Mary, my almost-ally, she was with one of the young folk; talking, cooking, drinking tea, "bonding." No fair. I needed a mother too.

Dinner that night was a repeat of last night and the kids devoured it just as greedily but the atmosphere was subdued. I was so tired; I didn't have the energy to go chasing after rambunctious boys and girls so I welcomed the peace. There was no attempt to sing around the campfire, no protests of "I never go to bed before midnight!" We just ate and collapsed. Mary took the new orange T-shirts and washed them in the hand basin in the toilet block, and then hung them on a line to dry. I thought this was a lovely idea and found the change in my purse to run them through the dryer instead.

"That way they're sure to be dry by morning," I said.

"A little extra money sure helps make life easier," Mary said. "Sometimes you're all right, Lou."

Absurdly pleased at the compliment, I wrapped my sleeping bag around my weary body. As I tried to doze off, though, I gradually became aware of little moans coming from inside the other tents and dragged myself out to go investigating. I shone my torch into the first tent I came to and found Melanie and Sara sitting on their sleeping bags, holding their heads and stomachs. I touched their foreheads and they were burning. I turned my tired brain back to the St John's First Aid course I'd done in high school and thought, "Heatstroke."

Amazingly, my diagnosis must have been correct. Most of

the juvies (Jason and Timbo's tent was the only one that remained silent) were suffering from mild sunstroke so I made myself busy providing fluids. I mixed a small amount of red cordial with a lot of water–no sports drink available here, mate!–and passed out the weak drink with Home Brand paracetamol (was there anything they didn't make?) and sympathy. I then dug hats and caps out of backpacks for tomorrow. The kids were all sound asleep before the first firefly appeared.

The camp was finally quiet but I was wide awake. I stood alone near the bus, drinking the last of the cordial, looking at the stars, looking at the universe. Able, at last, to forget the horrors of the day. I also forgot my loneliness. I was falling in love and allowed myself to enter the night as though I were entering my lover's boudoir. Looking around at this godforsaken desert under the moonlight, I even allowed myself to be proud of the behaviour that had resulted in this CSO.

"And fuck you, Your Honour," I toasted the judge with the last of my watery red drink and wished it were a nice cabernet sauvignon.

The darkness hovered around me like it was protecting me from unsuitable behaviour, teasing me with its hint of smells– maybe wildflowers, maybe a nearby billabong, maybe small night creatures. I found myself waiting for Warren, but he didn't appear and I got, oddly, the tiniest pang of neglect but was too tired to try to interpret or even regret these feelings. I finally crawled into my tent, donned my sleepwear, and lost consciousness without a single R-rated thought.

I dreamt about Sydney. I was on a yacht, in a race and we were entering the Heads a mile in front of all the others, and I could see my parents high on the cliffs, waving me in. Suzanne and Claudia were on the foreshore, both dressed in diaphanous gowns blowing like signal flags in the breeze, popping champagne corks and toasting my victory. I turned around and saw Dalby behind me, dropping the sail and turning the rudder. I frowned at him. He was deliberately slowing me down, allowing other yachts to fly past and reach the finish line ahead of me. It was my yacht, my decision to make, so where did he get off ensuring that I lost? I tried to protest but my voice wouldn't work. I shouted and shouted, but I was mute.

Then we were in bed together in his room. He above me, up on outstretched arms, holding himself off me, teasing me with his hard prick. I lay below him, ravenous for a root but he would not enter me. I begged and he grinned maliciously. Whenever I tried to touch him he pulled away.

"Don't fuck with me, Louisa," he said. "I am your future."

I woke up in a cold sweat. There was definitely something wrong with my brain and I wanted to blame this wretched Outback.

"Fuck you, your honour," I said again and tried to go back to sleep. Dalby and my future were too difficult to think about tonight. Besides, the sad fact of the matter was that I wanted Warren, not my fiancé, but Warren didn't want me and I feared, as I lay there in my pool of perspiration, that I was doomed to be frustrated every minute of my natural life. Why couldn't I have married Dalby when I had the chance, back when I had no idea how miserable my existence was?

CHAPTER TWELVE

AT DINNER THE NIGHT BEFORE, Warren had announced that we would try to make Kununurra by lunch time. He'd been his usual jovial self–jovial around the kids, that is.

"Of course, that's means an early start but, we can do it," he'd said heartily. "I want everybody up by emu fart. We can pack up while Mary is cooking another one of her delicious breakfasts and be ready to hit the road by 7:30. How's that for a plan?"

There'd been a few groans. Jason had hollered, "You betcha, Boss!" and Gazza had fallen backwards off the log he'd been sitting on, not even waking up when his head bounced on the hard ground. But, as the poet observed, "the best laid plans of mice and men gang aft aglae."

Emu fart came and went. Even the kookaburras had fallen silent by the time Mary had the sausages sizzling on one of the campground's gas barbecues. Kids who were accustomed to city streets dragged themselves through tent flaps, only to collapse on the ground when they tried to stand up. I fell back asleep after Warren sent Brooke to wake me, and I didn't emerge from my slumber until I smelled the toast burning.

"Oops, cooking the toast was supposed to be my job," I remembered as I sat in front of my tent, trying to lace up my damned hiking boots, still stiff with newness. I wished I'd brought sandals and the snakes be damned. Not really, but I'm very existential first thing in the morning.

I heard a harsh, hacking cough and looked up to see Corey crouching near the table, sounding as if he were coughing up a lung. One untied boot on a foot and the other in my hand, I rushed over in concern. Fortunately, I managed to avoid stepping on any early morning reptiles with my sock-clad foot.

"Hey, mate, what's up? Did you catch pneumonia in the river yesterday?" I asked as I thumped him on the back.

"Naw, it ain't that," he gasped as he tried to catch his breath.

"I reckon it's all this fresh air. The shit'll kill you!"

"Plus, he got a bit of toast stuck in his throat," Andreas volunteered.

"And no wonder! My body don't know how to digest food this early, 'specially when it's all burnt. I never eat before Macca's is serving their burgers."

"I could go a Big Mac right now," Andreas agreed.

McDonald's aside, the sudden image of these poor little city mice trying to become country mice hit my funny bone and I started laughing and couldn't stop. Warren had come over to see what the commotion was, heard Corey's remark about the fresh air, and slapped that disapproving frown across his face again.

"This is not a laughing matter, Miss Smith," he admonished, and then to Corey, "The fresh air is probably trying to clean all the tar and smoke from your poor lungs, mate. Be grateful."

He turned and walked away, ramrod straight. Corey and I looked at each other and laughed again. Poor Warren. Did he ever have any fun in his life? He took it all much too seriously. Andreas picked up Corey's sandshoes.

"Phew, these don't half pong," he said, holding his nose. Corey snatched them away.

"Yeah, well, they did get a bit wet yesterday and had to dry on my feet."

"Man, those poor shoes."

The boys walked off discussing the trials and tribulations of bush life. I stopped laughing. The flashback of Corey and the croc sobered me up and I looked around, trying to find a young life to save but nobody appeared to be in imminent danger. They were dragging their arses this morning, in no hurry to get going and not wandering far from breakfast.

Fat Gazza was the last to appear. Even if we all had been ready when Warren had wanted us to be, we couldn't have gone anywhere without the driver. I caught the sick smell of old alcohol oozing from his pores as he brushed past me toward the food. He must have got it from the other campers because surely Warren wouldn't allow him to keep his own stash. He was bringing the expression "sly grog" to a new level because there was no mistaking the sights, sounds, and smells of a chronic drunk who was still drinking. This morning at the food table he had to make do with the left over toast but it would be sticking to his ribs since he'd soaked up all the sausage grease with it.

He was, not surprisingly, bleary-eyed and unpleasant. I saw him eat four aspirin with his breakfast and hoped, for our sakes, that it would help. We were packed and in our seats by the time he'd finished whatever morning ablutions he engaged in. He grunted as he climbed the bus steps with the effort it would take to climb the Eiffel Tower. He dropped into his driving seat and bent over the steering wheel, panting to catch his breath. Just my luck, the old bastard would have a heart attack out here and leave us stranded without a driver. I wasn't sure my first aid skills went much beyond heatstroke so I wouldn't be any help if he needed reviving. He wasn't much, but he was the only bus driver we had and we were in the middle of the Never-Never. Finally, he managed to take a deep, cleansing breath, hawk a wad of I-don't-want-to-know-what out the window and gunned our vehicle into movement, spitting sand and gravel into the clouds of exhaust as it mounted the tarmac and took off down the highway. Warren stared silently out his window. Now that I was beginning to feel a responsibility for these kids, I had to take this behaviour seriously. I turned to Mary.

"That arsehole must have a stash of alcohol somewhere! Isn't that illegal on an under-age tour? Everybody knows he gets drunk every night. Why doesn't 'Officer George' say something or do something?"

"Haven't you heard? It's us Abo's have the problem with the sly grog, not the whities, and *certainly* not the coppers. Truth is, Lou, I don't reckon Officer O'Brien has drawn a sober breath in twenty years. Hell, he'd probably be more dangerous if he wasn't drinking. Don't you worry. Warren knows what he's doing." Mary's answer was too cynical to be reassuring. She opened her book.

"I wish I could believe that, Mary, but it's bloody obvious..." I tried to protest but she just shook her head and continued to read. Well, it was bloody obvious to me, and if it happened again tomorrow, *I* would bloody well say something! I was in my usual back seat and opened my bag, fishing around inside it for my paperback. I was a third of the way through a crime novel and the second corpse had been found just before I fell asleep last night. The kids were quiet and there were no vicious predators they needed protection from on the bus. I could just relax and pretend that my life was normal for a couple of hours.

That pretence was short-lived. The body had barely been lifted onto the coroner's cart when I became aware of small whimpering noises. I glanced up and saw Brooke, sitting alone in one of the rear seats, blubbering into her hands. Spider and Sara, several seats ahead, were watching her and sniggering. Warren, at the front, was sitting between Andreas and Caleb, pointing out the window and talking intently.

It'll keep, I thought, *no harm's being done.* I was really not good at dealing with tears–especially teenage tears–and I prayed silently for it to stop. Brooke was cute, the only one of the lot who didn't look anorexic. Her olive skin and almond-shaped eyes confirmed her Filipina background, and her plump figure suggested that she enjoyed a good meal. She had beautiful, straight, black hair that reached nearly to her waist. I remembered the pathetic tube top that couldn't quite cover her boobs and was silently grateful for her orange T-shirt. She definitely looked sturdy and self-reliant to me.

The restrained crying carried on, though. It was very disturbing and was reviving bad memories. At age fifteen I'd had problems with weight and complexion and I'll never forget those girls on the netball team. They took great pleasure in pointing out to anyone who would listen how ridiculous I'd looked in my short skirt, all fat thighs and bulging belly. It sounded so silly now, but back then...well, my stomach still churned when I thought of those days and had always blamed them on my inability to bond with any organized sport. *Maybe this is part of my "job,"* I thought with a big sigh. I noticed Mary glancing in Brooke's direction and decided not to await instructions from Warren. I placed a slim, silver bookmark between the pages, closed my book, and joined Brooke.

"What's up, girl?" I asked, putting an arm around her shaking shoulders. Brooke sobbed, Spider chortled, and I looked up, catching a sneer on Sara's face. I gave them both a severe look. They hurriedly faced forward and Brooke sniffed.

"It's nothing, Miss, truly. Guess I'm just homesick, ya know?"

"I know exactly what you mean. I'm homesick as well. What do you miss the most?" I asked, giving the girl a small hug. She was just homesick? This would be a piece of cake.

"It's not missing stuff, so much, Miss, it's more like I'm worried about my baby sister Bridget. She's just eleven, eh."

"Why are you worried about Bridget?"

"I'm scared that while I'm not there my dad'll get stuck into her."

Oh...shit. This wasn't going to be as easy as I'd hoped.

"Does your dad hit you? Does Bridget drink as well?"

She shrugged. "He hits us a bit, of course, but mostly I'm worried he'll go into her room at night and—well, you know how dads are."

A chill ran down my spine. No, in fact, I had no idea about dads like that. My dad could certainly make a nuisance of himself when he would decide to interfere in my social life and insist on driving me and friends to parties, and then picking us up at what *he* considered a suitable hour. I remembered feeling hurt and angry when he missed my first school play because he was overseas on business, but I didn't think these were the sorts of fatherly transgressions Brooke was talking about. In fact, I knew so little about dads like that, that I hoped I misunderstood her. Yes, that had to be it. I gripped her shoulders tighter but didn't know what to say.

"See, I'm older." She looked at me earnestly, trying to sound mature through her sniffles. "I'm fifteen and I've got sort of used to it. I can take it, but Bridget is so little. She doesn't know much, Miss, and I should be there to look out for her." She wiped her nose on her shirt sleeve.

"Of course, you should," I said automatically, finding a packet of tissues in one of my pockets, but *No way should you have that responsibility* was what I was thinking. "Don't you have a mother?"

"Yeah, of course I do, Miss," she smiled incredulously. "But she's pregnant again and she's pretty old and I don't think Dad likes her too much anymore. If he got stuck into her she might have a miscarriage or something."

"I see..."

What else could I say? I'd been struck dumb. I'd come forward to help plump young Brooke deal with how she looked in shorts. Now I so wanted time to reverse itself and go back to a few minutes ago so I could keep reading my book and not hear this story. Face it. There was nothing I could do about Brooke's family. I sure as hell didn't have any advice to give this poor girl so why shouldn't I go back to my seat now? Most of me wanted to but I couldn't.

"Good thing it's only a week," I said lamely.

"True," Brooke sniffed and wiped her eyes with a tissue. She glanced up at me with a small smile. "A week's not that long, and he probably won't even do nothing. Thanks, Miss, I reckon you'd understand dads better than I do, being old and all."

"Old?" I was liking this conversation less and less. I took the coward's way out and changed the subject. "Have you ever been on one of these Outback tours before?"

"No, well, because this is the first one ever. I've just had warnings about going into Juvie before, but this time the judge said it was high time I learned there was more to life than getting drunk and he reckoned this'd be better than detention." She gave a little giggle. "I think I prefer getting drunk, though, compared to falling in a river full of man-eating crocs."

"I think that's a pretty smart preference, Brooke. Well, maybe not getting drunk—but anything has to better than getting eaten by a croc!" I put my arm around her shoulder and gave her a little hug.

"You think I'm smart, Miss?" Brooke hung her head and peered at me timidly with those almond eyes.

"I think you're smart and strong and that you have a good heart, Brooke. I wish I had a sister like you."

She sat up straight, smiled, and heaved a large sigh as she used the tail of her T-shirt to wipe her face. "You're all right, Miss."

I gave her another tissue. "Why were Spider and Sara bothering you?"

"They're just being stupid, calling me a fat slope and saying my mum is a mail-order bride. My mum may be Asian, but AT LEAST *SHE'S* MARRIED!" She hollered that last bit at the backs of their heads and made a face at them. "Don't let them worry you none."

"I won't, and don't you let them worry you, either, OK? You are not a slope, you're a beautiful *Eurasian...*, and you're certainly not fat."

Giving council gave me an odd sense of satisfaction. How weird was that? I had no doubt that Brooke's tale would return to haunt me over and over again, but now, in this minute, we were both safe and smiling. We carried on chatting about nothing in particular until the bus pulled into a small roadside park for morning tea. The juvies, after sitting for two hours, flew through the door of their cage like a flock of birds suddenly set free. I moved far more slowly, leaning against a picnic table to stretch my back and hamstrings.

"I saw you having a word with Brooke." I hadn't realized that Warren was standing directly behind me and startled me so I nearly tore one of my hammies. "Any problems?"

I recovered quickly. "A couple of the others were giving her a hard time, that's all." Somehow, sharing my knowledge, even with the boss, would be betraying a confidence.

"Yeah, they do like to torment each other. It looks like they're OK together now." He nodded to where Sara and Brooke stood, holding hands and laughing. The sight made me smile, but when I looked up to share my pleasure with Warren he had disappeared without so much as a "Good job, Louisa." Once a bastard...I finished my stretches and tried to forget about his insolence, which was easy because things started going wrong.

The gas barbie didn't want to heat the water, a couple of the boys didn't want to come out of the toilet ("We're not doing drugs, Boss, we got the shits from all these veggies!") and then Melanie stopped to have a vomit so the twenty minute break turned into forty. At this rate, lunch would be mid-afternoon but schedules, like rules, were made to be broken, no matter how anal your tour guide was. He so needed to relax and I amused myself by thinking up any number of ways to help him expend his pent up energy. Most of them involved a red sarong and, once again, my fantasies got me in trouble because I wasn't paying attention to what was going on around me.

Mary had magically started one of her fires to boil some water, so I sat alone at a table, idly drinking a second cup of instant coffee, awaiting orders to move from the boss, lost in my thoughts.

Gazza drank several cups of strong, sweet tea and must have been feeling better. He displayed this change of mood by sitting next to me at the table and running his hand up my thigh. His touch shocked me out of my reverie but he was under my shorts and nearly at my panties before I reacted. I grabbed him by the thumb the instant before he reached anything strategic, and bent it back as hard as I could.

"Pain turns me on, Love," he grinned and reached with his other hand. Thinking fast, I knocked my hot cup of coffee into his lap and jumped free when he stood up, cursing. The kids, who were helping themselves to tea and bikkies despite their various illnesses, had a good laugh at his wet shorts as he tried to slap the heat away. He stomped off to the toilet block and Mary waved me over to the tap where she was filling a washing-up bowl for the cups.

"You be careful there, Lou," she warned. "That's one guy you don't want as an enemy."

"Well, I'd rather have him as an enemy than a lover!" I replied heartily as I dipped my mug into the soapy water.

I saw Warren, at another table, frowning and shaking his head, as usual. At me? At The Pig? At the general behaviour? Who knew? What I did know was that, as my supervisor, he should be taking steps to protect me from predators, both foreign and domestic. But he was doing jack and I was not happy about his inaction.

"If you think this behaviour is inappropriate, then why the fuck don't you do something about it?" I called to him.

"Please don't swear," he said and got up to wash his cup. I nearly threw mine at his head but pulled back just in time. If I injured the boss, I'd most likely have to finish the tour *and* do time in Berrimah when we got back.

Gazza came out of the toilets, shorts nearly dry. His mood was really filthy now and he boarded the bus angrily, flinging himself into his seat and grinding the engine to life.

"I'll have youse in WA in plenty of time for lunch but you better get your arses up here now!"

Tires dug holes in the track and the motor protested loudly as he pressed the accelerator with the clutch still engaged. Tea drinkers scrambled, tossing the rest of their drinks onto the ground, cramming whole bikkies into their mouths, and hurriedly dipping dirty mugs into the plastic basin Mary held. She dashed the dirty water onto the ground, shoved everything into the trailer, closed the latch, and then we all jumped onto the bus, nearly losing poor Melanie who had been in the toilet during Gazza's tantrum. She ran up just as the bus was beginning to pick up speed and Jason reached out a hand to grab her and fling her in through the still-open door.

The kids thought it great fun and whooped it up while Warren sat silent and I seethed. We sped along at a frightening speed. I'd heard that speed limits in the NT were flexible, but this was ridiculous. I watched Warren as he watched the desert fly past. Why didn't he man up? Nothing made sense to me and this guided tour was revealing more bloody layers of intrigue than I could cope with. I closed my eyes and tried to sleep.

"Just wake me up when we're dead," I said to Mary.

CHAPTER THIRTEEN

OUTSIDE KUNUNURRA (which we did, indeed, reach in record time) we passed a fish and chips shop and I awoke, alive, as Jason set up the hue and cry. "Aw, please, Officer George! Them lettuce salads are killing me. My body *needs* the grease."

"Oh, yes, Boss!" Spider joined in. "I grew up on the coast. I fuckin' need the fish. It's brain food, ya know."

"Too late for you, Spider," Warren replied with a smile. "And no swearing."

"Please, please, *please!*" Sara, Timbo, and the others joined in. "Tell him, Miss, explain how us growing kids need fried food."

OK, I'll admit it. I was flattered by their patronage. Yes, boys and girls, my affections can be bought. I joined in the begging until Warren stood in the aisle and raised his arms.

"All right, all right! I give in! Gazza, turn the bus around and we will feast on a lunch of fish and chips. But," he pointed menacingly at Jason, "this is a one-off and it'll be camp food, fruits, and veggies from here on out."

"Yes, Boss. You betcha, Boss. Health and fitness for us, Boss," Jason stood in the aisle and saluted. Warren cuffed him good-naturedly on the side of the head and everybody laughed. Even Gazza was in a good mood now.

He, no surprise, must have been craving a greasy meal as well because he had us pulling into the parking lot almost before I drew breath. Pity, because once those doors opened, I didn't get a chance to breathe for a very long time.

The eatery was part of one of those service stations cum mini-malls that dot the Outback and that are always named after somebody's well. Behind the buildings was a picnic area with, incredibly, a green lawn and shade trees. Somebody must have been using his well water to keep this little oasis going.

Ten boys and girls pushed each other out of the way, shouting orders, grabbing drinks, and downing them before any costs could be rung up and, generally, behaving like the young hooligans they were. At the height of the melee, Gazza, using his big arms and ham fists, pushed his way to the front of the line and ordered three pieces of fish and two servings of chips for himself.

"Don't forget your sunscreen and hats!" My own Akubra firmly in place, I stood to the side of the line distributing the caps most of the kids had left on their seats in their scramble for takeaway. Melanie grabbed the first cap and put it on backwards.

"I don't think wearing it like that will be very effective against the sun," I cautioned in my best motherly voice.

"I don't think wearing it any other way will be very effective against dorks!" was the reply and I shrugged. I'd made the effort. Even dork Warren could see that. Besides, I was starving and anxious to get the line served as quickly as possible, since I was at the end of it.

Inside the shop I kept an especially close eye on Melanie and Caleb, our light-fingered duo, but I didn't really trust any of them not to lift a soft drink or two. I removed several packets of chips and candy bars from beneath a few T-shirts and hoped that I got them all. The mayhem continued while we waited for the food, and then, once it arrived, the air was full of complaints of "This isn't what I ordered." I no longer wanted to be the hero so I distributed paper packets of food and ordered each child to consume what he/she was given. Each did, of course. No one really cared whether or not it was what he/she had ordered, as long as it was greasy and familiar.

The picnic area was a wonderful contrast to the diesel and dust we'd been living with and even the juvies must have appreciated it because when peace and full bellies finally reigned and Warren ordered them to pick up all the greasy papers and aluminium cans that had blown throughout the outdoor eating area and dispose of the rubbish properly, no-one objected. They cleaned the place completely and I, after the most exhausting meal of my life, was impressed. When we were back on the bus, I told them so.

"You people did a top job of cleaning up there. Why, you could nearly eat on those tables now!"

The juvies, obviously unaccustomed to compliments, only grunted and shuffled as if to break the awkward silence, and then Timbo farted loudly. At that they cheered.

"Now perhaps you understand why it's not a good idea to stop at take-aways," Warren whispered in my ear as he pulled a contraband candy bar out of Caleb's pocket.

"Perhaps." I couldn't believe he was speaking to me in a civilized manner and smiled up at him, but he was already concentrating on his microphone leaving me to waste my smile on thin air. *Fucking bastard won't ever give me a break.* I removed my hat, brushed damp curls out of my eyes, and went to the rear of the bus.

THE SMELL OF FISH AND CHIPS took me back to Watson's Bay. When I was little, my parents would take me, my older brother, and my two baby sisters there. We'd get on the Manly ferry where the salt air would whip up our appetites and Dad would buy us each a packet of crisps to tide us over 'til lunch. Once we arrived, we were allowed to run like wild Indians through the park, climb the overhanging fig trees until the green ants chased us down, splash on the beach, and race each other up the steps to the Sydney Heads. I suppose playing in the grass, climbing trees, and swimming in the bay could be considered associating with nature, but I'm sure Watson's Bay is so much safer than the Outback.

When I was older and went there with my friends we eschewed the park in favour of drinking Guinness in O'Reilly's Pub, staggering up the steps to watch the Sydney to Hobart yacht race begin, and then staggering back down to drink champagne because it was afternoon by then. One lovely summer afternoon while at uni, Suzanne, Claudia, and I went for a girls' Sunday Session to cheer up Claudia because her boyfriend had just dumped her.

"He was an idjit, anyway," I said, in keeping with the Irish theme, and ordered another pint of Guinness.

"He was an idjit," agreed a tearful Claudia, "but he was my idjit, and I didn't have to go looking for a lay in seedy pubs like you two."

"This is true," said Suzanne, "but Louisa and I have spent many a blissful hour looking for lays in seedy pubs. Much more fun and profitable than looking for a lay in an art gallery."

"This is true," I echoed. We were all being so very agreeable. "Although I must concede that looking for the lay can often be much more fun than the *actual* lay itself. Suzanne must know this already because she has never, *actually*, taken home one of these seedy lays. Or was it seedy pubs? Whatever, it is a sad fact that many men who spend their days in seedy pubs tend to make many promises they can't keep. I am here to tell you that Brewer's Droop is not an urban myth."

Claudia laughed at that, and then she and Suzanne went to the Ladies' to wash their faces and prepare their bladders to receive more Guinness. We had been quite pleased to discover that Irish ales are, in fact, very nutritious so we didn't have to eat while drinking them. While they were gone, a tall Viking with long, silky blond hair sat down beside me.

"Hi," he said in a Swedish accent, brushing the hair from his eyes. "My name is Sven."

"Of course it is." I smiled and forgot about my friends. By the time they returned, Sven had his hand on my breast, my hand was massaging his inner thigh, and we were discussing the chances of an Australian meeting a Scandinavian in a bar in Sydney.

"Does Sweden even have a royal family?" I asked, perversely proud of my ignorance.

"Of course we do, and I am the crown prince."

"I don't think he is, Louisa," cautioned Claudia.

"I don't think I care, Claudia." I threw caution to the wind. "These are my friends, Sven. Do you have any friends for them?"

He looked the girls over. Claudia is dark and petite, with brown eyes and long black hair which, that Sunday, was gathered at the nape of her neck by a green velvet ribbon. Suzanne is fair, tall, and buxom, to put it mildly. Her cup size is double D, but she wasn't wearing a bra. ("Not to an Irish pub," she'd explained. "Isn't one expected to look earthy in a place like that?") When she leaned forward to shake Sven's hand, her right boob tried to break free from her tight singlet. Sven's cock reacted and I tightened my grip.

"Hey, finders keepers," I said. "I suggest we leave these two to find their own men and you and I can go down to the beach and look for long boats."

His cock did a double take.

"OK. Those guys over there," he indicated two more tall blonds at the bar, "are my mates and I bet they would appreciate to know you. Lars, Ingmar!" he called and waved them over. He and I stood up as the other Vikings eagerly sat down. Sven's baggy board shorts hid what was happening in his knickers. We walked down to the beach, arms around each other until we found a private cove.

He pulled me to him and we kissed, tasting tongues and each other's Guinness breath. My hands went into his pockets to check things out. No Brewer's Droop there. His cock was long and hard and throbbing. I could feel its heat through the cloth but wanted to feel the skin in my palm. I unbuttoned his shorts, reached into his skivies, stroked his balls, and gripped his hot dick. He lowered me onto the sand, out of the sight of passing boats (I hoped) and undressed me. He touched my very wet pussy, kissed my very erect nipples, and licked my very swollen clitoris. Then he gave an impatient grunt and quickly slid a condom on. He lay over me, finding port at first thrust. He took me with the calm assurance of a Viking lord claiming his prize, moving slowly at first, and then, before I could come, he pumped hard and erupted with a cry. In the interest of safety, he reached down to hold the condom and exited quickly.

"I apologize to come so fast. Australia is a very passionate country."

"It's OK," I lied, trying not to sound too disappointed. I put my hand on his chest but he took it and placed it on his wet cock. Surprisingly, it reacted as soon as I touched it.

"I will be ready soon if you can suck my dick," he said, so I did.

It was still a bit flaccid when I put it in my mouth but tasted yummy and I sucked plenty. It was hot and hard again in a jiffy. I rolled a fresh condom on with my mouth and straddled him, grinding my fanny into his groin. His shaft was so long I could feel it in my tonsils and was forced to lean forward, my nipples caressing his fine, blond chest hairs, teasing him until I came, sitting up straight, arching my back, and crying out through the spasms. This excited him more and, when I was finished, he gripped my hips and moved in me with the smooth rhythm of rowing a longboat until he came again.

We were both stuffed by then and fell asleep, naked in the sun. Of course I had a pounding headache when we woke up and he remained limp under my helpful fingers, but he wasn't at all embarrassed and kindly fondled me 'til I came. What can I say? An orgasm is better than aspirin any day.

We got dressed and walked back to O'Reilly's to find the others waiting for us.

"Did you find a longboat?" asked Suzanne.

"Did I ever!" I replied. I never did ask Claudia how she enjoyed the session that had been meant to cheer her up, but since she and Ingmar are still together, I'm guessing she thought it went all right. I know that the memory of Sven is still one of my favourites.

Suzanne didn't really hit it off with Lars, but she and a comely Irish barmaid had become quite friendly and Lars had been happy enough just watching them.

I WOKE WITH A START when a body fell on me. I couldn't believe I'd fallen asleep again and hoped I hadn't done or said anything in my sleep that might have given my dreams away. I pushed the boy off me and sat up as the toilet door slammed.

"What in the name of all that's holy is going on here?"

"I gotta go really bad, Miss, but Timbo pushed me out of the way. He reckons he was first. Sorry about falling on ya, Miss."

"Don't worry about it."

I blinked my eyes and tried to wake up properly. I looked at the boy in front of me, all brown skin and big brown eyes and straight black hair. A single black eyebrow crossed his forehead and his eyelashes were long enough to hang a heart on. His lips were thin and his nose Roman. *Looks more Indian than Indigenous*, I thought.

"You're Caleb, right?"

"Yes, Miss, that's right."

He smiled, showing a mouthful of white tombstones for teeth and his eyebrow raised an inch or two. He looked pleasantly surprised that I knew who he was. I smiled back, Mary looked at us and smiled, Timbo came out of the toilet grinning, and we were all friends together. It might be a small thing to know one boy's name, but I found it extremely gratifying. Caleb went into the toilet and Timbo continued up to his seat, still grinning. I smiled at Mary and she gave me one of those famous, unfathomable looks and returned to her reading.

"I hope you won't be having any more of them dreams," she said quietly with a knowing chuckle. I blushed from my toes to my hairline.

CHAPTER FOURTEEN

AFTER KUNUNURRA we had turned south toward Lake Argyle and arrived at the campground in a flash, I suppose because I had slept through most of the trip. A Range Rover towing a silver caravan with a solar panel on its roof was already there and an elderly couple sat under its canopy, drinking mugs of, presumably, tea. They took one look at us and swore. I recognised them from the Gregory National Park and gave them a cheery wave. The glare I received in return would have melted steel but, hey, I'm just flesh and bone so it went straight through me. Warren must have seen the look as well because he guided Gazza to a campsite far away from the oldies.

We finally found a place to set up camp. The features I liked best were the enormous power lines, in whose shade we erected our tents. We might not have electricity where we were, but their presence reassured me that, somewhere in this troubled land, civilization and polite society ruled. Other than that, we had concrete tables and benches, boulders, some nice trees growing by the lake, and sand. Always sand. There was an amenities block with a couple of solar spotlights mounted on the roof which had showers and, at this time of year, the sun beating down on the pipes provided solar hot water between 7 a.m. and 10 p.m. meant that the showers were only cool enough to tolerate very late at night or very early in the morning. The toilets were *au natural,* composted by harmless chemicals, earthworms, or some other greenie thing. Anyway, this godforsaken place was so arid that every organic thing quickly mummifies, even, I'm guessing, our shit. As a chemical engineer I probably should have been interested but, in God's truth, my career was the farthest thing from my mind. I'd never included long-drop toilets in my career plan. The few times when I pictured my future at all it was in a pristine lab coat, working in a modern, state-of-the-art laboratory for some multi-million dollar conglomerate, maybe designing smudge-free lipstick for super models. My brother calls me shallow but what would he know? He's a guy, and besides, I've heard him complain about lipstick on his collar, especially when it wasn't his girlfriend's!

We all hopped out and gathered round our fearless leader to listen to his usual pep talk/warning.

"We'll be staying here for three days and four nights so things will feel a bit more permanent," he reassured us. "Daylong bus rides can get pretty boring, I know. You'll like it here. From the campsite we'll travel each day to visit some amazing, natural phenomenon."

"As amazing as Corey getting ate by a croc?" Jason had to ask.

"Right now, Boss, I think an amazing natural phenomenon would be somebody else putting up my tent while I sleep," said Timbo, scratching his head.

It is my belief that most people who wear dreadlocks do so because they don't like washing their hair. Timbo was no exception and I shuddered to think what creatures might be causing his scalp itch.

"Good one," the boss smiled, "but I'm afraid that's not the way it happens here. Look at it this way. Once you get the tents up they can stay that way for four whole nights! So, who can get their tent up the fastest? There might be prize in it for you."

Those kids must have been gamblers at heart because I could not believe how they scrambled to win the prize. Melanie and Sara were the first but protested mightily when the award turned out to be two apples. We all got a good laugh out of that. Then the rot began to set in.

It was the third day and their combined lack of fitness for the Outback was becoming glaringly obvious. Laurel was allergic to some biting insect and her lower legs were swollen and blistered. Her hair was naturally blond and her formerly pale complexion was now a high pink. Corey and Spider's mossie bites were infected from constant scratching, while the "cool" dudes who'd worn their baseball caps turned backwards were suffering from severely sunburned faces.

"I can't even get my shoes on, Miss," Laurel complained. "I'll have to wear thongs, and then I'll get bit by a snake!" I tried to be sympathetic, but when she and Timbo went off on their nightly forage for fuel, I made sure he wore snake-proof boots and gave Laurel a pair of my thick woollen hiking socks.

"Socks and thongs, Miss?" she protested. "Like, super-dork!"

"Like, no-snake-bite-dork," I replied.

"I can't stop scratching, Miss," Spider dug at the red spots in his arms. "These mossies ain't nothing like what we got in Darwin. I'm used to them."

I threatened to cut all of his fingernails right off and told Melanie that her red skin was sunburn, not an allergic reaction to fresh air.

"Get real, Miss. How could I of got sunburned riding in a bus?"

"You haven't been in the bus the entire day and I warned you about wearing your cap like that." I tried reason but reason was lost on the youngsters. They wanted relief from their discomfort and, most of all, they wanted to blame somebody else. I was in complete agreement, as long as they weren't blaming me. I still blamed the judge who'd sent them out here.

As I dug through the medicine kit, swearing under my breath and looking for lotions, ointments, and unguents, I heard someone vomiting nearby. Afraid it might be Melanie again I went searching. Looking behind a nearby gum tree, I found Jason bending over, holding his gut.

"Must have been too many chips," I said, placed my hand on his back, and tried to sound sympathetic without spewing myself.

"Must of been them salads," he answered when he could. "I don't know how anybody can call that shit healthy!"

"I'm no nurse, but maybe I can find something in the box that can help you."

"Don't bother, Miss. Better out than in, as they say."

I shouldn't have been surprised by his response. I'd always suspected that these kids knew how to look after themselves far better than I did. I sighed and returned to my ever increasing number of patients. I found bottles of Dettol, tubes of Betadine, and Paw Paw (whatever the hell *that* was) ointments, Tiger Balm, bandages, and plasters of assorted sizes. With a false bravado that was meant to inspire trust, I went to work but, when all was said and done, I'm sure that the cups of tea Mary handed out with her gentle smile were doing far more good. After an eternity I was free to wipe the sweat from my forehead and get my own cuppa.

"Funny how good this makes you feel, even on a day as hot as this."

"You're doing a fine job there, Lou," Mary said.

"You reckon?" Stirring two heaping spoonfuls of white sugar around a Home Brand teabag, I shook my head. "I feel like I'm going two steps backward for every one forward. I don't think I'm cut out to be a mother."

"Mothering usually starts with one baby, not ten teenagers."

"Do you have any children?" I tasted my tea and it was delicious.

"Lord, yes. Six, to be exact."

Just then Gazza slouched over to join us, looking like one of Dian Fossey's gorillas. If he'd slumped one centimetre more, his knuckles would have been dragging.

"When's dinner?" he grunted, scratched an armpit, and I snorted my lovely cuppa all over Mary.

"Aren't you still filled up from lunch?" she asked him as she wiped her face. "I don't know how you can be hungry."

That pissed him off. "Hey, you're the cook. It's not your job to decide when I'm hungry. How long before it'll be ready?"

"Give me an hour or so. It'll be something light after that big lunch. I don't think any of the kids got much of an appetite."

"You better make sure I get my meat! These bloody kids can eat what they're given." He stomped away in the direction of another campsite where several rough-looking men were gathered around a large Esky in the back of a Ute.

"He's going to get drunk again tonight." I couldn't believe it. "That guy may be related to the commissioner but surely there's something Warren can do!"

"Don't you be saying anything against Mr Warren, now." Mary stood. "Lou, do you really want that fat bastard sitting in the back of the bus with you, me, and the kids?" She shook her head and walked away, leaving me feeling inadequate again. Couldn't I get anything right? Sometimes it was like there was a conspiracy of silence around here. What was it they wouldn't tell me?

The few youngsters who weren't feeling ill sat under a silver gum with Warren, watching him draw something in the dirt. I took advantage of the calm to crawl into my tent and pray for the trip to end. I think, at one point, I was on my knees, hands folded. I just wanted out.

I must have fallen asleep praying (Corey was right, this fresh air was obviously trying to kill me by giving me sleeping sickness) because the call to dinner woke me with a start. I crawled from my tent, damp with sweat and dopey from sleeping in the heat. The others had already started, the picnic table nearest our camp kitchen was crowded so I got a cup of tea and a piece of damper and took it to an empty table on the edge of the grounds. I realized my mistake too late.

Officer Pig joined me with a plate piled so high I doubted he'd be able to eat any without spilling half. The overpowering smell of rum on his breath combined with the smell of onions and the slurping, grunting noises he made as he ate. For the second time that day, I wanted to vomit. When he took a drink from my own cup of tea, I shook my head and laughed hollowly at the outrage. The pig, obviously misinterpreting my reaction, laughed as well, his mouth full. I turned away and saw Warren watching us, anger clouding his face. He stood up and began clearing the plates.

Oh, great. He probably thinks I'm flirting with this fat bastard to get out of work, I thought bitterly. *That arsehole probably thinks it's whities sticking together.* Was there any point in trying to make him see the truth? I tried to get up but Gazza's hand was on my leg again. The thumb trick hadn't work and he'd finished all my tea. My mind, still a bit numb from the afternoon nap in the heat, was completely blank. Warren was slamming the plates together now. Good thing they were made of tin!

Gazza's finger was nearly up to my crotch and my fist was tightening around my fork when Jason saved the day by staggering over and spewing all over the bus driver's dinner.

"What the...?" The copper's face turned purple, his eyes bugged out and, best of all, he raised both his hands to reach for the hapless boy's throat. I jumped free.

I'd never been so happy to see a plateful of puke in my life.

"Oh, Jason, you poor thing!" I couldn't keep the glee out of my voice as I pulled him out of harm's way. "I'm going to give you a tablet and put you to bed. No more food for you tonight."

By the time I had him and the other invalids settled, Gazza was snoring in his tent and Mary was washing out his clothes. I noticed that she was also washing the orange T-shirts again. What a great idea! I had envisioned the kids wearing their shirts every day, getting grubbier and grubbier until, by the end of the trip, JD ROC would be as unrecognizable as the dream that had created it. That dream! As seriously as Mary and the juveniles took it, I found myself hoping it would come true, for Warren's sake.

CHAPTER FIFTEEN

BLOODY WARREN! I dried the dishes and wondered where he'd got to, starting to feel cranky again. He had to sleep with The Pig each night and if he, even once, had been nice to me, I might have spared him a sympathetic thought. But I couldn't be bothered. Those bastard boys could bond forever as far as I was concerned.

The campsite was clean, clothes hung on bushes to dry, Mary had gone to bed, and he still hadn't appeared. He must be asleep too I decided. I wasn't tired. The sleeping sickness must only strike during daylight. Perched on a bench away from our tents I sat in the solitude, nursing a cup of coffee, unable to keep speculative thoughts from forming.

I wished I could figure him out. I wished I could figure myself out. He was my boss, for one thing, and not even a nice one at that! So why did I want to touch him so much? Why did I want him to touch me? It's not like I got the hots for every good-looking guy I laid eyes on. I've never slept with a man I couldn't have a laugh with. Suzanne works for a modelling agency so I get full-on exposure to gorgeous men, particularly since she's use to it and doesn't seem to appreciate the largesse, but if there wasn't a personality to go along with the looks, I couldn't be bothered. (Don't judge. Sven's personality was in his pants. Plus he had that Mary and Frederick thing in his corner.)

There was just something about Warren, and I really wanted to know what it was and how I should handle it before things got out of hand. Four more days of this emotional turmoil might just kill me—and there were so many physical things out here that might just kill me. How many times could one person die? It occurred to me, not for the first time, that Gazza was the one I *should* have been concentrating on. That guy was serious trouble and not only for me. But why ruin a beautiful night dwelling on The Pig? Suddenly, I remembered that grubby little roach I'd seconded the day before. Walking out to a boulder at the edge of the camp, I pulled my boot off and fished around inside until I found it, slightly the worse for wear but that didn't matter. I'd heard that Darwin ganja could be hot shit...and I wasn't disappointed.

With one boot on and the other beside me on the rock, I sat to smoke my little bit of heaven in the peace of the wilderness nightfall. It tasted of red dirt and unwashed feet and filled me with a blissful, mellow feeling. All my anxieties about kids, co-workers, and responsibilities in general drifted away as I became one with the night. A dense cloud covered the moon and the stars came down to touch the earth. Night sounds filled the air and my problems with the men on this trip faded away.

Gradually I became aware of an eerie booming noise from the direction of the river. It must have been the combination of drugs and magic because I became a part of the scene, a character in the night's little drama. Totally without fear, and also without one of my boots, I arose and walked to the river to find the source of the booming. I stood on the bank, peering through the blackness, invisible and invulnerable. Suddenly the cloud moved off the moon...and everything happened at once.

I saw, less than a metre in front of me, a massive crocodile on the riverbank, his back to me with jaws stretched open wide. The moonlight glistened on the biggest teeth I'd ever seen. A tail that must have been three metres long switched back and forth over the dirt, dislodging rocks as big as boulders in its sweep. I was close enough to feel the breeze and dust on my bare legs. An involuntary squeak erupted from my throat and he began turning his gigantic head to see what was behind him. I stood paralysed. I couldn't move, and then, before I could even digest what was happening, something grabbed my singlet from behind and my body jerked back as I was dragged across the sand and into the scrub. Once clear of the croc, I was abruptly halted, pulled upright and human arms encircled me from behind. Now I knew what to do. I screamed bloody murder.

A hand came up to cover my mouth and a voice whispered in

my ear, "Don't wake the camp. You'll cause a panic."

Warren! Abject terror was replaced by relief that flooded my body. I twisted in his arms to face him. If he hadn't been holding me so tight I would have collapsed. Our pounding hearts thudded together. In a flash his mouth was on mine and we were locked in a fierce embrace. Fear turned into a ferocious passion. I had to have him inside me...now!

My hands reached down to clasp his beautiful butt and pull him against me. That's when I realized that he was naked. That red sarong must have been lost in the rescue. Oh, my—

God, this was good. My wetness moistened my panties. I could also feel his thick cock swelling against my thigh. If either of us spoke, the spell would be broken.

Instead, we kept their mouths busy sucking tongues, sucking tits, panting out animal grunts. When Warren pulled my shirt over my head and filled his mouth with my breast, my whole body shook in a small orgasm. He thrust his hand between my legs to hold me upright. His hand squirmed into my panties to collect my cream and spread it on his dick. While I tried to get my damn belt unbuckled to get my shorts off, I tripped and fell to my knees. His cock was in my face and I couldn't resist taking it in my mouth, running my tongue under the foreskin while pumping the warm shaft.

Now he was shaking. He pulled away. I was still trapped by my shorts and struggled to get them off over the single boot but, in the end, couldn't wait any longer. I turned and positioned myself on all fours, like a bitch in heat and raised my hindquarters for mounting. He dropped to his knees and entered me urgently, pounding his slick cock back and forth, not even trying to hold back until he came in a jerking flood, pulling out at the last instant to spill his seed in the dust. He knelt still, hands on my hips, flexing fingers into my flesh with each spasm of his dick.

At last he collapsed over my back and I fell forward into the dirt. I turned over and moved my cunt into his face. With an eager grunt, he grabbed my buttocks firmly and licked and nibbled and sucked until I couldn't stand it any longer and came in such violent jerks that he almost lost his grip.

Then it was all over–the most intense experience I'd ever had in my entire life. I was spent and, by the depth of his gasps, so was he. We lay side by side in the dirt, arms touching without holding each other, until we heard what sounded like moaning coming from nearby. We looked up to see Jason standing in the Spinifex. His hard, weedy cock stuck out of his boxer shorts, gripped firmly in his hand and covered with sprog. Where the fuck had *he* come from!

I grabbed at my shorts to pull them up, filling my knickers with dirt as they dragged along the ground. Warren sat up beside me, holding onto his knees to hide his nakedness.

"Sorry, sir," Jason sounded close to tears. "I just came out to take a whiz and I saw youse and couldn't help myself. Fuck. That was the horniest thing's ever happened to me!"

"Go back to your tent and forget about it...That's an order." Warren spoke softly, with a hint of regret in his voice.

"As if I ever could. Good night, sir...Miss." The poor boy turned and walked back toward the tents, stopping to empty his bladder along the way.

"Shit," I said, standing to get my pants on properly. There was always something to spoil every special moment on this whole freaking trip. "Did we just contribute to the delinquency of a minor?"

"Naw, he's nineteen." Warren stood up, brushing dust from his backside instead of looking at me. "He's just such a sad case that the judge felt sorry for him and sent him with us. There's no harm in him, really."

There was a moment of silence while I awaited acknowledgement of what had just occurred, but it never came so I had to ask, "So how did you know I was about to be eaten by a croc?"

"Because I have had to keep my eye on you since day one." Now he looked at me with a big frown. "Big city, rich bitches like you think that they are immune from danger as well as rules," he spoke in a hoarse whisper. "Especially when they've been smoking dope! Got any more?"

"Why, you want a toke?" I sniped back at him. Did he just call me a bitch?

"Lower your voice, woman. Do you want to wake the whole camp? I told you at the outset, no drugs. Now go to bed."

He was angry again and, brushing more sand and gravel from his beautiful bum, found his lost sarong and waited impatiently for me to finish adjusting my clothes. Nothing further was said as we walked back to camp, me limping as spikes of Spinifex pierced through my sock and stabbed my tender foot, and wondering what had just happened. He *did* call me a bitch. What was the story behind that? We left each other and turned toward our respective tents. After retrieving the other boot from where it was waiting on the boulder, I called into the women's showers where it took some fierce scrubbing to remove the red dirt from my knees. I relished in the pain while I had a conversation with myself:

"He watches over me...He cares!" The romantic schoolgirl in me sighed.

"Bullshit! He just knows he'll lose his job if you get eaten by a croc," the woman of the world replied.

"You're wrong. He wanted me as much as I wanted him."

"A male will always root when the female he's with is in rut. You know how angry he was once it was over."

"Maybe he's got a wife and he was sorry he'd been unfaithful."

"As if! Who'd marry him? You've already noted that he's not wearing a wedding ring. And he did call you a bitch."

"Don't be mean. Even you have to admit that that's the best fuck you've had in years and that you'd like more of it!"

The woman of the world sighed. *"I do have to admit that. But never mind. Just remember that you have ten children to look after. And, Louisa, you may not be a bitch, but you are a rich city girl. Maybe you should consider how he would fit into your world?"*

My world. Now that was a good question. An Indigenous policeman from the Never-Never transplanted onto Sydney's North Shore...not sure how well that would work. This was real life, not just Ernie Dingo playing a part. How would Suzanne and Claudia react? And my parents? Shit! Mum and Dad might be OK with my brother John's Pakistani girlfriend, but her parents own a manufacturing empire, she got her Masters at Oxford and is doing her PhD in childhood cancers. I don't think their racial tolerance has ever really been tested. The romantic schoolgirl was far too tired to worry about it tonight.

Before I could sleep, though, I had to make myself come just one more time. But this time I did it in the shower, not lying next to Mary.

CHAPTER SIXTEEN

I WOKE UP IN SUCH A GREAT MOOD. For the moment, the fact that Warren was disgusted with me was not a problem. I did not give a hoot that he'd behaved like the biggest, chauvinist, jerk idiot in history last night. I thought about what had come before. I felt fine and I knew why. It was a sad and sorry fact that for longer than I cared to remember, I had not smoked a joint, suffered a serious fright, or engaged in wild sex and last night's little episode had done me the world of good. Not only did I know I was alive this morning, I was glad of it!

Poor Jason had the misfortune to be walking past my tent to grab the tray of mugs for Mary just when I emerged, fresh-faced and eager. His eyes rolled back in his head and he made small mewing sounds. I thought he was going to have a fit but he only ducked his head and hurried away on his errand. I had pity for him but was also petrified he wouldn't be able to keep his mouth shut.

He ignored me during breakfast but his face was such a bright shade of red that all the others kept up a constant, teasing abuse about his sunburn and telling him to get "Miss" to rub something on it. I was so sure that he would crack that I tried, in a show of forgive and forget, to have a private conversation with him after breakfast, but when I threw an arm around his shoulders to guide him away from the others, he got a stiffie. Spider and Timbo hooted with laughter, shouting, "Oh, mate, don't even think about going there!" Poor Jason blushed and ran to the showers while I scolded the other boys for their mockery.

"It's natural and it will happen to you someday as well. If you ever grow up, that is. Now you can wash the dishes if you want a good laugh." I was still smiling when Gazza, late for breakfast as usual, grabbed my arse. I was so happy that when I stabbed him with a fork I didn't even break the skin.

"I told you, I like a woman who plays rough." He chuckled,

causing Warren to look up from the plates he was gathering to take to the washing-up bowl. He caught my eye and I couldn't keep the smile off my face. He shot me a hateful scowl and shook his head. I began to think that the wind had changed and his face was now frozen in that expression. In a single gesture my beautiful morning turned sour and I had to blink away the tears. *Stop that, girl! He doesn't matter! It's still a gorgeous day and it's up to you to take advantage.*

"Hey, Miss," Brooke called, "come over and have a look at Melanie's bracelet. It's brilliant."

All the girls were hovering around Melanie's outstretched arm. The sun reflected off her glasses and last night she'd finally washed her hair—with some of *my* shampoo because she hadn't packed any. I smiled and joined them. It was a chunky bracelet made of large polished stones in green, blue, and red, with small white pebbles strung between. I admired it and forbore to ask light-fingered Melanie how much she'd paid for it.

Despite the small traumas after breakfast, the day began in a fairly relaxed fashion since there was no packing up to do, no bus to catch. A small herd of brumbies grazed along the lake's edge, fat and free with their coats shining in the sun. While the boys washed the dishes, the girls went in the shower block using the extra time to get their makeup just right. I helped Mary put the food away, locking it into animal- and teenager-proof containers, ensuring that the little portable fridge was plugged in and keeping the perishables cold, and then securing its door with a padlocked chain. We had Gazza's appetite to worry about too. I surveyed our surroundings. For a campground it was serviceable—just. Have I mentioned that I am not a great fan of living in the great outdoors?

I sighed and turned back to speak to Mary, but she had disappeared. I found her inside our tent, looking for her book.

"So, I understand we're here for three days. Isn't that going to be a bit expensive for the NT criminal justice system? They'd have made more money if they'd let me pay my fine."

Mary found her book, backed out of the tent, and answered me. "Naw, this whole trip'll still be cheaper than putting us all in the watch house. Anything's better than that hole, even in this fucking heat." She'd also got her sleeping bag and was dragging it over to the shade of a large gum tree. "Actually, these juvies would have had to be put into some kind of care, and let me tell you, those facilities are busting at the seams in Darwin."

I followed along with more questions, thinking it slightly odd that I should even care about the answers. "I've never actually got the point of this trip, communing with nature and all that. What are we gaining by being eaten alive by mossies and other animals?"

"This whole thing was Warren's idea. I hear he put in a grant proposal to some funding body and to the Juvenile Justice system and got the money and permission to trial this alternative approach. I think it's something like four trips in a twelve-month period. Of course, Juvenile Justice approved. What with the grant it means they're not paying one cent on these kids and, if it don't work out, they got old Warren to blame. It's win-win for them." Mary found her shady spot and proceeded to make herself comfortable with book, thermos, and a few bikkies hidden in her blouse.

I crouched in the dirt beside her. "Do you think it will work out?"

"I surely hope so. It'd be a great way to do all my CSOs."

"How often do you have to do CSOs! What in the world do you keep doing to keep getting arrested?"

Mary laughed and leaned back against silvery tree trunk. "I think you gotta be a blackfella to understand. When the weather's good, I like living in the park with all me mates. I like having a drink with them and don't like spending what little money I have on fines. To tell you the truth, Lou, I'm gonna like coming to WA as well. My people come from the Kimberley."

"But what about all those six kids? Who looks after them while you're away?"

"Family, of course. Got plenty of that in Darwin. None of mine are babies, anyway. Why, girl—I got grandbabies!"

"You don't!" I dropped down on the ground and stretched out beside her. A very light breeze made the shade feel cool. "Christ, you don't look more than thirty-five!"

"Thirty-eight, actually, and I do. Four of them that I know of. My oldest boy is a bit wild with the girls. Maybe he should come out on a trip like this, eh? It's good to get away once in awhile you know. Gives me a chance to catch up on my reading. Them novels from the library are the only romance in *my* life these days!" She laughed and I gasped. Darwin had a *library*!?!

"Well, whatever floats your boat. I know I miss my home like hell." Stretching out, I laced my fingers under my head and stared up into the pale green leaves. "I still live with my parents, *and* with my two sisters and brother in the house where I grew up, right on the most beautiful beach in the world. I miss my family, I miss my friends, I miss the shows, I miss the traffic and the coffee shops, and there's this little Turkish place that does kebabs to die for...Oh, Mary, I want to go home!"

"How'd you end up in Darwin, anyway?"

"That's a long story and relates to a night I spent drinking with some of my friends. I don't regret coming up North, but I sure as hell regret that I can't leave."

Mary opened her book and I closed my eyes and thought about that fateful night.

IT HAD BEEN BLOODY FANTASTIC! My new friends and I had come for our usual meeting and there was a special guest speaker present. He was gorgeous and passionate and his dark curls kept falling into his face as he gesticulated wildly and told us what we needed to do—NOW! The epitome of an anarchist. He even—God help me—wore a Che Guevara T-shirt. Not that I knew anything about Che Guevara or what he stood for, but my brother had gone through a period of pasting Che posters on his bedroom wall so I'd heard the name and seen the photo and knew it was kind of cool. Our speaker's reckless enthusiasm impassioned us all and, after coffee and baklava, none of us wanted to let him go. We went to a hole-in-the-wall pub at the end of a cul-de-sac off Glebe Point Road to carry on. At 3 a.m. this gypsy, Georgio was his name, and I were the only ones left and we were drinking retsina on a swing set in some desolate playground.

"You must come with us, Louisa," he urged in his deep, velvety voice. "The satisfaction you will feel you will never experience doing anything else. Not even sex can make you feel so good."

"Not even sex?" I was dubious. I'd had a good life, full of positives, but it was hard to remember anything that made me feel as good as a really fine root did. Maybe Georgio's experiences weren't, shall we say, as enlightened as mine.

"Do you have a girlfriend?" I asked.

"Yes, I have a fine woman waiting for me in Cairns. I have not seen her in a very long time and I am lonely, Louisa."

His fingers crept inside my blouse, under my bra, and I was weakening. The idea that men are easier to arouse physically than women would be, in my case, a fallacy. Fondle my breasts and I'm yours. Electric impulses shoot from tit to twat and I am totally turned on, my mind empties of conscious thought. I must be satisfied, I must be laid, and I will not be delayed.

Georgio didn't need to do much to have me crazy on the see-saw within minutes. We ducked behind a concrete wall painted in primary colours. I found an old condom packet (for emergencies only) in my purse and ripped it open with my teeth, hoping that I wasn't damaging the rubber itself and covered his thick, Slavic cock while he made small protests, asking why I wasn't on the pill. Vaguely confused by his mutterings, I shut him up by sticking my boob in his mouth and he suckled at it like a grateful child. Men can be so easy to please. While he was busy doing that, I got into position on the concrete slab (I'd rather have the rash on my butt than on my knees. Everybody can see the knees and then everybody knows) and guided him in. It was great for about sixty seconds, and then it was over for him, and apparently, for me as well. The sex was sudden but I learned three things about my anarchist. Firstly, Georgio considered a woman's G-spot to be a myth perpetuated by foolish women's magazines; secondly, it violated his manly, Eastern European nature to go down on a woman; and thirdly, he still satisfied me better than Dalby had in a long time. Of course, he had first inflamed my emotions with his impassioned rhetoric, and nothing says "good sex" like inflamed emotions. I've heard that it's the make-up sex that keeps foolishly optimistic women coming back to deadbeat men.

I spared a thought for the woman in Cairns, adjusted my knickers, and let him hail me a cab. The next morning, waking up alone in my bed in my father's house, my now-sober mind recalled the promise I had made during my moment of need.

Louisa Mayflower Smith, sensible and stable, should have recanted there and then but, somehow, she didn't want to. She didn't mind that Georgio was leaving today. She had got what she needed from him. Something deep inside of her had been awakened and she was going to the Northern Territory with her new friends. There was work to do.

CHAPTER SEVENTEEN

"HEY, LADIES, CAN YOU INTERRUPT your secret women's business and come over here, please?" Warren called out and I opened my eyes. I was surprised to see the sun so high that the morning shadows were almost gone. He stood at the head of the picnic table with a map spread out in front of him. Nine of the youngsters were seated around him and Jason was emerging from his tent, adjusting his clothes with a damp tissue clutched in his hand. No prizes for guessing what secret business he'd been involved in. I had the good grace to blush and hoped that nobody noticed. Good ol' Warren took no notice of anything but his job.

We ladies left our shady resting place and joined them. I squeezed in next to Laurel whose face was bright red and puffy. No blisters yet but I made a mental note to dig out the sunscreen as soon as this meeting was over. Meanwhile, I reversed her cap so that the beak shaded her face. We smiled at each other and turned to our tour guide.

"The plan is to spend three full days here, exploring a different area each day. Today we'll see the Ord River Dam and Lake Argyle." He tapped the map masterfully to make sure we knew where "here" was. "Tomorrow we'll take the bus down to Purnululu Park and see the Bungle Bungles." Loud snores from the direction of his tent explained why our bus driver wasn't with us now. "The third day, well, we'll see what happens. That'll be our last night so plan for a big barbecue and maybe a little disco. Maybe fancy dress, eh?"

The mention of the disco brought loud cheers and applause from the group and the girls began to jabber about what they would wear.

"Whadya reckon, Caleb," Andreas said. "Old Sara wouldn't have to dress up at all to look weird!" The boys fell over themselves in hilarity, Sara picked up a rock to throw and I caught her wrist just in time.

"You can't throw rocks! A rock could hurt somebody."

"I know! That's *why* I was gonna chuck it. To hurt somebody—Andreas." She poked her tongue at him and Caleb, and then turned to Brooke. "They're gonna so beg us to dance and we won't dance with them once, OK?"

"You bet, Sister!" The girls locked arms and leaned their heads together, Sara's black curls contrasting with Brooke's very straight hair, pulled back in a long plait.

I shook my head. Were they immature for their age or had I really gotten this old in a mere seven years?

"Settle." Warren gestured for silence. "There will be no throwing of stones or calling of names. We will respect each other and we will respect nature. That is what I'm going to talk about now so listen up, all of youse."

"So listen up, all of youse." Behind Warren's back Caleb mimicked him silently, shaking his finger at the crowd, his other hand on his hip. Andreas and Corey snorted but I sent warning looks to all three and they straightened up quickly. Warren took no notice and carried on.

"First, the sun. How many of you got sunburned and a bit of heatstroke yesterday?" No hands went up but fingers pointed.

"Of course the whities did," Timbo, who had very black skin himself, volunteered.

"You might not have got burned, Timbo, but I saw Miss Louisa looking after you. That headache and weakness you experienced was sunstroke. It doesn't matter what colour you are, the sun will kill you if you don't respect it. Rules for sunshine. One. A hat worn properly to shade your *face*—and you wear them from dawn until dusk—no exceptions. Two. Sunscreen for everyone—this means even you, Sara and Timbo. Everybody gets protection under my watch. Miss Louisa will hand it out when we're finished here. Three. Plenty of fluids. Each of you will carry a water bottle and Mary has plenty more drinking water for refills. I want each of you drinking at least two litres of water per day."

"Two litres! I'll die of drowning," Spider objected. "Now, if it was two litres of beer..."

"Yeah!" "You bet!" "I'll drink to that!" was the not-unexpected response.

"Water will do, thank you. Next, the air is full of biting insects. We have repellent so come to Miss Louisa or myself if you want it. The hills and deserts are alive with dangerous creatures. We've already had an encounter with the crocs, but there are also poisonous snakes, lizards, scorpions, you name it. Wear shoes at all times, and I don't mean thongs. It should also be remembered that the large animals like the camels, the brumbies, kangaroos, dingos, et cetera, are all wild animals and should not be approached at any time."

"A dingo ate my ba-a-aby!" Jason cried out in a high falsetto, bringing the house down again.

"Lucky baby," Warren joked back. Bet he wouldn't have thought it was funny if *I'd* said it. "One final rule never to be broken or even bent. It is very easy to get into trouble or lost out here. No-one, and I do mean no-one, must ever go off alone. You find a buddy, stick with the group, always tell one of the adults what you're up to and where you're going, all of the above. Never be alone out here, OK?

"Now, enough of the lecturing. Who's for a swim before we go on a boat trip?"

"A swim?" I couldn't believe what I was hearing. "There are *crocodiles* in that water!"

"Shit, Miss, this is the Outback," Corey laughed. "There's crocs in *all* the water, even the beaches in Darwin. We checked for their slides earlier, but, and there ain't none around here now."

I allowed myself to be placated as I wondered what the hell a crocodile slide was and the youngsters scattered, diving into their tents to change into shorts, singlets, togs, whatever they had that would pass for swimming costumes. No-one wanted to wear his or her DJ ROC T-shirt into the water and I was impressed by the almost reverent ways they were folded and put aside. Had Warren noticed it too? Did it make him feel proud?

As I dug out a large dispenser of sunscreen and Mary began to fill water bottles, I kept remembering how Warren's voice had sounded each time he'd said "Miss Louisa." I was beginning to think that I was no more mature than the fourteen-year-olds.

When Warren emerged from his tent, dressed for the beach, my heart stopped and my juices started leaking again. Would I never have dry undies when I was around him? He wore stubbies instead of the Speedos I'd have liked to have seen him in, but his firm, muscular chest and legs, and his slim waist where it disappeared into the low elastic band, all looked every bit as wonderful as it had felt last night. My groin actually ached when I thought about last night and I had to look away quickly. It was time to smear the sun-factor 30+ on the backs of my young charges. Warren let Mary apply his.

My jobs were finally finished so I ducked into my tent and pulled on my bikini, grabbed my towel, and raced down to the water's edge. Bugger the crocs! I was dying for a swim and if the kids could do it, so could I. I shouted as I dove headlong into the cool, brilliant blue lake and swam underwater until my lungs nearly burst. That water was unbelievably nice. I popped up with a *whoosh!* and nearly knocked over Warren in my enthusiasm.

"Oh, my God, what are you wearing?" He stood as if rooted in the waist-deep water, looking all agog.

"My swimmers, of course," I answered, adjusting my strap. "Why?"

"Take a look around you."

I did. Jason, Timbo, Corey, Spider, Caleb, and Andreas stood in a semi-circle on the bank, mouths wide open and hands covering their crotches.

"This," Warren whispered harshly, indicating my bikini with his eyes, "*is* contributing to the delinquency of *several* minors. Go cover yourself—now!"

Amid a veritable smorgasbord of emotions ("He remembers last night!" "What right does that bastard have telling me how to dress?" "I'm only twenty-three, practically a minor myself!" "I never got arrested in Sydney for wearing this!"), I left the water, bowed grandly to the awestruck boys and stalked to my tent. Mary was there, rummaging around in her stuff, looking for her ubiquitous book.

"Mary," I asked as I dragged an oversized black T-shirt for sleeping in over my head. "Does Warren hate all women or just me?" I pulled silk boxer shorts, also for sleeping, over my bottom, trying not to kick the other woman. Our tents weren't very big.

"Are you sure he hates you?" she asked from the depths of her bag.

"It sure feels like it. Maybe some other woman broke his heart," I said, half-hopefully.

"Maybe...Found it!" Mary sat up, triumphantly clutching her book. "See you later," she said as she backed out of the tent.

Still full of unanswered questions, I returned to my duties. It was difficult to swim as the shirt ballooned around my head and got tangled in my legs. I tried knotting it to keep it in place, but in the end I gave up and just lay in the shallows to keep cool while feeling very pissed off. Apparently, I was not allowed to have any fun at all.

Water, as it does, had a calming effect and I was smiling by the time Brooke came over and told me that Mr Warren said it was time to get ready for the boat trip.

"Oh, Brooke," I sighed happily, "what does this water in Western Australia have in it? Bondi was never like this."

"Bondi? Isn't that, like, underwear?"

I grinned, jumping up and playfully grabbing at her long plait.

"You must be nearly able to sit on this. Must take a long time to wash and comb."

"White men like long hair on us Filipinas, eh," was her unexpected reply.

"How in the world would you know something like that?" I blurted without thinking, and then wanted to bite my tongue, but Brooke just laughed.

"From me dad, of course! He goes rank every time Mum gets hers cut, but I think she does it 'cause she's tired of getting pregnant."

Jesus H Christ! I'm never going to get used to these people, I thought as I herded the girls into their shower block.

At 11 o'clock we went down to the small wooden jetty where we boarded another covered, flat-bottom boat for a cruise of the lake and under the dam. Hats had been adjusted, drink bottles filled, sun block spread, and Mr Warren had warned, "There will be NO climbing on the roof of this boat. This means you!" Growling playfully, he pointed at each teen. They giggled and agreed to behave. Whatever that meant.

"Isn't he such a total dork?" Laurel asked Melanie, but the adoring looks they gave him told a different story.

There was another ranger in khaki, younger than the last one and better looking. Almost too good-looking. He smiled at me and took my hand to help me into the boat.

"Watch your step, ma'am."

Ma'am! Crikey! I was no older than he was, maybe younger. I moved quickly away, feeling damaged, but when I saw how he smiled at Warren it was suddenly easy to understand his attitude toward me. I wasn't damaged, just superfluous. *You've got no chance there, Charlie,* I told him silently, basking in my afterglow. Warren didn't notice a thing.

Caleb took a seat beside the ranger, Corey and Andreas sat together on a bench near the aft and I, not prepared to take any chances this time, plopped myself between them. Corey, at sixteen, was small for his age and looked as if he was waiting for puberty to catch up. He had red curls, blue eyes, a big overbite and freckles all over his sunburnt body. He was a likeable lad, with teeth too big for his mouth so that his lips were stretched into a perpetual grin. That grin widened when I sat down beside him.

Andreas was fourteen, on puberty's cusp and when he arrives–watch out! He was all big feet and hands, elbows and knees, and his voice was breaking. His skin was black, his hair was curly, and he had a shy smile that always took a moment to reach his eyes. Brooke was the only juvie on this trip with any meat on her bones, but I had to wonder how any poverty stricken parents could afford to feed even one of these ravenous teens? Mary spent her days in camp struggling to prepare enough food to fill them up. I noticed, for the first time, a thick keloid scar running the length of Andreas's right calf.

"What happened there? It looks like it was pretty serious."

"Not that serious. I didn't even go to hospital or anything."

"Not even for sutures? Why not?"

"Well, in the first place, I was doing what I shouldn't of been doing. I'd knicked one of the men's hunting knives and was practising how quick I could pull it out of me boot. I found out that it was sharper than what it looked. Shit, did it bleed!"

"So why didn't you get it stitched up?"

Andreas sighed and spoke slowly, as if explaining to a small child. "We were at the camp, all the men were drinking and talking about men's business and stuff and they were pretty pissed off with me for cutting myself like that so none of them would drive me into the hospital. They poured whiskey on it, but, so it wouldn't get infected or nothing and wrapped it up real tight and, when we come home about a week later, I could stand up and hop around with a stick so there was no need for a doctor then."

"His old man's always drinking, Miss," Corey volunteered. "His old man's famous for his drinking."

"Yeah, well at least I got one. Corey's oldies took off years ago, Miss, and he's got no clue where they are." Andreas leaned forward to glare at the other boy.

"They're dead, smartarse." Corey returned the glare. "And at least my brother would take me to hospital if I got hurt that bad."

I sensed a fight building but, before I could intervene, Andreas's fist whipped around my body and landed with a thud in Corey's gut.

"Whoof!" Corey turned a deeper shade of red and bent double. I grabbed Andreas's wrist and held it clasped under one arm while I wrapped the other one around Corey's shoulders.

"My God, are you all right?"

"I'm OK, Miss," he answered between gasps. "Old Andreas couldn't hurt a flea."

"There will be no more punching, whether there are fleas or not!"

"Croc to the starboard!" the ranger behind us called and all quarrels were forgotten. Both boys leaned over the side as far as they could with me gripping frantically on to each orange T-shirt.

"Watch it, Miss, you'll stretch it." Andreas tried to brush my hand away but I wasn't letting go. "Coo, that one's nearly as big as the one that almost got Corey."

Not as big as the one that nearly got me last night, but of course they didn't know about that and this wasn't the time or place to recall that little escapade.

"That was about the scariest blooming thing I have *ever* seen," I remembered not to swear.

"Too right, Miss," Andreas stood up, his eyes glowing at the memory. "That was so exciting, I reckon it was better than any homebake I've ever had."

"What's homebake?"

Once again, Andreas sighed and explained, again sounding like he was addressing a child. "Homebake, Miss...speed...*you* know."

"Oh, yeah, sure, I know." I actually had no idea what he was talking about but I was tired of feeling like the idiot here.

"So, anyway, Corey and me decided we'd like to be crocodile hunters, like Steve Irwin and all. We always knew he was a great man and all, but now we know the truth even better."

"Too right," Corey agreed. "When we get back we might get jobs at a crocodile park and go into training. That would be so cool."

"Deadly, man."

They were so earnest and cute. I couldn't resist resting a hand on each boy's shoulder. Maybe they were learning that there could be more to life than fights and drugs. Glancing up, I caught Warren watching us with a little smile. When I tried to return the smile, though, he frowned and turned away. The prick! What did he want from me? I'd like to use *him* as crocodile bait.

Caleb appeared to be talking the ranger's ear off, Timbo, Spider, Laurel and Melanie were seated in the front with the boss, but Brooke and Sara looked at me so I beckoned them over. At least the kids seemed to accept me and were honest about their likes and dislikes. They didn't fuck me one night and then fuck me over the next day.

Two hours later we returned to the jetty and the girls were jumping onto its planks before the boat was even secured.

"Jeez, Miss, you can't make us drink all that water when we don't even have a place to pee!" they shouted in protest as they ran for the toilet block.

My bladder must be really strong, I was congratulating myself, but then I picked up my own water bottle and realized it was nearly full. I hoped nobody else noticed. It wouldn't be good to get caught breaking my own rules!

By the time the cruise had finished we were famished and the rest of us hurried back to camp to eat. Mary had mountains of sandwiches waiting; ham and pickle, ham and cheese, cheese and pickle; not a lot of variety but we were too hungry to notice. I managed to gobble down a couple before the whole stack disappeared. Whatever physical complaints that had been ailing the kids last night were well and truly healed and their energy was boundless. Spider kicked a soccer ball into the air and it was game on.

It was Jason and the girls against the rest of the boys, Warren and I were in the goals, and Mary was the cheer squad. Gazza was missing again. In fact, he hadn't even been there for lunch. Maybe he got a day off because he was a real copper. Whatever, he was sure to be drunk when he did turn up and I'd have to be on my guard. He gave off a dangerous vibe to me. Just then, I caught an unintentional header and nearly got whiplash again so I turned my attention back to the game.

Warren's shirttail was slipping out of his shorts, his white socks were tumbling down his legs, sweat gleamed on his face, and he looked so hot in every way. He was watching me so I deliberately pulled up my singlet to wipe my face, exposing belly and bra. Brooke kicked one right past him into the net.

Ha! So you think I'm hot as well. Deny it now, you bastard. You'd be shit lucky to get into my knickers again. It must have been the adrenalin talking. One look from him and I knew those knickers would be history. He jumped up, stretching to catch a high ball and I got a fleeting glimpse of the trail of tight black curls that led down to his delicious cock. I could see myself just reaching right down to grab it.

CHAPTER EIGHTEEN

WHEN THE GAME WAS OVER, Warren led a group into the nearby desert to throw a boomerang. I looked around and saw Sara trying to coax a scorpion into a slim-line tampons box. A scorpion! So it *was* true! They *did* hang around out here in WA! I didn't think. I just reacted. I picked up a rock and smashed the exotic creature into the next star sign.

"What the fuck didja do that for, Miss?" Sara shrieked and picked up another rock, drawing her arm back to let it fly in my direction. "You're nothing but a horrid, selfish, racist murderer!" She dropped her arm and burst into tears.

I stood stunned, rock in hand, shocked at my behavior, but more shocked at Sara's. Racist? I dropped the offending stone and tried to put my arms around the girl but was beaten off with weak, pathetic blows.

"What did you do to that child?" Mary came running to investigate the noise.

"Saved her life, is all. She was playing with a scorpion. Those things can kill you."

Mary sighed. "They won't kill you, Lou." She put her arms around Sara and the girl snuggled, sniffling, into her shoulder. "They can make you feel right crook, but, so you probably shouldn't play with them. Stop your blubbering there, girl."

Sara straightened up, wiping her nose with the back of her hand. "You're as bad as she is. You should be on my side, Auntie."

"I'm on nobody's side. I'll fix us all a cup of tea while you apologize to the young missy, here." Mary left us to it.

"You don't have to apologize, Sara," I shrugged and shook my head. "Just tell me what I did that was so wrong. I didn't mean to upset you, OK?"

"Well..." Sara wiped her eyes and sniffed. "Maybe you didn't mean to, you being from Sydney and all and not knowing nothing."

"I know a little..." I tried to protest but Sara carried on.

"This is my first time in the desert but this is where my people are from. I need to learn the ways so I can live out here."

"But touching a scorpion..."

"I wasn't touching him, and he wasn't going to sting me, anyway. No bug or animal or spider or nothing has ever turned on me since I was born and that's the truth. Me mum used to tell me I had the gift and I always had pets when I was little."

"Is your mum looking after your pets when you're out here?"

"No, Mum's passed on and, anyway, I don't have none anymore." She scooped the smashed scorpion into the little box and looked at it sadly. "Poor thing." She closed the box and carried it over to a nearby picnic table. I followed. We sat and she continued.

"I've never been allowed to have any kind of pet since I went into foster care. They don't like you to have nothing of your own. They probably figure looking after a stray kid's bad enough without looking after its animals as well." She peeked up at me through long, straight, black lashes and giggled. "I used to fool 'em, but. I'd play with the cockroaches at night and even give them names sometimes."

I had never even seen a cockroach until I was six and the thought of playing with those disease-carrying menaces turned my stomach. I didn't want her to see my disgust and smiled sweetly. I was timid about the next question but I had to ask.

"Sara, do you think I'm racist?"

"Against scorpions, for sure!" she laughed. "It goes with the territory, you know, being white and rich and all but I gotta admit, Miss, most of the time you've been alright."

"To tell you the truth, Sara, I know nothing at all about life in the Northern Territory and need all the help I can get."

"Duh!"

Mary came over with tea and bikkies.

"Are lizards poisonous?" I asked but it must have been another stupid question because Sara whooped with laughter and Mary choked on her biscuit.

"No, Miss. Not in Australia, anyways."

"I didn't think so." I defended my ignorance. "OK, then, Sara. Can we make a compromise?" I asked. "Can you please leave scorpions, spiders, and snakes alone and, if you can catch a lizard, you can keep it."

"OK, Miss, I'll do my best but, I'm telling you, you don't have to be scared."

"I'll do my best as well, Sara, but, like you pointed out, I'm just a dumb city girl."

We all laughed and I didn't know why I had such a warm glow inside. The campfire tea was strong and bitter and had a slightly medicinal taste, but I was drinking it like a drowning man. The desert was absolutely silent and empty, nothing like the noisy crowds I loved. The distant hills and trees were outlined so sharply they might have been carved in relief from the land and sky with a painter's knife while the edges of my world had always been blurred with sea mists and smog. And don't get me started on the smells of clean dust and daylight as opposed to the exhilarating fumes of exhaust pipes, hot tar, and multiple ethnic eateries. A beautiful calm melted through my body.

"Sydney is a very long way away from here," I said quietly, "but that's OK."

"It sure is," Sara agreed and Mary gave me her funny look again. Sara grabbed up a handful of bikkies and wandered off in search of company her own age. Mary left to get started on our dinner and I took my cuppa and returned to that shady spot, which was now on the other side of the tree.

AFTER MY ILLICIT NIGHT with the gypsy activist from Cairns, I had sought out Dalby, feeling a bit guilty and anxious. Guilty about the gravel rash and anxious because my last ever final exam was scheduled for the following week and I very much needed his support. After all, engineering was my chosen career and he was my chosen partner. He'd given me a ring last New Year's and we'd sealed it with an engagement party on January 26, Australia Day.

Mum had taken three weeks off work, complaining madly the whole time that I should have given her more warning. Then she would see a photo of Dalby and me together (on a yacht, at the Opera House, at Darling Harbour, they were all over the house) and she'd burst into tears and hug me and forgive every transgression I'd ever committed in my entire life.

"Oh, Louisa, I just can't believe it. You've made me the happiest mother in the world!"

Then my brother John might walk in. He was single but doing his surgical residency at Sydney Children's Hospital and *he* made her the happiest mother in the world as well. She'd have to grab him and cry too. We both suffered a lot of wet shoulders during that period. We had the engagement party on our own beach. It was so big that people I didn't even know were there congratulating me. Everybody was so happy for me I thought I must be happy as well. Ten months later, I needed him and was trying not to have second thoughts.

"Where were you last night?" he asked when I found him at a coffee shop near the university.

"At my meeting. You knew that." Hoping to deflect his questions with my surliness, I pulled out a chair and sat down. He scooted his chair a little further away.

"I suppose you'll be wanting a coffee?" he said but his tone said *I'll match your surliness with my aloofness.*

"Yeah, thanks. You buying?" I smiled at him, pretending not to notice what a jerk he was being, trying not to say that I wouldn't need new friends if he paid more attention to me.

"Why? Haven't you been home to collect your allowance yet?"

That barb really stung. Did he think I'd been out all night? My raw backside prickled but I wasn't game to rub it and draw attention. Instead, I looked pitiful and said, "Don't be mean, Dalby, I've been looking everywhere for you. I'm practically *living* at the library lately. My final's next week and I'm not prepared."

"You might be if you didn't waste time with those troublemakers."

"I don't want to talk about it." For more reasons than one. That guy's aftershave had been so Eurotrash I was afraid Dalby might be able to smell it on me despite my thirty minute perfumed bath! He never wore cologne but had plenty of foreign students who did. Dalby didn't have much money but he had plenty of *je ne sais quoi* and bought his linen trousers, tweed jackets, hemp shirts and woven leather sandals from the Lifeline in the elite suburb of Newtown, just a few blocks up from the University. Fortunately, there was very little risk of him seeing the rash on my backside before it healed. We hadn't had sex in ages.

"Dalby," I played with the sugar bowl, wearing a cute little pout. "Please don't be like this. You know I love you, and I'll spend all this week with you. I promise."

"Only because you need help with your studies," he said but he was relenting and allowed his body to relax. He signaled a waitress to bring another coffee. "As soon as we've finished here, we'll go to my flat and drag out the books." He leaned over and kissed me with more interest than he'd shown in weeks. He didn't appear to notice Georgio's scent. Maybe I would have to make something up about my sore bum.

Once we got back to his flat, though, when I held him close and tried to carry on what we'd started at the coffee shop, he put his hands on my shoulders instead of around them.

"We need to hit the books," he said sternly.

"We can do that later." I tried to sound sultry and rubbed my hips across his groin. His cock responded and I grinned, lowering my hand to caress it through his trousers. He leaned his head back and moaned, becoming large and hard in my hand. We hadn't done this in so long; I was getting a bit excited myself. When I tried to unzip him, he moved my hand away.

"There will be plenty of time for that when we're married," he said. "You put the jug on and get out the books we'll need. I got to go to the john."

Trying not to show my hurt and frustration, and not wanting him to see the flush of humiliation burning my face, I turned quickly into the kitchen. After all, he was older (twenty-nine at his last birthday) and wiser. He knew so much more about engineering than I did, and he probably knew more about marriage as well. I boiled the water and got the mugs out. Did he want coffee or tea? I went to the bathroom and opened the door to ask him. There he stood in the shower, his back to me, masturbating!

Shocked and still hurt by how he'd rejected me moments earlier, I backed out, closing the door quietly. I crept back into the kitchen and made tea, wondering what was wrong with me. Why did he prefer sex with himself when I was right there and willing? Why was he withholding what he used to give so freely? Maybe he was trying to punish me, but I didn't dare confront him for fear of losing him.

I'd worked very hard to get my degree and knew I needed his help to finish it. Daddy–and Dalby–had invested so much in my education; I couldn't let them down now. *That's it,* I consoled myself, *he has my best interests at heart and I'm sure he hates acting like a controlling jerk as much as I hate him doing it.* I measured out two teaspoons of tea, added one for the pot, and poured in the boiling water, hoping and almost believing that it would change as soon as uni was finished. I knew how happy everybody was for us and how we were such a great couple...

CHAPTER NINETEEN

GAZZA RETURNED AT DINNER TIME. We never ate before 7 o'clock, preferring to wait until the sun had set and the heat of the day was beginning to settle. The sun, as always out here, was a blood red orb of fire sinking behind the hills, turning the sky yellow and pink and orange with the hills becoming midnight blue in their own shadows. The brumbies had returned to the water's edge, sturdy silhouettes in the dusk as hordes of waterfowl flew in from who knows where to settle on the lake for the night. Flocks of swallows hunted evening insects before coming to rest on bushes and wires, and hundreds of squawking lorikeets, pink galahs, and black cockatoos appeared in a riot of colour, sound, and bird droppings. Another reason to delay dinner.

When Mary called us to eat, Warren stood at the head of the queue to give us, as usual, the agenda for the following day.

"We're off the visit the Bungle Bungles in the morning and they are at least an hour away by bus." He spoke in that deep voice he likes to use when he's being authoritative. "Rich tourists may fly to the Bungle Bungles, but those of us who are socio-and-economically disadvantaged have to drive."

"Let's hear it for the Social Misfits!" Timbo cheered.

Warren shook his head, but couldn't hide a small smile. "Be that as it may, what it means for us that tomorrow will be an early start. Now, let's eat!"

Jason, looking like a Minister of the Dark Arts in that black tailcoat and ghostly white skin (no amount of sunlight was going to change his colour) said grace. It was the same one he said before every meal. "Birds are great, birds are good, as long as they don't shit on my food!"

Tonight Gazza, unusually jovial, slapped him on the back like a pile driver and it very nearly drove Jason's face into his food.

"That's a good one, son! That's bloody bonza! Now let's

fuckin' eat!"

Officer Pig took a plate and filled it with five chops and three baked potatoes. He had to eat the chops with his hands before he had room to cut open the potatoes and slather them with butter.

I looked at Warren, hoping to see some sort of acknowledgement of the pig's unacceptable behavior, but Warren, seated at another table with Mary and three of the boys, stared at his plate, eating quietly. His shallow, rapid respirations indicated that he wasn't happy. I couldn't help wishing he'd do something, hierarchy be damned! Our little group was balanced precariously enough in our little boat and this man was a rocker. I ate silently, and then Mary surprised us all.

She brought out a bush plum tart she'd made for dessert and placed it triumphantly before Warren. I'd been at the girl's table, but rushed over to admire this work of art.

"How in the bloody—sorry, I mean—great wide world did you do this on a camp stove!" I couldn't believe my eyes.

"You can thank Sara and Laurel and Timbo for the fruit. They gathered it all for me. The cooking's the easy part."

"You are too modest, woman," Warren said as he handed me a piece.

I took a bite. The sweet pastry and tangy filling lit up my tongue like neon. "This is fantastic. How come you're not a chef in a restaurant?" I asked while shovelling more into my mouth.

Mary laughed. "Who'd hire a fat old black thing like me?" Everyone lined up for a bit and not even fat Gazza was allowed to cut ahead.

"Hey, when we get back maybe you and me and the girls could open a café or something that sells bush tucker!" Timbo sounded excited, which didn't surprise me. The way that boy ate it would take a restaurant kitchen to fill him up. Why not own one? Sara and Laurel joined in with more ideas.

"Yeah! And we could do, like, hospitality courses at the TAFE and art courses and decorate the place with Aboriginal paintings and all like that!"

"Sounds good to me," said Warren. "I'd be eating there every night, for sure."

"Open your eyes, you losers," Gazza guffawed. He'd finished his piece in a single bite and gazed hungrily at Laurel's. Timbo stepped between them. "Look at yourselves. Youse're ex-cons and kids! What chance could you possibly have with a restaurant in a place like Darwin? Maybe in Humpty-Doo..."

The girls looked shame-faced and Mary shrugged, glancing at me as if to say, *See what I mean*?

Timbo stepped up and squared off in front of the driver. "You take that back, you fat old fart!"

Gazza gazed at him unperturbed. "Watch your mouth, Boy. I'm the law out here and don't you forget it. Your file is in my hands."

"Mr Warren..." Timbo turned to the tour leader for help. Warren sighed, stood up and placed an arm around Timbo's shoulder.

"He's right about one thing, Timbo. He is the highest ranking officer out here. But he's wrong about your restaurant. I reckon that would be a goer in a place like Darwin. Now, sit down and have some more tart." Amazing Mary had brought out a second one.

Timbo, only partially placated, rejoined his mates. The kids finished that tart off in ten seconds flat, and then disappeared before it was time to clean up.

Gazza shot Warren a menacing look through narrowed eyes and Warren averted his. Anger burned inside me. I fought down a scream and moved closer to Mary.

"How much more of this shit is Warren going let him get away with?" I asked in a hoarse whisper.

"Just leave it. There's plenty you don't know and, remember, Lou, you're one of the crims as well. Besides, we don't need those two fighting it out while we're stuck out here in the Never-Never. Are you going to drive us back to Darwin?"

She was right again. I may be clever enough at driving my BMW around Sydney's streets, but get behind the wheel of *that* vehicle on *these* roads? I don't think so. Then I remembered my NRMA Roadside Assistance membership and got the glimmer of an idea. They could tow us home when I got stuck...

I turned to Mary with cunning. "Hey, what do you think they would do to me for killing a Northern Territory cop in Western

Australia?"

"I'd give you a bloody great medal."

Mary rose and began gathering empty plates. When she took Gazza's, he playfully tugged it back, touching her breast when she was pulled forward. Mary didn't react. I saw Warren watching the incident but couldn't read his expression in the fading light. He certainly didn't interfere, though.

"Come here, Miss," Melanie called out, breaking into my feelings of impotence and rage. "Me and Brooke got something to show you."

I dug out a smile from someplace, put it on, and went over to where the girls stood under the spotlight outside the shower block.

"See?" They held out their hands, showing off their fingernail art. Brooke's nails were bright red with blue moons while stars and rainbows glittered across each of Melanie's.

"That's fantastic, those look great!"

"We done our toes as well, and we've got make-up. We were wondering if maybe we could practice on you? Please?" Melanie twisted her head around and gave me her best puppy-dog-begging look. Her eyes looked so big behind her glasses and her straight, orange hair was caught up in elastics on either side of her head. If she'd barked I wouldn't have been surprised.

"Oh, yes, Miss, please, please, please?" Brooke pleaded. "You got such beautiful skin."

"You don't need to bribe me with flattery, although I love it." I laughed. "Of course, I'll to be your guinea pig. I haven't had make-up on in over a week and I'm going into withdrawal. Where do you want me?" I am so easy in so many ways. I wanted the approval of these street kids as much as they wanted mine—more, probably.

"There's a chair in one of the showers. We can do it there by the sink."

We all trooped inside the concrete block building still holding the day's heat, and I was seated ceremoniously on a steel-backed chair, surprised to see that Caleb had followed us in.

"Whadda you want?" Melanie asked impatiently.

"I just wanted to watch. I'm not hurting anybody."

"Just wanted to watch make-up? You're so gay!"

"Am not!" he shouted defiantly. "Indian men wears heaps of make-up for ceremonies and stuff." His lower lip quivered as he turned to go.

"Caleb..." I tried to get up to speak to him but firm hands clamped me back in the chair and he was gone before I could say anything more.

"Well, now we can get down to business." Melanie said as she opened her bag full of blushes, lipsticks, eye shadows, lotions, and sprays from Max Factor, Calvin Klein, Chanel, Stella McCartney, you name it, and it was expensive. I chose not to ask the young girl how she could afford these brand names because I was pretty sure I knew the answer!

"I got all these at that flash boutique on the Esplanade. They're super expensive, you know."

That, I knew, but what I didn't know—I stopped myself...Darwin had a flash boutique!?!

"I just love fashion and beauty," Melanie said with a sigh as she massaged exfoliate into my face and Brooke began brushing my hair, removing the sand and grit that accumulated daily. "I would so love to get a job in a salon but I need a certificate for that."

"Why don't you get one?" I asked without moving my lips.

"I can't do nothing 'til my kid's in school, and by that time it looks like I'll probably have another one. You know what men are like!"

"You...have a kid?" This time my lips moved.

"Sure, he's one this year and I'm late again, not to mention the morning sickness!" So it wasn't the fresh air and vegetables making Melanie puke. "I can't take the pill and my boyfriend don't like condoms."

"You're fifteen and you'll have *two* children? I can't believe it!"

"Believe it, Miss, but I'll be sixteen before this one's born. Then I should get a break 'cause my boyfriend'll be in jail. The car he stole this time wasn't that flash but he ran over a magistrate's dog while he was driving it." Melanie laughed and I tried not to cry. It would ruin the mascara. "Now let me finish this, Miss, and then Brooke'll do your hair. Brooke's really good with hair."

Yeah, especially the long kind that men like. I sat still and thought about when I was fifteen and my girlfriends and I had make-up parties, financed by our parents; when we'd drive the expensive cars we'd been given for our birthdays; when the girls who "got caught" were discreetly sent to specialists for early abortions, and then sent on overseas holidays to forget. I'd never had a termination, but I also knew that was due more to luck than to judgment. Getting pregnant was not a part of the master plan and would have ruined everything. My father had paid for my degree in chemical engineering so that my studies wouldn't be interrupted by something so plebeian as work and, when I got back to Sydney, I had three job offers to choose from whose starting salaries, including benefits, would approach six figures. Somehow, wanting to earn a living by applying make-up and washing other people's hair didn't sound like an unreasonable dream.

When Brooke started on my coiffeur, my back was to the mirror so I couldn't see what was happening, but from the tugging, the feel, and the smell, I knew that there was a lot of gel involved. I've always been a great fan of beauty salons but, in the sort I'm used to, the fragrance in the air is more likely to be patchouli-scented incense, not burnt onions from the barbecue, and the attendants are slim, soft-spoken men and women in form-fitting silk-weave tops embroidered with the salon's oh-so-posh logo, not gum-smacking girls in big, bright orange T-shirts whose nasal voices could shatter glass.

I was having so much fun in this toilet-cum-beauty parlour!

When I was finally allowed to view my hair style, I shrieked, "Oh my God, it's red!"

"Don't worry, Miss," Brooke said. "It's only a spray-on colour."

Then the girls brought me out to show the others my long eyelashes, arched brows, pale cheeks, black lipstick and scarlet fingernails, all topped off with a bright red Mohawk–my sides were gelled flat and my top curls gelled straight up.

When we stepped into the light, the kids cheered and even Warren smiled at me. He had a dazzling smile for such a weak, spineless bastard. Why did he keep avoiding me after what we'd *done*! Anyway, I couldn't help smiling back and did a little sashay, parading up and down, arms and hands extended.

"Hey, that's a bit of all right!" a rough voice called out. "I'd have you in my lock-up anytime."

I realized, with deep disappointment, that Pig Gazza was still there. He hadn't gone to find his drinking buddies yet. He surged forward, jiggling his balls and making obscene pumping gestures. He grabbed my hand and stuck it between his legs. "My dick likes having black lips suck it."

Trying to pull my hand away, I clenched my other fist and was ready to let fly when Warren stepped in and grabbed it before I had the chance.

"Hey, you two, there are minors present. Keep it clean." He continued holding my hand, sending unexpected shocks through my body before pushing me gently away. "Look after your charges." I moved back, he let go and turned to Gazza.

With a comradely arm around the big man's shoulders, Warren led him away and chatted to him quietly like they were best buddies. I couldn't believe it! He'd done it again! Choosing The Pig over me! I stood, both fists clenched, trembling with lust and loathing. They were both arseholes! Fuming, I joined the juvies who had retreated and clustered around the table. Jason stepped bravely forward.

"If you ever need protection, Miss, I ain't afraid of no cop!"

"Thanks for that, Jason, but maybe you should be. I can take care of myself."

"But he's a big one," Caleb added. "You don't want to mess with him."

"No, I don't want to mess with him and, right now, I don't have to." We all stood around in an awkward little group, unsure of how to move the night's festivities forward. I looked around at their sad, angry faces and appreciated a little of the impotence they had to live with every day. *No wonder they strike out*, I thought, *I'd have smashed that bastard's face and enjoyed it*! Time to move on. I was supposed to be helping these kids learn to avoid trouble–not encourage anarchy.

"I've got an idea!" I said with forced enthusiasm. "Why don't we ask Mary to make us a big pot of tea while we build a bonfire and find out who can tell the best ghost story?"

"All right!" was the immediate response and I was impressed by how quickly and thoroughly they were able to put the earlier unpleasantness behind them. Within minutes, those boys had an enormous fire blazing away and we were all gathered amid its shadows, listening to stories of min-min lights, bunyips, and most popular of all, backpackers who got sliced and diced. This lot were way too gruesome for poor little me. Mary brought over the tea and leftover damper with golden syrup but only listened for a moment before throwing up her hands and turning to leave.

"I hate this kinda shit. I'll leave you to it, Lou," she laughed as she left us.

At last, suitably frightened and sleepy, the youngsters went to bed. Mary had long since retired, The Pig was snoring loudly, and Warren was nowhere to be seen. I needed a shower to remove the make-up and the memories. The night was warm but I wanted the water hot. Under its sharp jets, I lathered the soap and washed my face and worried about Melanie's babies. Thoughtfully, I rubbed the lather over the rest of my body, down my long arms, my smooth legs, my trim belly, and over my firm buttocks. I always enjoy rubbing my nipples and breast with soft, sweet-smelling bubbles, relishing in the warm tingles it sends through my belly to my fanny. When I reached down to wash between my legs, though, it wasn't Warren's hand that came into my mind, but Gazza's.

With sudden revulsion I scrubbed my labia raw, digging my fingernails through the pubic hair in a panic to wash clean any thought of his defilement. That was rape! He had raped me! I suddenly realised, understood, and appreciated what generations of women have been fighting against. I couldn't take it anymore. Exhausted by the emotional overload, I collapsed against the shower wall and sobbed for my old life, my old friends, even my old Dalby.

"Old Life!" My God, I only left it three weeks ago and already it was a distant memory. Something very strange was going on out here.

I dragged myself back to my tent, my skin still hot and sweaty. I left one half of the flap raised and lay upside down on my sleeping bag, pressing my face against the screen to catch any wayward breeze. While I watched the stars dancing on the hills, Warren emerged from the men's showers, ubiquitous red sarong in place. As he walked past the women's shower block he stopped, bent, and picked something up. In the light I could see that it was my soap! I must have dropped it. He looked at it, sniffed it, looked around at all the tents, silent and asleep (except for mine but he obviously didn't know that), and sniffed it again.

He carried it over to a boulder at the edge of the camp and sat down, his back to the camp, legs slightly apart. Holding the bar of soap close to his face with one hand, he reached between his legs with the other and I watched as his arm moved up and down rhythmically. It moved slowly at first and I imagined his face– smiling as he drank in my scent and remembered the taste of my body, and then quickly as his needs became urgent until his back suddenly stiffened and he sat very still. After a few deep breaths he stood, adjusted his sarong, picked up a handful of dirt, and scrubbed something from the rock. He walked a bit stiffly back to his tent, placing the soap on the picnic table as he passed.

I knew it, you prick, I thought smugly. *I knew you were hot for me. I don't know who your first bitch was, but I'm the one who's haunting you now!* Even though Mary was snorting, asleep, I crawled into my sleeping bag for privacy. I could have a cold shower in the morning but tonight I wanted to savour what I'd just seen. I curled under the down cover and gently rubbed my secretions into my sore labia until they stopped hurting and thought of Warren wanking. Rubbing the juices into my clitoris, I remembered how his back had stiffened when he came, and I came myself.

Once wasn't enough. This place was turning me into a nymphomaniac. I turned on my back, straightened my legs and rubbed again, my fingers trapped between my thighs. I stroked harder this time and the delicious jolts travelled from my toenails to the roots of my gelled hair. I nearly suffocated swallowing my pleasure squeals. Who knew what would wake Mary? I'd never had sex–even with myself–while lying next to another woman. That taboo turned the excitement up a notch.

CHAPTER TWENTY

I WAS BLISSFULLY ASLEEP when the crash of breaking glass followed by whispered shouting woke me up.

"You dickhead!"

"You're the dickhead! Now shut up before you wake up the whole camp."

It was the unmistakable voices of teenage boys doing something they shouldn't. Wide awake, I dressed and was outside in a flash. Spider and Timbo were near the bus, both staggering, and Timbo held a broken bottle. I ran over and grabbed it from him. He looked at me, surprised. The smell of alcohol overwhelmed me and brought tears to my eyes.

"What you doing here, Mish?" Timbo slurred, trying unsuccessfully to whisper and blinking hard as though that would improve his focus.

"Wasn't me broke that bottle, Mish, it was 'im!" Spider's speech was no better. They both wobbled and shared a difficulty in focusing. I looked at what was left of the bottle in my hand....that had once contained a litre of OP rum!

"Where the bloody hell did you boys get this and how much did you drink?" I demanded to know, keeping my voice low with difficulty.

"Not that mush. Maybe half." Spider continued to defend himself.

"More like half eash!" Timbo corrected him.

They thought that was hilarious and fell against each other, laughing. I noticed that the bus door was open and the light was on and began to get suspicious. I grabbed Spider by the collar with my free hand.

"Tell me right now where you got this bottle!"

Spider, face as red as a beetroot, suddenly looked worried. "Aw, Mish, he didn' mean to break it. You won't tell Mr Gazza will ya?"

"Didn' mean to break it...but we meant to *drink* it," Timbo said and they were laughing again.

"Where did you get it?" I was getting angry and shook him hard, which wasn't difficult since he was so wobbly already.

"I think I know," said a voice behind me. I turned.

Warren took the bottle from me. He entered the bus and I saw that the driver's seat had been lifted, revealing a hiding place. Reaching into it, Warren pulled out another unopened bottle of OP rum. So this was where Gazza kept his stash! How many more bottles were in there, I wondered? The boys watched Warren.

"We seen that old pig getting stuck into this the other arvo when he thought we was off exploring so me and Timbo figgered why not us? Didn' figger he'd notice just one bottle missing. Then old Timbo had to go and break it..." Spider, barefoot, lurched toward his mate and nearly stepped on the broken glass. I yanked him back in time.

"I don't want any slashed feet." I looked up at Warren. "I'll get these boys cleaned up and into bed. You are going to do something about it now, aren't you? Before somebody actually dies?"

Without waiting for a reply, I marched the boys over to the men's showers and shoved their heads under the cold water, and then grabbed a towel off the line and dried them vigorously while they moaned and giggled.

"Had a drink *and* had a shower with the Lady Boss," Spider slurred. "Thass awright, I reckon!"

"We might jus' do this agin. Watcha reckon?" Timbo just didn't know when to shut up. I gave his head another dunk and didn't dry him off this time.

I then threw them (they didn't put up a fight) into the tent they shared with a final warning. "There will be NO vomiting...and don't call me Boss!"

By the time I'd finished, the bus was shut up and dark and Warren had disappeared. I returned to my sleeping bag but sleep eluded me. I was still awake when the first shadows woke the birds and the brumbies.

The brumbies! Sharp whinnies and thundering hooves had never been part of the dawn chorus before! What was bothering the brumbies this early in the morning? Dingoes? All our mob should still be fast asleep. Not eager to come between wild dingoes and wild horses, I curled up tight inside my sleeping bag and listened hard for signs of imminent danger. I didn't want any stampedes through my tent, although I had no idea how I would stop one if it started. Gradually I became aware that it wasn't barking dingoes I was hearing but the muffled voices of humans. *Not teenagers again!* I thought in despair. Once more, I dressed and exited the tent in a flash.

My worst fears were confirmed. It wasn't grey nomads disturbing the herd but a couple of dingo kids named Andreas and Laurel. Sweet Jesus! Where were the men? Why was it always up to me to save the children from the ferocious beasts? Where was that fucking judge? Bet he'd never even seen a brumby, let alone have to save anyone from an entire mob of the creatures!

Laurel stood at the edge of the small herd, her blond hair flying, waving her arms like she was trying to shoo them into the water while Andreas was in amongst them, trying to grab onto a mane without being bitten or trodden underfoot. As I rushed forward, he succeeded in his endeavour and catapulted his small body onto the back of a sleek black horse. I stopped short, rooted in terror, as the frightened animal bucked desperately to dislodge the foreign object from its back. Laurel screamed encouragement while I just screamed bloody murder.

Suddenly the brumby was off and running, faster and faster away into the desert scrub, Andreas still clinging to its back. The rest of the herd, rearing and shrieking, set off after them. Laurel sobbed, "Andreas, come back!" as I regained use of my legs and feet and gave chase. I'm not sure which part of my addled brain thought that I could outrun a herd of wild brumbies, but what I lacked in intelligence, I made up for with confidence. Until I tripped on a small thorn bush and sprawled flat on my face.

Warren grabbed an arm and jerked me upright. "Was that Andreas on a brumby?" he hollered into my face. He was wearing his swimming stubbies and a blue singlet which, I imagined, he probably slept in. At the moment, though, not even the thought of Warren's sleep wear could arouse me.

"Yes, yes–Andreas! You've got to save him!" Since another adult was finally there I allowed myself to give into hysteria. "Go—go now!" I screamed at him. "Go get Andreas before that damn horse kills him! He could die out there, Warren! He could get killed and die!" I wanted to be sure that he understood the gravity of the situation.

He must have because he pushed me back down in his haste to get away but not before I heard him say, "Shit, Louisa, shit!"

The entire campground was awake by now and Warren rushed over to another campsite where a Jeep Cherokee was parked. After hurried negotiations, the grey-haired man who must have been its owner and Warren jumped aboard and sped off in the direction of the brumbies. They weren't much more than a cloud of dust by this time. I dusted myself off and limped over to Laurel, who was sobbing madly. I put my arm around her shaking shoulders.

"Wanna tell me about it?" I asked quietly. The need for screaming was over.

"He loves them horses," she answered jerkily as her sobs turned to hiccoughs. "Said his grandpop was a stockman. Taught him to ride when he was little. Said he knew what he was doing. Oh, Miss..." She raised red, wet eyes to mine. "Do you think he'll be alright?"

"Of course he will," I reassured her with more bravado than I felt and hugged her shoulder. "He's got Mr Warren to save him, doesn't he?"

"I just hope that's enough." Jason had come up behind us. The concerned look on his face made him appear surprisingly mature and even almost handsome. All the other juvies were there, as well as Mary.

"Come on, youse," she said, always the practical one. "We can't do nothing standing around. Let's go get cleaned up and ready for breakfast." We followed her sombrely back to our tents.

I noticed the absence of Spider and Timbo so I, rather unkindly, sent Jason to get them up. They were subdued but knew better than to argue, especially once they'd heard the story of Andreas.

I poured steaming tea into various cups, noticing that no-one commented on the faint, but still evident, scent of whiskey on the air. Looking up, I saw the Jeep in the distance, returning to camp. Everyone stood still in dreadful anticipation until it arrived and gave a tremendous cheer when young Andreas, looking scratched but otherwise unharmed, climbed from the backseat. Warren followed, turned to thank the other man profusely, and then pulled Andreas from the clasp and questions of his mates.

"Enough of that. Andreas," he snapped, "go get cleaned up." He turned to the rest. "He is not a hero and I don't want anybody treating him like one. A stunt like that could have killed him in a heartbeat, don't ever think differently. Now, I am going to get changed and ready for today's *scheduled* events." He walked away, shoulders slightly slumped. I sighed and finished pouring tea. Nobody spoke as we waited for him to reappear, signaling a return to normal.

When Warren had warned us last night that the morning would need to be an early start, I'm sure he hadn't meant *this* early, and I know he didn't mean this dramatic. He'd just been trying to prove that he was the one in charge of this guided tour and that we shouldn't forget it, but I'm guessing that Andreas and Laurel had put Warren in his place this morning, not to mention those two last night. For once, I couldn't help but feel a twinge of pity for our fearless leader.

CHAPTER TWENTY-ONE

FINALLY WARREN AND ANDREAS, washed and dressed, joined us and the tension released. I noticed, for the first time, the distinct lack of razors in the group. Every male past puberty was sprouting facial hair and Spider's head was now covered in a reddish-brown baby fuzz. I also noted that Warren's black stubble made him even sexier. Have mercy!

Mary cooked breakfast, I desperately drank coffee (bitter and chewy), and Warren, as though the incident of the brumbies had never happened, took the young ones into the desert to measure shadows or some such nonsense. Andreas had cleaned up just fine and, although I was a bit surprised when the culprits from last night joined in, I also realized that despite their tender ages, they had probably already recovered from more hangovers than I'll have in my entire lifetime.

"Let's hear it for the social misfits, indeed." I smiled recalling Timbo's words. Maybe these kids weren't as bad as I'd once thought. Maybe this trip wasn't that bad, either. Wait a moment...did I really think that? Was I drunk on the fumes of OP rum? My brain cells certainly weren't synapsing the way I thought they should. I had to sober up. If it wasn't the OP rum, it had to be the effects of adrenalin surges before breakfast. Shouldn't be allowed.

I sat quietly, finishing a third cup of coffee and watching the rest of the group explore a small, nearby billabong. The kids followed Warren around like he was the Pied Piper. He always spoke respectfully to them, but it was more than that. He treated each one with dignity. Hell, he even treated The Pig with dignity, which couldn't be easy most of the time. *Warren's a real gentleman,* I thought, and then with a smirk—*although what we did the other night didn't feel very "dignified."* I allowed myself a pleasant moment of introspection.

Suddenly, a tickle on my un-waxed leg made me look down to see a tan lizard, about eight centimetres long, climbing up my shin. At the sight of that creature I very nearly screamed but stifled it at the last minute, remembering Sara. Taking a very deep breath, I reached down and grasped the reptile.

"Mary! Mary!" I screamed. "Quick, I need a box or jar or something. Hurry! Please!"

Mary, having no idea what was happening, panicked and grabbed a jar with salt in the bottom and ran to my aid.

"What's happening, Sister?" she asked as she removed the screw-top lid.

"A lizard for Sara. Yuck!" I gave a little screech as I dropped it with relief on top of the salt and Mary quickly recapped it.

"That salt will kill it. Never mind. I'll get a proper container." Mary walked away with the jar, and then stopped and turned around. "Good on you, Lou."

I gave a smug little grin. Easy to feel good as long as Mary had the lizard.

When the others returned I proudly presented my catch. Sara was ecstatic, and Warren was incredulous.

"*You* picked up a lizard?" He couldn't believe it. Hell, *I* couldn't believe it!

"She did," answered Mary. "I seen it with me own two eyes."

I shrugged as if capturing wildlife were commonplace. "It was nothing. They aren't slimy at all."

Warren chuckled, shook his head, and walked away, rounding up the youngsters, telling them to wash their hands before breakfast. I got a warm glow in the pit of my stomach. I'd actually gotten the guy's approval! My reason told me that it was long overdue and not that big a deal, but, nonetheless, I couldn't wipe the smile from my face. Not until breakfast began, that is.

Gazza, having missed the entire ordeal earlier, was last out of bed and first at the breakfast table. Unfortunately, the kids, apparently ravenous after having witnessed the earlier ordeal, crowded in so quickly that I was forced to sit next to the greasy pig. The stench of alcohol exuded from his pores and his breath could stop a camel. He never took any notice that his clothes had been washed. Either that or he just assumed his laundry would be done for him if there were an Aboriginal woman nearby.

I could face only the pancakes. Eating a sausage would be too much like eating him, and as much I wished someone would cut his dick off, I didn't want it to be my teeth that did the deed. Despite the bus driver, it was a gorgeous morning, all ten juvies were safe and healthy (at the moment!) and The Pig was too busy eating to notice that I was beside him.

Things were going well and dumb ol' me was naïve enough to believe that they would continue in the same vein. Later I would learn the truth about wishful thinking.

As we boarded the bus at eight o'clock, the heat of the day was already beginning. Gazza turned the on air con full bore and Jason and Laurel decided to lead the group in song which made me wish desperately for my iPod. Warren was trying to use his phone (must have been satellite) and moved to the back of the bus to hear over the singing.

"What?...What? I can't hear you," he said into it while walking down the aisle. He gestured impatiently to me. I was sitting, as usual, in the last seat.

"In Kununurra, you say?" He frowned and placed the phone against his chest to speak to me, sounding irritated. "You can sit up front with them this morning. I've got work to do."

"Like I don't." I said it just to hear the sound of my voice but moved forward anyway, wondering where his good humour had gone. Spider and Timbo invited me to sit with them. I decided I would hate Warren and become one of the crims again. I didn't want to get too up close and personal with Timbo's nits so I sat sideways on the bench in front of theirs, hung over the back, and chatted.

"Where did you get a name like Spider?"

"Me mum says I used to crawl around on me hands and feet instead of me hands and knees and I looked just like a spider."

"Your own mother called you Spider?"

"Only when she wasn't calling me Shithead." That got a big laugh. I doubted that their blood alcohol would even have reached the legal limit yet but, what the hell? They weren't driving and we were having fun.

"So where's your mother now?"

"She got a new boyfriend last year and whenever he thumped her, I'd thump him so they left and went to

Townsville. That's OK, but, because I can stay with me dad or me sister or friends or whatever."

"When you're not in the juvie lock-up, that is," said Timbo and they laughed again. "It happens to him a lot. He's a very noticeable kind of guy."

"You betcha." Spider flexed his tattooed biceps and looked pleased. "I'm gonna get some tatts on my head when we get back. I'm lucky I'm not too black and tatts show up real good on me."

They made it sound like getting tattooed got you sent to juvenile detention, but I didn't think that would be true. Not even in the NT. Spider's ABH charge was sounding justified to me. I mean, if your mum loved a man who thumped her more than her own child, wouldn't that encourage you to thump people? I might have to discuss this with Claudia, if I ever get back, that is.

"Have you ever been in juvenile detention?" I asked Timbo.

"Just the once, and that was only a couple of weeks. It ain't hard for a blackfella to avoid being noticed in Darwin, so long as you stay where you're supposed to."

"You mean like at home or in school?" I was being serious but everybody who heard me laughed at my question. Everybody was in such a good mood this morning while dumb ol' me still tried to find the jokes. Oh, well, they were less trouble when they were happy.

"No, Miss, I said 'blackfella.' I mean like the park or the Aboriginal Housing or places like that." He high-fived Spider. "They picked me up this time because I was spending the day in the Art Gallery and stood out a bit."

I zoned out for just a second...Darwin had an *art gallery*!?! And it was for Whites only? None of this sounded right.

"You got arrested for being in an art gallery?" He had to be exaggerating.

"There was this big exhibition of the Aboriginal desert artists, you know, and I fucking love that shit. If I had the money, I'd spend the rest of my life painting pictures. Back when I was in school my teachers said I had talent, eh."

"But why..." I persisted.

"Oh, that...Well, there was this particular painting that fit perfect into my pocket...Turns out it was by Albert Namatjira. Man, I coulda learned so much from that picture."

"So why don't you go back to school?"

Timbo looked at me with a straight face. "You're kidding, right?"

"You gotta be able to read if you wanna go to high school, ain't that right, Timbo?" Spider laughed and swiped the other boy across the top of his head.

"You can't read?" That was hard to believe. "You went to primary school, didn't you?"

"Yeah, but in Grade Five they told me I was disconnected..."

"Dyslexic?"

"Something like that, and then the headmaster told me I'd never amount to anything so what was the point in trying high school?"

"And the boy is still totally disconnected!" Spider said.

"You should talk." Timbo grinned and they high-fived again.

I settled against the seat to contemplate the vagaries of life in general and Darwin in particular. The joviality of Spider and Timbo could be explained by the OP rum circulating through their systems but I also wanted to believe that the cheerful atmosphere of the whole group was related to the improvements in their general health. Sunburns were turning into tans, the infected bites were healing, and their stomachs were adjusting to healthy eating.

This was an all day trip and Mary had come along. She sat in front with the kids as well, allowing Brooke and Sara to plait her hair into corn braids. Those two had become fast friends. Caleb and Melanie had their heads together, deep in conversation, his straight black hair mixing with her orange locks. About make-up? Jason, Corey, and Andreas were checking out leaflets about crocodiles and I certainly hoped they weren't planning to catch any. Laurel was in the front seat, leaning over and chatting with Gazza. Her skin had turned from pink to a soft tan, her blond hair was pulled back in a pony tail, and with her sparkling eyes she looked eager and attractive. The way our driver smiled at the girl made me uneasy but I chose not to intervene. He was the policeman and maybe I was wrong about the look on his face.

We'd been travelling for a couple of hours and finally arrived at Purnululu Park and turned into a picnic area. As always, the youngsters flew off the bus and jumped around as though they'd been let out of prison. Mary had brought along thermoses of hot tea and a family size packet of biscuits for our morning tea break.

"I made extra damper last night for smoko today, but that's what youse ate for the ghost stories last night. Still can't believe none of youse had nightmares."

I couldn't believe none of them had bellyache after eating a big dinner, plum tart, *and* damper. "I'm sure the biscuits won't matter," I said. "They've got the great outdoors to work off their energy in today." I noticed Laurel going into the ladies toilet and followed her, planning to give motherly advice.

"You and Gazza had a lot to talk about," I tried to sound nonchalant as I went into the stall next to hers.

"You're not wrong, Miss! He reckons he could get me into the police academy." Her eager voice echoed from inside her stall. "That would be so cool. I could get a car, a gun, everything, and my oldies would be so proud. Even my uncle—and he's a bad crim. I reckon he'd be glad to have a copper in the family. Officer O'Brien's not so bad, Miss, once you start talking to him, like."

I heard the flush and she stepped out to wash her hands.

"That's great, Laurel. I think you'd make a fine policewoman." I didn't know what else to say. "Although maybe you should have practised on Andreas this morning?" I teased as I emerged from my stall. I splashed her as I washed my hands, she splashed back, and the mother-daughter role vanished.

CHAPTER TWENTY-TWO

I WANTED TO ENCOURAGE Laurel's ambitions but I couldn't lose the uneasy feeling about The Pig. He stood outside talking to Warren. It was a pretty safe bet that he hadn't noticed that his stash had been raided yet. There was a hike down Piccaninny Creek scheduled for 10:30 a.m. and, as it was getting underway, I realised that Gazza would be leading the hike. I didn't know what to think about that decision, but he sounded sober enough and, what the hell, the fresh air and exercise might do him some good. That was the whole point of this journey, wasn't it? Warren climbed onto the bus and retrieved his laptop. I got a sudden idea and ran to find Mary.

"I'll give you two packs of my Beedies if you'll go on this hike for me, Mary. I'm feeling really tired and want to rest before we start climbing this afternoon." That part was certainly true after last night and this morning, and I tried to make myself believe that's all there was to my request. I had almost convinced myself but Mary was having none of it.

She looked at me, looked at Warren on the bus, and then back at me.

"Yeah, I'm sure you're very tired. Make it four packs and you've got a deal."

"Four! That's all I have left."

"Take it or leave it." She looked again at our tour guide, bent intently over his computer. "If I were you, Sister, I'd leave it."

For one split second I considered the pleasure of smoking against the opportunity to be alone with Warren. I could catch up on my sleep another time. In actual fact, it felt awkward smoking in front of the kids and I only had the odd cigarette late at night now. I probably wouldn't even miss them.

"You aren't me, Sister. I'll take it."

A brief handshake and Mary followed the group down to the dry creek bed and I hid myself behind a boab tree. *Oh, God, you're such an idiot*, I chastised myself as I waited, sweat trickling down my neck and prickling my eyes. *You don't even have the nerve to let him know you're here! What are you going to do? What are you going to say*? While carrying on that heated argument with myself, I suddenly realised that he was no longer sitting on the bus. Searching around in a panic, I saw him walking toward a cleft in the hills, a towel slung over his shoulder. Breaking his own rules, going off alone. I could not allow him to be hoisted on his own petard, could I? So I followed, feeling smug and suddenly calm. A little self-righteousness can go a long way.

He quickly disappeared among all those bloody rocks and my panic returned. Hurrying forward into I knew not what, I rounded a bend and saw him. I stopped, heart in my throat, aware that I was experiencing a secret moment, a pivotal occurrence, and if I did not turn back now, I would be forever lost. He stood, tall and naked, at the edge of a small swimming hole, arms outstretched, hands raised, palms upward, forming an intimate part of the landscape. His back faced me, its muscles tensed and sharply defined. His straight spine formed a trough down to the cleft separating his firm, round buttocks. He stood with his legs apart, thigh and calf muscles rigid as he raised himself to his toes. For the second time, I watched as he sensed my presence and turned to face me, arms remaining outstretched. He wasn't surprised to see me, but looked straight into my eyes. He gave a broad smile, nostrils flared and pupils dilated. His beautiful, black, uncircumcised penis thickened and cocked, beckoning me to him.

My blood heated and raced throughout my body, washing away all conscious thought. I removed my clothes as I walked to him, slowly but without hesitation, my shorts slipping easily over the thongs I'd worn to follow him. It was a morning for breaking rules and many more were about to be shattered. I stepped into his arms and we held each other tight, not speaking, allowing touch to give rise to forbidden feelings. His cock pressed against my navel, its tip already moist with desire. I leaned my head back and looked into his green eyes, spinning through my own private universe until I sank into their black holes. My desire equalled his. My blood slowed in my veins, my fanny ached with need, and time lost all meaning.

He leaned forward and kissed me gently, lips closed, as soft as I knew they would be. I melted into his embrace, kissed him back, and suddenly our mouths were open and hungry, each attempting to devour the other. Our hands desperately searched hidden passages and the tropical sun that burned my back was cool compared to the fire welling up inside me. His finger found my clit and I nearly collapsed, my cries muffled by his lips.

Without loosening his hold, he walked me backward down a gentle slope and into a deep pool of the clearest water I had ever seen. We swam easily to the centre, and then we were tightly clasped in each other's arms again, my legs wrapped around his waist. He entered me. I heard him gasp and I groaned as the power of the penetration surprised us both. Kicking to stay afloat he let me ride him until I came, hanging on for dear life. I admit, it didn't take long. Then I spread my arms wide, lying back in the water to laugh in pleasure, legs still tight around his hips and holding his hot cock firmly inside. I thrilled to his first spasm and wriggled encouragement but was a bit disappointed when he grabbed my legs, wrenched them apart and pulled out to ejaculate into the pool.

I watched his cock throb again and again under the water, spurting his cream. I reached down to grab his hard handle, milking out the last of his come as tiny fishes darted in and out of the jism cloud, nibbling frantically.

Then, unbelievably, he was hard again and back inside me, sliding in and out, in and out, working up a friction that burned as hot as fire. I don't know how we didn't drown. He grasped me by the waist and kicked to shore, still inside me. He carried me from the pool and we collapsed onto his towel to finish. Once again, he pulled out before he came and, once again, I was slightly disappointed. Gasping, we lay side-by-side. Looking up, we saw the Bungle Bungles all around us like giant phalluses, dancing a shimmy in the shimmering heat.

The sight made my vagina swell yet again and I found I wasn't finished. Tender, yes, but horny as hell. For some reason, I just couldn't get enough of this guy. I took his fingers, put them into my mouth, and then onto to my swollen clit.

He understood my need. With me spread out like a lizard on

a rock, he smiled as he used his whole hand, fingers inside, fingers outside, juice running down my thighs, me wriggling. I came softly this time, on account of the heat and my exhaustion. Tingling suffused my body, travelling down my limbs, up through my belly, chest, neck, and face. I stiffened for a moment, and then gently settled, eyes closed and smiling. In that instant, my life was perfect.

Suddenly Warren removed his hand and jumped to his feet. I opened my eyes and saw him standing, his back to me, staring into the distance.

"What's up?" I asked, still smiling.

"Please go now," he said. I rolled over and shook my head. I couldn't believe what I was hearing from the mouth that had so recently been sucking me to heaven and beyond. I sat up. I wasn't going to take this lying down.

"This is the second time you've done this to me. The first time you did this to me, I thought it was because you were just feeling guilty about Jason finding us. So what the fuck's your problem this time?"

"It doesn't matter," he replied without turning. "You're no different than she was. Now, please, just go and leave me in peace. Gazza will be back soon. You can go to him." He walked to the water and plunged in.

Me?...Go to *Gazza*? Enraged and confused, I was afraid that I would burst into tears if I tried to respond. And who the hell was "she?" At least he hadn't called me a bitch this time, but was that supposed to make me feel better? I was at a loss. I gathered my clothes and walked away in the dust and heat, praying fervently that he would drown or, at the very least, be mauled by a crocodile.

I was fully clothed by the time I returned to where the bus was parked, and I sat inside, nursing a bottle of water and a badly bruised ego. At this point, I didn't know which was worse; Warren hating me or him thinking that I wanted Gazza. That belief, more than his rejection, proved that he had no respect for me. But there was little time for self pity. I heard a shout and looked up to see the explorers returning from their expedition.

CHAPTER TWENTY-THREE

SPIDER, TIMBO, and Caleb had painted their faces with something red, three of the girls had covered their arms and legs with dust, and crazy Jason had numerous feathers stuck in his tangled hair.

"Hey, Miss, we gone Indigenous on ya!" the former Goth yelled and their joy infected me. I put aside all thoughts of that arsehole at the swimming hole and bounced out of the bus to hear their stories. Mary was dragging her feet a bit but looked happy.

"Oh, Lou, I'm too old for this!" She laughed and shook her head, collapsing onto a nearby bench. "I probably don't have enough breath left to smoke them Beedies of yours. Brooke, quick, bring me water!" She laid her head on the table and Warren, looking fresh and clean as always, joined us.

"It serves you right, Mary. Trading CSO-assigned duties for forbidden cigarettes was very naughty." But when she cast a knowing smirk in his direction he hastily averted his eyes. "Where's Gazza?"

"I dunno. He was behind us a minute ago but he wasn't looking too good," said Corey.

"And where's Laurel?" added Timbo. His query surprised me a little because I was certain he liked to make a point of avoiding her. So why was he missing her now?

Warren looked at Mary, exhausted by the excursion, and then glared at me as though I were the worst thing that had ever been created. The bastard was accusing *me* of dereliction of duty! As if he'd never been anywhere near that swimming hole!

"Don't waste your breath blaming me," I shouted and took off running down the dry creek bed. "Just fucking find her!"

All the guys started running back the way they had come. I guess none of them trusted that pig any farther than they could throw him. Were we going to find that he had finally gone too far? Around the first bend we found them, Gazza sitting on a large rock, panting, sweat pouring off his bright red face, and, more worryingly, hanging onto Laurel. His arm was around her shoulders and his fingers were millimetres from her breast. She looked up when she heard our shouts.

"Thank goodness you're here! Poor Mr Gazza is nearly collapsed with the heat frustration."

Warren arrived first and roughly removed the driver's arm from the girl's body. "OK, Laurel, thank you so much for your help. You go back with the others and I'll look after Mr Gazza," he said sternly.

"But, I was just—" she protested, unsure of what she'd done wrong. I came up and took her hand.

"I know, Laurel, you were helping him and we're all very grateful." I led her away. "But now we're here and Mr Warren's strong enough to get him back and I'm the one who has the first aid kit. You go on with the boys and let Mary get you something to drink, OK?"

The boys were glad to assist pretty Laurel back to our picnic area, but I hung around for another minute, curious to see how Warren would handle this. I didn't doubt that Gazza was hot and tired, but I was certain that he could have made it the last few metres if he'd wanted to. I'd seen the leer on his face fade to disappointment when we appeared on the scene.

"Come on, Miss," Jason called. Warren saw me and waved me away, his forehead wrinkled in a frown. When the two men joined us a few minutes later they appeared to be best buddies and Warren gave the other a big bottle of water to drink and bathe his head in. Fucking men!

Mary had an Esky full of bread and sliced meats and salads that she carried over to a picnic table. I went to help her make sandwiches for lunch but was trembling so much that she took the knife away.

"Man trouble?"

"*Men* trouble. I hate both of them so much, Mary. I've got to get out of here before I go crazy or kill somebody."

"You don't hate one of them too much. I can smell him on you."

"Oh, shit!" I'd left Warren in such a hurry I hadn't thought to clean off the evidence. There were no showers around, and I certainly wasn't going to go swimming with him after he'd ordered me away. I picked up a plastic knife and furiously began slathering butter on the bread.

"I hope you at least washed your hands," said Mary.

"I bet you don't!" I grinned wickedly, but of course I had. Out here I always carried Wet Ones in my pocket.

"I'm just saying, girl, you be careful."

"*They'd* better be careful." I brandished the plastic knife. "The way I'm feeling right now, even this is a deadly weapon."

Once again, my appetite was ruined so, while the kids ploughed their way through the 500 sandwiches we'd cut, I took an apple and returned to the water hole. I hadn't meant to linger, just a quick ablution on the edge, but the crystal blue pond was so still and inviting that I stripped off and jumped in, ducking my head under its cool depths, trying to wash away more than the cum. My brain went black, crammed full of anger and frustration and uncertainty and violent desires. I don't know how long I'd been there when the sound of a splash made me look to shore. Warren stood there with his hands on his hips. He had chucked a rock into the water to get my attention.

"We're about to leave," he said in a flat tone. "This isn't only about you, Miss Smith. Kindly come back and do your work." He turned on his heel and left. "And don't forget to put your clothes on!"

I screamed "F-U-C-K!" to the pelicans in the pond. They paid no attention. They'd been witness to the morning's activities and knew what a fool I was. I got dressed and returned to work.

A long hike around the amazing beehive domes they call the Bungle Bungles was the afternoon's agenda. Warren would lead us, giving a commentary about the history of the area, and I was the sweeper, the one who walked behind, picking up stragglers and making sure nobody got lost. Also to make sure nobody ducked away for a secret smoke or nookie. There will be no illicit pleasuring on this guided tour, thank you, ladies and gentlemen, boys and girls! There'd be no more for me, either. Mary had my cigarettes and Warren had my self-respect.

Was that Warren's problem? Did he think I was leading him astray, off the straight and narrow? Well, if I was in the lead, he had certainly been eager to follow and had no right to blame me. I had to say it again: *FUCKING MEN!* Only this time I could only scream it in my head. Mustn't frighten the children! I kicked my boots in the dirt, feeling very sorry for myself.

The hot and dusty trail with the sun directly overhead made shadows few and far between. It was probably not the best time of day for an excursion like this. Mary and Gazza had chosen to stay behind and were most likely sitting in the bus with the air con on. I tried to imagine what that would feel like but the heat was so dry that I could feel my skin cracking. I'd forgotten my hat in my hurry to "get back to work" and the sun bore down on my head like a helmet of fire.

I'd finished my water bottle within the first half hour and now my feet were starting to drag. I was doing my job taking up the rear really well. I spotted a small patch of shade and stopped for a moment. The rest of the group disappeared through the rocks. I meant to follow straight away, of course, but must have dozed off just a little. I don't know how long I'd been sitting there when a shout made me look up. What I saw made me jump up in a hurry.

Jason and Brooke were on top of one of those rocks, dancing and waving their hats to me.

"You idiots! How did you get up there?" I hollered.

"We climbed! It's easy! You should come up and see the view, it's awesome!"

From thirty metres below, I panicked, scrambling around, looking for a trail. I was so sure they would fall. What I found might have been called a trail by well-rounded adventurers, but to me it was a goat track in every sense of the word. And I was no goat. While reaching for handholds and searching for footrests, I climbed as quickly as I dared while shouting, "Come down immediately, you two!" The good Lord only knows how I thought I'd be able to get them down once I got up there.

She died with her juvenile offenders. Would that expunge my CSO? Would that make my parents proud?

Somehow I made it up to where they were. Jason reached

down to give me a hand up, Brooke danced backwards, slipped—and fell! In horror, I watched her hurtle down the rock face, bouncing off it once, and then disappearing into a chasm with a blood-curdling scream.

"Brooke! Brooke!" I screeched, wringing my hands hysterically, afraid to approach the edge myself. "Oh, God, can you hear me? Are you all right? Are you conscious?"

I leaned over as far as I dared but could only see a foot in a red sandshoe, gripped tightly between two rocks. I heard moaning so at least she was alive but for how long? What sort of injuries did she have? She had fallen down the side of a sheer cliff. We'd have to go back down the way we'd come up and try to find a way to get to her.

"Oh, shit, Jason, we have to move quickly. You go back down that trail I just came up and run for help. I'll try to find out exactly where she is."

Before I could move, though, Jason, like the mountain goat I wasn't, was somehow running upright, down the dome, and toward the place that had swallowed Brooke, black coattails flying out behind him like wings. I slid down the trail, all the way back to the ground and ran around the rock to see if I could see them. I met Jason, dirty and bleeding from numerous scrapes and scratches, coming around a corner. He carried Brooke, whose right ankle was swelling rapidly. She was groaning and gripping his neck tightly.

"It's OK, Miss, I got her. I'll be carrying her back to the bus."

He took off at a trot with me following and he didn't slow up until we arrived at the picnic area twenty minutes later. I'd been sure we were lost and had no idea how he knew, so unerringly, which way to go.

When Mary saw us she dropped her book and hurried forward to meet us. She'd been lying on a blanket under a tree and Jason placed Brooke there. He went over to a spigot to get a long drink of water while Mary and I examined the poor girl. The first thing I did was gently remove the red sandshoe from the injured ankle and Mary got a paring knife to cut through a black-and-gold football sock.

Brooke's sobbing had subsided, and she only winced when we touched her sore places. She had lumps and swellings and scratches, but, other than the ankle, appeared to have escaped any serious injury. Once again, I racked my brain to remember details of that high school first aid course and, since she could wiggle her toes, I suspected she had a bad sprain rather than broken bones. I ran to the bus, grabbed the first aid kit, and searched for bandages while sensible Mary got a bag of ice from the Esky. She elevated Brooke's foot on another rolled blanket, and then wrapped it in the ice.

"We'll bandage it later, and we probably won't need that sling there, Lou."

I looked down at what I carried and realized that I'd grabbed the first thing that was made of cloth from the box. I remembered how hysterically my mother had laughed when, at age ten, I'd told her I wanted to be a nurse.

"Maybe not this time," I said ruefully and tucked it away in my back pocket. "What the *bloody* hell am I doing here?"

"Learning." Mary smiled and turned back to her patient. I gave her the Panadol I'd also found in the kit which Brooke swallowed gladly.

"How's she doing?" Jason had come up behind me. Dropping everything I whirled around and threw my arms around his neck.

"My hero!" I cried. I was still hugging him and he was bright red when Warren appeared.

"What did you do this time?" he barked at me but saw Brooke and rushed over. I let go of Jason and hung my head and hands. As if I didn't feel bad enough. I didn't need his blame as well.

"Just the usual, Boss. I fucked up big time."

He glanced up at me. "I wish you wouldn't swear."

"And *I* wish I hadn't been forced to come on this fucking trip!" I'd been so frightened, trying so hard to do something I'd never been trained for, and this arsehole just wouldn't let up. Tears pricked at my eyes but there was no way I'd let him see me cry. A flash of my temper dried them before they fell. "And you can just bloody well get fucked!"

I stomped off, going God knows where, ignoring the juvies who'd gathered round to watch the fireworks. The last thing I heard as I disappeared from view was Warren complimenting

Jason and Mary. I didn't resent them because they'd both been brilliant, but Warren hadn't been stroking their bodies a few short hours ago. I couldn't sulk alone for long, though, because poor Brooke had to be taken to Casualty in Kununurra and that was a fair drive. Hiding behind a large rock, I smoked a bedraggled Beedie I'd found at the bottom of my bag, and then returned to my charge.

Warren and the others were still gathered around her. Warren the Prick was chastising her about following Jason up the rocks. "You know he's not reliable, Brooke. What on earth convinced you to go with him?"

She shrugged weakly. "Dunno, Boss. Guess I'm getting to like nature too much, eh? And he *did* save my life."

Warren patted her cheek. "He did do that. I'm glad you're all right. Now," he said and stood up and turned to the others, "let's all give Brooke some air and get ourselves something to eat and drink. Then we better get back to base."

He strode over to the Esky and began pulling out cold cartons of flavoured milk and juicy red apples, which were eagerly grabbed up and noisily consumed. Some things were changing around here. I knelt by Brooke.

"You should be nicer to Mr Warren, Miss, even if he *is* a pain in the butt sometimes," she whispered.

"I'll do my best, Brooke. Now, let's look at your ankle."

Once again recalling my tenth grade St John's Ambulance course, I applied a bandage (firm not tight) in a figure eight pattern around her injury. The pain killers she'd taken earlier were beginning to kick in and all six boys volunteered to carry her onto the bus. Jason, of course, did the honours in the end. He laid her across the back seat with so many blankets and packs beneath her foot that it was higher than her head. All the others then crowded into the nearby seats, trying to cheer her up, and by the look on her face, I suspected she'd never received so much positive attention before in her whole short life.

I was glad for her and took my place in one of the middle rows. For the first time, it never occurred to me to isolate myself from my juvies. I hadn't realized how tired I was, but the day and previous night must have been too much for me because I was fast asleep, head resting on the first aid box before we left Piccaninny Creek and didn't wake until Gazza lurched us into the campground, jerking to a stop that exacerbated my whiplash. As if I didn't have enough pains in my neck to deal with.

CHAPTER TWENTY-FOUR

USING HIS SATELLITE PHONE, Warren had arranged for an ambulance to meet us at camp. They quickly transferred Brooke into the back, Warren jumped in as well, and they were off. Our mob of twelve stood watching the ambulance disappear into its own cloud of dust, feeling lost, forlorn, and inexplicably, abandoned.

He'll be back, I told myself, *and if you have to have a crim in charge, you're lucky that it's Mary.* Gazza had disappeared into the Grey Nomads' camp as soon as we arrived. *Meantime, Louisa Smith, you've got work to do.* Big fake smile plastered on my dial, I turned to my surviving children. "Don't anybody worry. They'll be back before you know it! Now, chop, chop, we have lives to live here."

I hustled us all back to the tent area and got busy with my usual evening routine: listening to stories, kissing boo-boos, taping plasters onto cuts, and rubbing ointments into bumps while Mary got busy with dinner. Suddenly, Gazza reappeared, his face so dark I thought he might be having a stroke. I could have cared less, and then it hit me.

Oh, Christ! He must have discovered the theft of one of his bottles and, now that Warren was gone, he was going to find and punish the culprit. Trembling with fear, I went up to him.

"Is there something you wanted?" I hoped my voice sounded stronger than my nerve.

I held my breath as he stood there, panting, clenching and unclenching his fists. He must have realized that punching a female detainee is never a good idea because he grunted and shuffled back to the other campers.

Expelling an enormous lungful of terror I looked around for last night's drinkers. Timbo was nowhere to be seen, but Spider's usually brown face was the colour of chalk.

"Thanks, Miss," he whispered and crawled into his tent. The boys had said there were "heapsh" of bottles when they'd been in Gazza's stash last night but looked very angry for having lost just one bottle. Had Warren gotten rid of the rest? Was he that strong? I hoped so and smiled.

The sun was beginning to set when we gathered to eat. Spider and Timbo were looking as healthy as young Olympians and I envied them their resilience. I've never been able to drink like that and recover so quickly but, then, I guess practise makes perfect. The conversation, naturally, turned to Andreas, Laurel and the brumbies, and the story Warren hadn't allowed them to tell that morning. The others sounded full of admiration which, unfortunately, I suspected it was my duty to kerb. Didn't want any repeat performances.

"Andreas, dude," Spider began, "Since when did you become a cowboy?"

"Me pop was a stockman," he answered casually, intent on slathering butter and barbecue sauce onto his bread. "Shit, I could cut a horse and ride it by the time I was six."

"Don't swear," I said from habit but wanted to hear the story as much as anyone.

Andreas grinned at me. "Yes, Boss. Anyways, Pop got sick and lost his job so the family moved into Darwin. Never been on horseback since. When I saw them brumbies it was like something rose up inside a me and I just had to ride again. It's just like Mr Warren said it would be, eh?" he said seriously. "Being out here takes you right back to your roots, where you oughtta be."

I was absurdly gratified to see Spider and Timbo exchange a guilty look when he said that. Were they actually having regrets about writing themselves off last night? I was almost sorry that Warren wasn't here to witness a small justification of his project. I cast a sidelong glance at Mary and her warm, fuzzy smile told me she was feeling the same.

"Yeah, but Andreas," Laurel asked, "how did you get off without getting hurt or trampled to death or something? How did the men find you?"

"Yeah, how?" Melanie and Sara echoed.

Everybody's plate was filled with salad and sausages on bread and we all settled in to listen to his tale while we ate, but Andreas wasn't much of a talker so it didn't last very long.

"Well, actually, I was a bit nervous once she took off running, didn't know where I'd end up, Alice Springs or what, but she was a smooth runner and her smell and the wind in me face and all that...I sorta didn't want her to stop, but she did, of course, and stopped so quick that I slid right over the top of her, landed in sand, and then I heard the jeep honking and the herd took off again and, well, here I am!" As if to prove his existence, in case we had any doubt, he crammed half his sausage sandwich into his mouth and chewed happily, sauce dripping down his chin.

"So, why were you there, Laurel?" Timbo asked in a funny kind of voice and she didn't look at him when she answered.

"Oh, I don't know. When I got up for a pee the brumbies were there so I was wandering over to have a look. That's when I saw Andreas and come over to see what he was doing and thought I'd see if I could help him, that's all. Got any more snags there, Mary?"

"Can't get enough of those snags, eh, Laurel?" Jason asked in his could-I-be-a-bigger-dickhead? voice, Laurel threw a spatula full of coleslaw in his face and then it was on for young and old. To me the reaction was unexpected, but I put it down to the traumatic circumstances of the day and to the absence of the big boss.

The fracas was just getting sorted when The Pig turned up, unsteady, laughing too loudly, and smelling of grog. Apparently he'd found some mates to cheer him up. He cornered me, yet again, after dinner. I was scraping the plates and some of the kids were carrying the dishes over to Mary to help with the washing up as others packed away sauce bottles. I decided to ignore him but he had his own ideas.

"I hear you like black cocks, eh?" he slurred, falling against the table and knocking a stack of plates to the ground. I stood firm, not picking them up as I was unwilling to bend over with him so close. I guess Jason hadn't been able to keep his mouth shut after all. "If you can fuck that Abo, I reckon you'd suck my dick, eh?"

He grabbed my breast and leaned his hairy face into mine. But I too had been having a really bad day and I, like Laurel, had a knee-jerk reaction. My knee jerked–three times–smack into his groin. He fell to the ground, gonads choking him, and I stepped over his writhing carcass, suddenly feeling absolutely fabulous. A perfect end to an incredible day!

"Outstanding!" cheered Mary as I high-fived her.

The Pig dragged himself into his tent muttering threats and the kids stood speechless. They hadn't seen his moves, just mine.

"Remember that, girls," I said. "As long as you've got a knee handy you don't need a self-defence course."

"Wasn't that a bit harsh, Miss?" Laurel asked.

"Hardly harsh enough!" grunted Timbo while the others agreed with him loudly.

"Youse just don't understand him!" she shouted and flounced away. I didn't follow her. I was too busy thinking how great I was.

It was well and truly dark by the time the Brooke and Warren returned to camp. They had got a lift back from one of the Grey Nomads who'd gone into the town for supplies. None of us had had the energy to build a fire and were, instead, draped in various positions over benches, tables, and eskies. We'd picked the plates up off the ground and the dishes had been washed and put away and we were gabbing on about whatever while awaiting the wayfarers' return. They'd eaten at Macca's in town and the good news was that there were no bones broken. Brooke had crutches—those short metal ones with arms grips—which the others thought were, to use their term, "deadly." They did look like they could be used as weapons. Jason took one of Brooke's arms to help her, Sara hurried up to take the other, and, as if reading my mind, Corey and Caleb each picked up a crutch and began fencing. I retrieved the foils before any permanent damage was done. We didn't need any broken bones in this mob.

It was late but no-one could think of bed. This day had been far too eventful (and they didn't even *know* my story). Sleep was a faraway country. Warren built a nice campfire and we sat around it playing "who's had the worst injury." I'd already heard Andreas's story but the others were really impressed by the blood.

Melanie grossed us out with her stories of childbirth.

Apparently the head hadn't quite fit through the opening and she was stitched from "arsehole to breakfast" (her words).

"Yeah, but that's nothing. I delivered a baby once," Timbo announced.

"Get out!"

"You never!"

"What makes you tell such lies?"

"It's true," he protested. "It was me sister's. I was only ten back then and didn't even know she was pregnant. She'd never told nobody and I just thought she was getting fat from too many pies and chips. I don't know what our mum thought. Anyway, I come home from school one day and heard her crying in her room and she sounded real sick so I went in to see what was happening and she was lying there in her bed with all this blood around her and a baby coming out of her fanny so I took hold of it and helped it out. It was really tiny, premature, they called it, and I didn't know how to cut the cord back then or nothing so I just called triple-0 and wrapped the baby in me jumper. It was a boy."

"Deadly!"

"Holy shit!"

"That is so cool, man," Corey said. "So how's the kid now? Can't be too good having you as an uncle, I bet."

"Aw, he didn't make it." Timbo looked down, picked up a small stick, and began drawing in the dirt. "Too little, ya know? But my sis has had four more kids since then. I'm a bit over being an uncle."

I sat speechless. I wanted to hug him or something but was sure any reaction would be inappropriate. Holy Hell, I wished they'd stop telling me their stories. Who could make up this shit? That this could be anybody's "normal" life was more than I could deal with right now. Didn't I have enough problems of my own?

That turned out to be the last tale of the night. The others patted Timbo on the back as they got up and made their ways to the showers. I decided to wait until the girls had vacated the toilet/shower block before going in there. Much as I hated to do it, I had to think.

CHAPTER TWENTY-FIVE

ONE MONTH—a lifetime—ago, I had opted to stay at Dalby's flat for the rest of the week until final time, and he was brilliant helping me study. The class was in waste management and Dalby knew every trick in the book for circumventing government regulations. He knew the top five Third World countries for dumping waste economically and knew which chemicals were the cheapest to recycle. He also knew, for bonus points, which NGO's (like Greenpeace, Australian Conservation Society, World Wildlife Fund and so on) were the easiest to manipulate.

When I was with him, all the activist rhetoric I'd been listening to faded into meaningless slogans. Our passion had faded almost before it had burned, but we were great friends and isn't that what they say marriage is about? He obviously wanted me to succeed and I was lucky to have him. I knew this because he reminded me of it all the time. During that entire week, however, I was relegated to the spare bedroom. "Think of it as being in training," he said. When he went out at night, I was told to stay home and study. Dalby may be only five years older than me but he was worse than my dad had ever been. I accepted it as what was required to get my degree.

"You're not going to act like my father after we're married, are you?" I asked jokingly one afternoon while he was watching the cricket.

"Like your father? What makes you say that?"

"You're not going to boss me around, are you? And we *will* share the same bedroom then, won't we?"

"Do you share a bedroom with your father?" He looked aghast but gave my hand a kiss when I hit him playfully.

"You know what I mean."

"I'm not sure I do. Why would I boss you around? Louisa, I'm not in charge and it hurts me to hear you say things like that. As your husband, of course I'll be concerned about you and help you make the right decisions. What a silly question. Now, don't worry your pretty little head with such nonsense."

I remembered Daddy saying that to me when I was six when I asked him what a mortgage was. An involuntary shudder passed through my body. I kissed his ear lobe and laid my hand on his chest.

"Let's sleep together tonight, Dalby. I get so horny when I'm tense."

He patted my hand. "Not a good idea until after the exam."

"I'm not in physical training and orgasms stimulate blood flow to the whole body, including the brain. Mine needs all the help it can get."

"I'm sure you don't mean that, my dear. You are, really, very bright."

God help me, I was flattered that such a brilliant academic would consider me bright.

"I respect you too much to risk your whole future on one night of pleasure," he continued. "Plenty of time for romance later." He patted my hand again, rested his head against the back of the couch and stared dreamily into space. "I can't wait until we're married and have a little girl just like you."

I reasoned that we would have to sleep together to get this daughter he wanted. Can't married people just enjoy sex for its own sake? The way my mum and dad messed around sometimes, much to the humiliation of their children, I was pretty sure that they still did. *Don't worry, Louisa,* I chided myself. *You can work it all out after the wedding.* For some reason that thought did not reassure me.

"Hey, look, lunch break's over." Dalby pointed to the television where a bunch of guys in baggy greens wandered around a pitch, patting each other's bums. It was far too manly for little old me.

I went into my room, feelingly powerless and irritated that I couldn't be more forceful around my fiancé. Would being married change that? I certainly hoped so. Meantime, I took my newly purchased vibrator from the drawer, climbed into my single bed and relieved my tension while increasing the blood flow to my brain.

By the end of the week my final exams were over and I was

confident the results would be favourable. I gave Dalby a chaste thank-you kiss and returned gratefully to my parents' house. For some reason, I didn't even want to screw him. He wanted to take me out for a celebratory dinner but I was too busy packing for the NT. I see now that I was learning to be a passive-activist, the first step in changing my world.

DESPITE THE FACT that this had been the longest day in the history of my entire life, longer than the all nighters I pulled before exams, longer even than the girls' weekenders that used to begin after class Friday and end at sunrise Monday, by the time everyone else had crawled into their tents, I was on my second wind and couldn't sleep. I dragged my sleeping bag out into the cool(ish) night air and lay down on it, wakeful and thoughtful beneath the velvet sky, watching stars, planets, and satellites. I caught sight of the faint blinking of an aircraft as it passed overhead at an impossible height and suddenly I was crying. All the tears I'd been holding back all day splashed out as I thought about Sydney and my friends and my need to be back among familiar sights. At least in the city I knew where I stood. The Australian Outback and its people were too freaking enigmatic for me.

This Outback...it attracted me like an unsuitable lover. It moved me to alarming emotions, yet I could not understand it and felt so very lost and alone. I lay there, awash in my tears, thinking I might die of confusion before my CSO finally finished. If I were still alive, the very second it did finish I would be setting up camp in the departure lounge, waiting for the first flight out. Even life with Dalby was looking good at the moment. It would be boring and predictable but, right now, that's what I wanted.

I heard a snuffling noise and sat up to see dingoes circling the perimeter. Their lean and hungry looks set my already-fragile nerves on edge and I was glad I didn't have a baby in my tent. The more I watched them, though, the less they frightened me and I couldn't help sympathizing with their hunger. What could they find to eat in this barren, godforsaken landscape? I wiped my wet face and dug into an Esky, found the sausages we'd saved for Brooke and Warren, and began tossing them to the dingoes.

Without realizing what was happening, I slowly advanced on the retreating creatures until I was well away from the protective area of the campsite. Suddenly I became aware that the dingoes had stopped retreating and were now circled around me, just out of reach but watching me closely with yellow eyes.

Oh, shit. When would I stop being the biggest fool that ever lived? Tonight, probably, once the dingoes had killed and eaten me. Backing slowly, I tried to walk through their line but they closed ranks, not allowing me to leave. I was out of sausages and they still looked very hungry. My pulse raced, sweat poured off me, and my legs threatened to give way, too weak to stand.

I was just about to scream when a figure ran towards my circle of death, waving a flaming stick. The dingoes disappeared into the night and I collapsed into a pair of strong arms.

"You fucking idiot!" Warren cried as he clasped me to him. "You fucking, stupid, fucking idiot! Don't you know they're wild animals? Do you have any idea how dangerous they can be, especially if you hand feed them?"

"Oh, Warren," I cried as I clung to his neck. "I don't know what I know! I don't know why I want to be part of this bloody barren desert, I don't know why I love you so much, I don't know why you want me and hate me at the same time! Oh, Warren, I want to go *home*!"

I collapsed into tears as he held me tight and kissed my hair and face and neck, and then suddenly he was crying too. We remained like that for a long time. At long last he pulled away, dried my cheeks with his red sarong (which, unfortunately, was draped over his fully clothed shoulder) and gently guided me back into camp.

When we got to where my sleeping bag lay in the dirt, he stopped and let go of me. "Go on to bed now," was all he said, and without looking at me, walked away.

I held my hands out, begging to his retreating back. "Warren, please tell me what's going on. I can't get my head round this shit you keep pulling. Do you want me or not?" I didn't care who heard me.

He stopped and half turned. "Things happen out here. People do and say things they don't mean." He still wasn't looking at me. "It's the spirits...or the bones or whatever you want to call it, but you'll forget all about it once you get back to the city. You did well with Brooke and Jason today, Louisa. Just leave it at that and go to bed now, eh."

Before I could answer he had disappeared into that mysterious night. I dragged my sleeping bag into my tent where I surprised myself by sleeping until dawn.

CHAPTER TWENTY-SIX

DAWN OUT HERE IS PRETTY SPECTACULAR—and this is from one who's been watching the sun rise over Sydney Harbour all her life. First, the horizon turns scarlet, and then pure gold as the hills turn purple. The ground glows red and every rock, bush, and tree stripe the landscape with long, skinny shadows. It's the only time of day when there's any humidity in the air so it holds the moist, earthy fragrances of eucalypt and lake bed. I stepped out of my tent and took a deep breath. Beauty is as beauty does, like my Gran used to say, and the day had just begun.

At breakfast the focus was on Brooke again and she lapped it up like a kitten at a saucer of milk. Kids tripped over themselves trying to be the first to see to her needs, but there was an anxiety in the air I couldn't identify. Finally Corey, his pale face blotched with emotion, burst out with the question they all wanted to ask.

"Are we gonna have to be going back early because of Brooke's ankle?"

"Yeah, are we?" Sara repeated, head bent, dark eyes anxious.

"It's not like it's broke bad or anything." Caleb smiled hopefully, his big teeth gleaming bright in the sunlight.

"Yeah, we can help her out and all! I could carry her wherever she needs to go," Jason said.

Sara's head jerked up. "She doesn't need you *carrying* her, you Gothic jerk! She walks perfectly good on the crutches and *I* can help her in the loo and the shower and stuff."

"Us girls don't mind taking over her other jobs," Melanie added.

The clamour continued until Warren raised his hands for silence.

"Do youse *want* to go back early?"

"Bloody hell, no way! Oops, I mean, no thanks, Boss," Jason

answered for everyone. Warren shook his head in disappointment at the lad's slip of the tongue, but smiled.

"That's just as well because, no, we aren't planning on returning before schedule. Brooke will have it easy from here on out, but some of you slackers aren't nearly tough enough yet. I hope you're all ready for a gruelling day today!"

"Maybe not Spider and Timbo," Jason called jovially. "They're looking like a couple of total slackos to me!"

Did anything happen around here that Jason didn't know about?

"To you and who else, boofhead?" was Timbo's reply and they sparred happily until Warren came between them. Any trace of the thieves' hangovers had long since disappeared and everyone looked ridiculously relieved that Darwin was still two days away.

Everyone but me, that is. I'd been on this roller coaster, body and soul, since the moment we'd left and the ride couldn't end soon enough for me. As Warren avoided me this morning, I avoided thinking about him. It obviously wasn't worth fretting over, trying to sort out my feelings. My indecision reminded me of the night of my engagement party earlier this year.

MUM HAD OUTDONE HERSELF and it couldn't have been more beautiful. From our lounge room, French doors open onto a terraced lawn where marble steps lead down to a mosaic patio, designed in an American Southwest pattern and surrounded by various potted succulents. Abutting the patio, there's a swimming pool lined in fractured tiles of varying shades of blue and surrounded by a wrought iron fence. Between the pool and the beach is a Bacchii lawn. Trees, native and imported, tastefully enhance and/or shade our different recreation areas. That night everything was draped with about twenty kilometres of fairy lights. One open bar had been set up on the patio and another on the beach. Two lines of torches led down to the sand, bonfires had been carefully stacked above the water line, and lovely young men in white jackets tended them, and the bars, and the never-ending trays of food to serve the 150 guests who'd turned up to wish us well. There was a pianist in the lounge room and a jazz trio by the pool. It was a dream come true. What girl wouldn't want to become engaged in a setting like that? I was so happy.

Dalby turned up looking like a wet dream dressed like a collegiate. You know what I mean: black linen trousers, a crumpled white linen shirt, embroidered African waistcoat, and brown penny loafers in that expensive, slovenly look that shrieks, "I'm an intellectual!" with his unkempt hair flopping over his glasses. It was his plan to teach engineering once he completed his dissertation, rather than getting his hands dirty doing actual work. He was the perfect partner to my co-ed costume of a cotton pinafore over charcoal spencer and knitted leggings. Mum had despaired when she saw my outfit but I knew what I was doing. I'd been going with the guy for two years and knew what he liked.

Claudia and Suzanne and the rest wore things like chiffon, sparkling diamonds, and glittering heels. The most important outcome was that the guests of honour (me and Dalby) should stand out like a centrepiece, which we did. Perhaps it was shallow of me, but that was what I'd been after. And then Suzanne nearly stole the show.

Claudia came with Ingmar. He was still on a tourist visa but they were trying desperately to secure residency status for him. He was a medical student in Sweden and had been enlisting my brother's help. It looked like he had a good chance if he was willing to go to someplace like Queensland, and I had to smile when I imagined Claudia in the provinces, but she was in love and blind. And from what I'd heard about Queensland, there was big need for social workers up there. Sven, I hasten add, was ancient history.

Suzanne, on the other hand, chose that night to walk out of the closet and onto my beach. Not that I was completely surprised when she revealed herself as a lesbian. Claudia and I had discussed the possibility with each other several times, but we'd never had the nerve to approach her about it. I still don't know how you're supposed to ask your best friend, "Are you a dyke?" It didn't matter to me but maybe it mattered to her.

Anyway, she managed to upstage me at my own engagement by arriving with Jo, a woman whose sexual preference left no doubt. Suzanne, as I have mentioned, is a tall, blond model. That night she wore a form-fitting gown in something that shimmered gold and all dicks stood to attention as she walked past. Jo, on the other hand, had short dark hair, a monobrow, and a scowl that said "hands off, she's mine!" She wore tattered jeans and a plaid sports jacket. Her arm never left Suzanne's waist and Suzanne had to lean down to kiss her lips, which she did, frequently. This behaviour might have contributed to the amount of champagne consumed by my mother and her friends, but, hey, this was Sydney and Mardi Gras was only a few of weeks away.

"I'm sure Jo's a very nice girl, dear," Mum said to me as she collared a passing drinks waiter. "But don't you think Suzanne could have found her some nicer clothes? Do they have to do that here?" she added as the girls fed each other cakes, licking each other's fingers greedily.

"What a waste of a beautiful woman," Dad said as he watched them closely. The next thing he said was "Ouch!" when Mum punched him.

It was well past midnight when Claudia and I finally got Suzanne alone to grill her about this apparently new lifestyle. I wanted to know *how* new it was. Meanwhile, Jo was bonding with the jazz band (she fancied herself a guitarist of the first order), Dalby was drinking with my brother and Ingmar, and we were by ourselves on the sand in the glow of one of the bonfires. Well, alone except for the white-jacketed young man who kept the chilled champagne flowing.

"Suzanne," I said, clutching her arm with one hand and my crystal flute with the other. "Jo? When? Where? How long? Do tell!"

But the girls were having none of it and accosted me instead.

"Never you mind about Jo," Suzanne admonished. "Let's talk about you. Of course we want to congratulate you, darling Louisa, but before we do, are you absolutely sure that this is absolutely what you truly want to do?"

"Marriage is for a very long time," Claudia added.

"What do you mean 'what I want to do?'" I was surprised. Dalby and I had been together for so long now, what did they think was going to happen? I drained my drink, they did likewise, and then we all held out our flutes as the darling young man refilled them.

"Look at him," I said. He was leaning casually against the bar, dark wavy hair falling across his high, handsome brow, his glasses absent-mindedly sliding down his nose, his strong chin jutting out thoughtfully. My heart fluttered when I looked at him. Aren't dreams always preferable to reality? "Isn't he gorgeous?"

"Yeah," Claudia conceded and Suzanne even nodded. "But is he the one you want to spend *the rest of your life with*, Louisa?" she asked gravely.

I was drunk and my life was perfectly planned. This was my engagement party so how could I not be in love? This was hardly the time to be sorting out one's feelings! Surely everyone knows that!

"Of course he is."

They looked at each other and shrugged.

"OK, girlfriend," Claudia said. "We just wanted to be sure that you were sure. No doubt you see qualities in him we have yet to discover."

Thank God I was too drunk for self-doubt or to notice the dig. I hugged them and thanked them for their support and promised that they would be godmothers to our many children. The ones I was going to have while pursuing a serious career.

We sat in the sand, leaning against each other, and toasting marriage and life and babies and Gays and anything else we could think of—including the waiter with the never-ending supply of champagne. And then Claudia, the fucking social worker, had to ruin it all.

"Do you know what 'cognitive dissonance' is?" she asked.

"Yes. No. Not really." I answered sullenly, not liking the tone of her question.

"Isn't it when you keep on doing something you know is wrong?" Suzanne offered helpfully.

I was worried about the direction this conversation was

taking so I stood up, staggered across the beach and joined my fiancé by the bar where he was drinking congratulatory toasts with each one of the 150 guests. He threw a happy arm around me and nuzzled my neck for the boys. He loved showing me off. But unfortunately, Brewer's Droop prevented him from consummating our engagement later that night.

CHAPTER TWENTY-SEVEN

LAST NIGHT I'D TOLD WARREN that I loved him but, in the cold light of day, I couldn't honestly say if that were true. I was too strong a woman to be in love with someone who despised me, and it was easy to believe that he'd been right last night when he said all magic would disappear once we returned to civilization. Whenever that would be.

Another boat trip on Lake Argyle was planned for this morning. It was just as well that the events on our itinerary were kept short and sweet because getting ten law-breaking teenagers in the same place at the same time took a lot more skill than I had. Maybe if we'd had two nuns, a priest, and three long switches... Naw, I don't think even that would have worked, but more than once I did wish for a pistol, a whip, and a chair.

They all got fed eventually. Mary said it was easier to leave the cleaning up to her and we gathered at the lakeside. Brooke had protested that she was well enough to go but Warren voted her down. I suspect that she was looking forward to having Mary one-on-one today. Unfortunately Gazza, at the last minute, decided he would come along.

"Since I'm here anyway, I might as well have a look, eh?" He tried to smile but he hadn't shaved in a week nor, I'm guessing, brushed his teeth in a year, so that thing he did with his mouth would have frightened a crocodile.

We were introduced to Rangers Mike and Stacy and climbed aboard.

"There are two of us today," Stacy explained, "because we have something special planned. Dancing crocodiles!"

"All right!" Andreas and Corey high-fived each other. I pictured the dancing hippos from the movie *Fantasia*. Would the crocs be wearing tutus? I also couldn't help being suspicious that Warren had organized for Stacey to accompany us to ensure that I kept my hands off the khaki. If he had done that, maybe he cared. Not that I cared if he cared, of course. Or maybe he had the hots for Ranger Stacey, whose khaki shirt was buttoned suspiciously low, revealing breasts suspiciously large. Not that I cared about that either.

Once in the boat, we settled into our usual patterns, Warren up front with the boys while Mike started the engine and Stacey busied herself with plastic tubs full of something gross and fishing lines. I was in the middle with the girls–except for Laurel. I looked around, expecting to find her with Ranger Stacy but, instead, saw her deep in conversation with Pig Gazza. He'd showered and put on clean clothes today (wrinkled but clean) but he was still a pig and showing far too much interest in Laurel. Sixteen might be the legal age, but when the other guy is in his forties and in a position of care, it shouldn't be allowed to happen.

I looked at Warren who was looking at Laurel and wondered what he would do. When he turned away, he caught my eye and frowned with a small shake of his head, as if saying, "Stay out of it." Didn't he care? Was it because Laurel was white? I was going to keep a close eye on that copper and let "Officer" George find out what I would and would not stay out of.

"Hey, Miss." Sara tugged my arm. "Miss, can you ask that Stacy how they make the crocodiles dance?"

"Sure. I'd like to know that myself." I beckoned her over and Andreas and Corey joined us as well.

"We need to learn the tricks of the trade if we're gonna be opening a crocodile park." Corey explained away their association with the women. Soon everyone, male and female, crowded around the pretty young ranger, hanging on her every word. She explained how she would climb to an enclosure on top of the boat and from there dangle pieces of meat over the water. Hungry crocodiles will jump full length out of the water to grab it.

"You hold the meat with your hand?" Andreas's eyes nearly popped out of his face.

"No way." Stacey assured him. "I dangle that meat at the end of a very long and strong pole!"

"Whew!" Andreas and Corey looked very relieved.

Once we were a fair distance from the shore, Stacey climbed

up to her enclosure, Mike turned on some music, and we all crowded to the edge. Once those prehistoric reptiles began leaping, though, I moved quickly to the back of the boat and sat close to big, burly Ranger Mike. At least he had the outboard motor in his grip in case he had to fight them off. Laurel shrieked like a girl and Pig Gazza laughed and put his arms around her. I shuddered and watched in case his hands went where they shouldn't.

Despite all my early morning resolve, I had a hard time keeping my eyes off Warren. His black, curly whiskers gave him a rugged look that even his white knee socks couldn't detract from. He was so lovely with those poor, neglected boys. He treated them like young men and listened sincerely to everything they said. I was discovering that if you actually made the effort to listen to what teenagers were saying, you usually find out that they weren't just talking crap. I'd have to try that on my sisters when I got home.

Home. When would I get back there? Would Dalby be waiting after he heard about my criminal record? Did I actually give a shit if he was waiting or not? I was beginning to suspect that the compromises I'd been willing to make to secure home, family, and status might turn out to be a step too far. Wasn't life for the living? Wouldn't life with Dalby be as dead as his dick?

My family, on the other hand, *was* important and I was learning just how precious a gift they were each day. I thought of the first time I'd decided I hated my dad. I was fifteen, my curfew was 10 p.m., and one night when I wasn't home by midnight he'd got in his car and came looking for me. At one point, while he'd been searching a park, frantically calling my name, my girlfriend and I had been hiding in a nearby ditch, laughing at him. When I wasn't home by 2 a.m. he'd got the police involved. When they'd finally found me at 7 a.m., hiding under a pier with my girlfriend and two boys from Grade Twelve, they inflicted the ultimate humiliation by bringing me home in a patrol car. After hugs and tears and reprimands, I was grounded for a month and Daddy went to work after having been up all night. Funny how, over the years, I'd chosen to forget about that episode. Funny that my dad was still even talking to me.

"This is awesome, Miss! You gotta come closer." Brooke and Sara started dragging me away from the safety of Ranger Mike's motor. But when cavernous jaws and a huge, smooth underbelly erupted inches from my face, I screamed and dropped to the floor. There I stayed, eyes covered, trusting the other adults to looks after the littlies until the show was over. The crocodiles stopped dancing and I tried to look nonchalant as I brushed boat dirt from my clothes.

We returned to camp to laze around the shore and play in the shallows while Mary prepared lunch. She had Brooke to help her today so I took a break, after reapplying sunscreen to all and sundry. Nobody protested anymore and even Timbo, who had the blackest skin I'd ever seen, took his turn in line. Warren always rubbed his own lotion into his strong arms, but I watched covertly and found myself fantasizing about rubbing lotion into those hard to reach places...

Oh, my God. My panties got wet just thinking about touching him! My body was letting me down. I hated him and wanted nothing to do with him ever again, full stop.

I dove into the water to cool off but that didn't work. He was demonstrating something to Spider and Caleb, standing with his back to me, his legs wide apart. When he bent over to pick up a rock, I had to run from the lake and into the shower for a quick wank. I was getting good at doing this standing up. Hanging onto the shower nozzle with one hand, I filled the other with my juices and worked them into my hot clit. I thought about his fat, black cock with its hot, red head and my fanny throbbed with wanting it inside. The hardest part was not grunting when I came, just in case someone else walked into the shower block at the crucial moment. Oh, Warren, if only you knew the sacrifices I make for you!

I lifted my fingers to my face and inhaled deeply. His scent was still mingled with my cum and I couldn't get enough of it. I experienced an overwhelming sense of loss at the thought that he would never be there again. The energy boost I'd got from my orgasm slipped away. I didn't deserve to have these desires about a man whose interest in me was nil. I tried to think about Dalby but I couldn't even remember what he looked like, much less what he had felt and smelled like.

I sighed, found a sliver of soap in the dish, and washed away all evidence of my transgression. I joined the others for lunch, smiling as though nothing had happened.

"What were you doing in the shower, Miss?" Melanie had to ask.

"I suddenly got an awful itch in the lake and had to wash it off with hot water."

"They got sea lice in Lake Argyle?"

"Was it that kind of itch?" Bloody Mary couldn't resist a snipe.

"Don't know what it was, Melanie." I ignored Mary. "Brooke, did you really make this beautiful salad yourself?"

"Hire the handicapped!" Jason said and we all laughed when he picked up Brooke's crutches and hobbled ridiculously around the table. They got tangled in his coattails and he fell with a crash.

"Don't break them!" I said sternly as I retrieved them and gave them back to Brooke.

"No, Boss," Jason answered from the ground.

"And don't call me Boss!" I joked but was serious later when I accompanied Mary over to the communal sink to help her wash up. I needed to speak to her alone.

"I'm concerned about the attention Gazza is paying to Laurel. Surely Warren must have noticed it too? Why doesn't he do something, Mary?"

"And just what would you have him do?" she asked. "Punch out a senior officer? You still don't understand how it is with us, Lou." She watched the detergent bubble up under the tap.

Cut me some slack here, I thought. *In one week, I'm supposed to become an expert on wildlife, teenagers, and all things Indigenous?* Aloud, I said, "So tell me. I do understand rank, but I also understand right and wrong." I picked up a towel and began drying the cups.

Mary spoke thoughtfully as she washed. "Warren got into the police academy, no worries, but he had to drop out before he finished when his dad took sick and wanted to go to Queensland where his country is. Later, when his dad died and Warren came back to Darwin, he took a job as a Police Liaison

Officer but a lot of the coppers think that's just a gammon job. If Warren interferes with a pig like that Gazza, why, he'd likely get thrown out on his ear. Him and his grant."

"So Warren is risking these kid's lives for the sake of *his* job?"

"Nobody's dead, nor likely to be. Warren is a good man, Lou, and these kids adore him. Don't you underestimate him." Mary picked up a pan that was black from baked-on grease, plunged it into the washbasin and scrubbed so hard I got splashed. Her defences concerning Warren were up again. I stepped back and looked around our campsite. I heard laughter and horseplay and saw a small crowd of kids in bright orange T-shirts looking relaxed and happy, as kids should be. *Him and his grant,* I thought. Perhaps lives were being saved. I was silent for a long time. At last I spoke. "If only we could take Officer O'Brien out of the equation."

I dried and stacked the last mug and Mary dried her hands and walked away. Had I pissed her off again? It was so frustrating! One minute Mary was my best mate then, the next, she was pushing me away, relegating me to the isolation of my perceived social status. It wasn't my fault where I came from, and it sure as hell hadn't been my choice to be here! The judge had hardly given me an option in my sentencing. I regretted my misfortune at being well-educated, wealthy, and white and went back to work.

CHAPTER TWENTY-EIGHT

THE TOUR WAS NEARLY FINISHED NOW. Two more days to go. I decided to concentrate on the juvies this afternoon and leave Warren to do his own thing. It wasn't difficult. They were really beginning to grow on me. I couldn't help it, I liked them all. I thought of the teenagers I knew in Sydney, loudmouthed smartarses who thought they knew everything. They had all the latest gadgets–iPhones, iPads, Palm Pilots, websites, you name it, and lived their lives on social networks. But they were Internet smart, which translates into, as Jason would say, "dumb as dog shit." With my upbringing, I couldn't believe I was even *thinking* a phrase that crude.

These kids were rough but they were the genuine article. Sure, they sometimes broke the law in their attempts to live halfway decent lives but, if they got caught, they didn't whine to their rich daddies, they took it on the chin. They did their time and appreciated the three squares and the clean sheets they got while they were "inside."

We went exploring the surrounding countryside. I was amazed there was so much to see in a land that was so empty. We climbed rocks, skinned our knees, found deep dark caves, frightened the bats and ourselves, spotted croc slides into the river, and tried to name all the birds we saw (we didn't get much past crow and parrot). We ran around like halfwits and had the time of our lives. Even Warren stopped acting like an Elder and joined in the fun. Gazza came along and showed surprising agility for such a big man. He started puffing before long, though, and Caleb found him a sturdy walking stick. Eventually everyone was starving to death so we counted heads and started back.

For afternoon tea Mary and Brooke had made a damper to die for–crispy on the outside, fluffy in the middle, perfect for soaking up melted margarine and Home Brand honey–and handed pieces out with hot mugs of steaming brew. I drizzled honey on my damper and had just sat down gratefully to enjoy my smoko when somebody asked, "Where's Laurel?"

"She was with us when we left to come back," I said through a mouthful of tea and food, grabbing a paper towel up to my face to catch the soggy bits of sweet damper that were being sprayed over all and sundry.

"Where's Gazza? Didn't he go with youse?" Mary asked.

I looked around. The Pig was not at his trough. He was nowhere to be seen.

"Holy shit!"

Dropping mug and damper, I took off running, back the way we'd come. Warren had gone into the toilets (he'd been drinking plenty of water) and hadn't heard this conversation.

"Tell Warren as soon as he comes out!" I shouted as I ran but noticed Corey and Timbo making a beeline for the toilets, obviously not content to wait for the tour leader to finish whatever it was he was doing.

Not too far down the path but out of earshot, I came around a boulder and there they were. Laurel was pinned by Gazza's fat belly up against the cliff face, her eyes wide in terror. One of his meaty fists was clamped across her mouth and the other one was trying to yank her shorts off. His walking stick had been abandoned on the path.

Before either of them saw me, I picked up that stout stick and whacked him as hard as I could across his kidneys while screeching "WARREN!" at the top of my lungs.

Gazza jerked back, releasing the girl when the first blow landed and raising his arms in defence.

"What the...?" he cried and stepped away from Laurel but my adrenalin was in full flow and I didn't stop swinging. I landed one on his head and two on his legs before he was able to turn and grab at the stick, reaching wildly and falling to the ground as he did so. Warren appeared just in time to see him go down.

"Louisa, what are you—"

"You deal with him! I'll look after Laurel." No-one argues with that tone of voice. Warren stood speechless and stunned. I thrust my weapon into his hands, hoping he would use it to beat the bastard senseless, and stalked over to where poor

Laurel now crouched in a quivering heap, clutching her torn clothing tight around her body. I held her close, protecting her from the thug in the dirt, heartily sorry that I hadn't remained sufficiently alert to have prevented the incident from ever occurring.

"She wanted it." Gazza squirmed in the dirt, grovelling at Warren's feet, trying to defend his behaviour. "She's been asking for it for days, the fucking little cock tease."

I think I saw a light dawn in Warren's eyes. "Get up," was all he said. He lifted the walking stick and threw it as hard as he could. It sailed, javelin-like, into the treetops where it lodged. Gazza got up, didn't even bother to dust himself off, and the two men left together.

Laurel and I sat on the ground, my arms around her shoulders. She pulled her orange T-shirt over her knees, hugging them tight. The elastic had been removed from her hair so it hung like a curtain around her pinched face.

"That's a lie, Miss," she said. Her voice was so small. "I never said I wanted it."

"I know you didn't, Laurel. He's a rapist. And if you want to bring charges when we get back to Darwin, I'll back you up all the way." My rage made my voice loud, which probably sounded threatening to the poor girl.

"Oh, no, Miss, I could never do that!" she cried out in fear and tried to pull away. Maybe I was moving too fast for the traumatised child. Sixteen might be legal age, but Laurel was just a little kid to me and she didn't want to think about anything yet. I tightened my embrace and lowered my voice.

"It's OK. We won't talk about it now. We'll sit here, and when you're ready, we'll go back to camp. They've got a bonza smoko waiting for us." Did I really just say "bonza smoko?"

It was nearly dark when we came back. Mary met us with a flowered sarong to wrap around Laurel's ripped shorts. Nobody else had witnessed what had happened back there, but everybody knew the details. Bush telegraph? The poor girl didn't want to eat anything or talk to anybody but I insisted she drink a cup of sweet milky tea, and then she let the girls come and sit beside her. The boys stayed together in a group and kept glancing at her. I could tell they were angry and just waiting for her to give the word so they could thrash the copper. Gazza was nowhere to be seen, either keeping a low profile in his tent or, more likely, off drinking with dero mates he'd found somewhere. Warren was noticeable by his absence too.

"He made a phone call when he came back," Mary told me. "Later a bloke came in a car and they took off together. He just told me to make sure youse got back before dark and here you are."

Where had the coward had slunk off to this time?

CHAPTER TWENTY-NINE

IT WAS OUR LAST NIGHT in the Outback but nobody was in the mood for a celebration. Mary cooked us up a barbecue according to plan because that was the food we had on hand. She and Brooke had also made fruit cakes and thawed out some custard from the bottom of the cold box. The kids couldn't help it; they ate like they expected The Famine to start tomorrow, but there was mumbling instead of singing around the campfire. Even Laurel, in her fragile state, succumbed to the irresistible aroma of frying meat and onions and nibbled on a sausage. Brooke and Melanie hand fed her small bits of fruit cake while Sara kept her mug full of sweet tea. Bedtime came early and all four girls crammed into one tent together.

"It'll be fun, like a sleepover," was the response to my raised eyebrows. As long as it helped them feel safe. I was a little envious of their bond. More like hurt that I hadn't been invited. Mary had retired with her book. She had said very little to me ever since I'd accused Warren of looking out for his job rather than these kids. The boys remained huddled in the light outside the shower block for a very long time before giving each other the obligatory "good night" punches. I was left on my own, again, sitting cross-legged on a picnic table, beneath a black velvet sky full of stars and a waning moon.

I was waiting for Warren but Gazza turned up first, drunk as always. I stayed very still but he saw me anyway and staggered over to where I sat.

"You think you can judge me, slut? You think you're better than me but you better remember that you're the crim and I'm the copper, you uppity, shit-faced slut," he slurred through breath so foul I gagged.

"Let me tell you something..." he continued when I didn't answer him, but I wasn't in the mood.

"Fuck off," I said ominously, looking him straight in the eyes. He must have remembered me with the walking stick because he did, stopping only to puke in front of his tent.

I stayed where I was, thinking. Tomorrow night my CSO would be over. I'd be a free woman on the red-eye to Sydney and life as I'd always known it. I'd be back among the museums and art galleries and theatres and universities and wine bars. I'd be with people who used correct English, who conversed knowingly about books and plays and paintings and who never talked with their mouths full. I'd take a good job in a research-and-design department and have an office with a Harbour view. I'd get my BMW out of storage and, after a year on a top salary, I'd buy a condominium on the North Shore, and then perhaps, I'd finally marry Dalby...or somebody like him. We'd have 2.5 children who, of course, would go to the best schools and mingle with the best people and never, ever get arrested. I had left this life only a few short weeks ago. Why was it feeling so alien and empty to me now? Why couldn't I just go to bed and sleep through the final few hours of this tour from hell? Why did I think I needed to talk to Warren, that loser who had made it clear that he only wanted me in secret?

Face it, Louisa, you don't know what you want! It was Grade Six all over again when I wanted Apollo Popodopolis to kiss me. Apollo was bad, but beautiful. He was expelled before the end of the year, but not before I got that kiss. Had I chosen to marry a respected citizen of the Empire such as Dalby just to save me from myself?

I heard a car door slam and saw Warren walking toward me. The car drove off into the night. Poor Warren. His blue shorts were no longer creased nor his black shoes shiny. I could have almost been sorry for the man if that damn love/rejection thing hadn't kept getting in the way.

"It's about time you turned up," I said in a flat, emotionless voice. "Poor Laurel thought you'd abandoned her."

Instead of giving me his usual order to leave it out and go to bed, he climbed up and sat beside me on the table. I was wrapped in an icy aura of disappointment and hurt and the heat of his presence couldn't penetrate it. He clasped his hands and looked straight ahead.

"I'd never do that. I take my responsibilities very seriously. She's probably been abandoned enough in her life."

"Why did you leave, then? Why didn't you beat the shit out of him?"

"Because it wouldn't have helped. If it makes you feel any better, though, I sure wanted to." He glanced at me and gave a sly grin. "Besides, you were doing a beaut job of that yourself."

I refused to be distracted by discussing my fighting skills or his smile. "When did you start caring how I feel?"

He turned away. "The first time I laid eyes on that snooty little arse of yours."

I hadn't expected that answer and shifted, breaking the aura of protection. I gazed at his sober face, silhouetted against the light of the shower blocks and my shield fell like broken glass all around me. I took a deep breath and touched his knee. He turned to me, looking heartbreakingly vulnerable.

"Last night..., did you say that you loved me?"

"I think I did."

"Was it true?"

"I...I guess." My heart filled my throat making it difficult to talk. "I don't really know."

"It would be nice if it were true."

"Why? You hate me."

He shook his head. "Never. The truth is I'm very frightened by my feelings for you. You remind me of my mother."

"Your *mother*!" I can't tell you how unexpected *that* was. I took my hand off his knee. "How did she get into this conversation? Don't tell me you've got an Oedipus complex as well!"

"As well as what?"

"Never mind." I couldn't say that I suspected he was just as racist and weak spirited so I repeated, "Your *mother*?"

"Yes, my mother." He stared off into the night and told his story. "She was like you, only American. Another rich, snooty, white bitch who thought she knew everything and came to Australia to save the poor Aboriginal from—whatever. She didn't understand the Outback, either, and, like most white folks, she let herself go completely wild. You know. She thought there were no rules or restrictions so she broke every one of them. Anyway, she met my dad and overwhelmed him. She seduced him and decided to start this new life with the people who were 'real.' Except then she got pregnant and gave birth to a little piccaninny and didn't *that* change everything. No way was she going to spend the rest of her life hanging around a blackfella's camp with black babies hanging off her titties."

I cringed inwardly. Would I be the same? I didn't think so, but the thought of spending the rest of my life in a camp with *anything* hanging off my titties was decidedly unpleasant. In my defence, that stupid woman (better not call her that to Warren's face) had come out here of her own accord, looking for—and finding—something that existed only in her own mind. I, on the other hand, had had this life thrust rudely upon me, and then got tangled up in it while trying to get out. These people were no more or less "real" than my beloved family and friends in Sydney, but they possessed a spirit I longed to get closer to and a land I knew I could help protect. But I would absolutely need to do these things from a home base in Darwin. A sudden image of my mother in her designer clothes visiting her grandchildren in a blackfella's camp flashed across my mind and I suppressed a smile.

"What happened?" I asked quietly, not looking at him. It was good, having a real conversation with him and I didn't want it to end. I unclenched my fists, resting my arms on my knees.

"The usual. She was off back to the States before her milk dried up, leaving my dad broken-hearted and me motherless. It's not going to happen to me, Sister." He leapt off the table and stood with his back to me. "Don't worry. You'll forget all about me, the kids, and this place the minute you touch down at Kingsford-Smith."

His words struck my solar plexus knocked me like I'd been king hit—deflated with a single punch. The biggest reason why I wanted to stay was telling me to go.

"So why do you want me to love you if you think it's all for nothing?"

"Dunno why I said that. Dreamtime talking, I guess." He turned toward me. "Just do me a favour and start forgetting us—now. I'm happy to start forgetting you."

That's not fair, painting me with her brush," I murmured, too hurt to speak louder.

"Life wasn't meant to be fair." He laughed harshly. "It was

one of our illustrious Prime Ministers who said that, wasn't it?"

"Yeah, the one who was caught with his pants down in Memphis. Not the first person I'd be looking to for direction in my life."

"Go to bed, Louisa." He sighed. "We've got a long drive tomorrow." Head down, he walked away.

I sat still as he faded into the night. A lump rose in my throat but I wasn't going to cry. If love and hate are so closely related, maybe it would be easy to change my feelings into hate before morning. Most of me still thought he was an arsehole so it couldn't be that hard to do. I stretched out on the picnic table, watching the moon obliterate stars as it wandered across the sky. I saw myself as was one of those stars, bright, and then growing dim until finally disappearing behind the light of another object. In Sydney I'd been one of the bright young things but started losing some of my luminescence when I joined that group of do-gooders (oops—meant to say "concerned citizens") and started realizing that, just maybe, the whole world wasn't about me. By the time I'd been arrested and given this Community Service Order I was fading fast, and tonight, all alone, I was finally invisible.

In that instant I knew that I didn't want to go back to Sydney and Dalby and the job of a lifetime.

I wasn't invisible in the morning, though, when Jason found me sound asleep, still stretched out on the picnic table.

"Morning, Miss." He shook me awake. "Is this how you get the biggest breakfast?"

"Oh, shit, Jason!" I was so stiff I could barely sit up. "I'm not sure what happened here."

"I don't know, either, but I bet it was Mr Warren, am I right?" He rubbed my shoulders vigorously, putting some circulation back into them.

"Don't mention Mr Warren." I suddenly remembered that I was pissed off with both of them. "I'm really disappointed in you, Jason."

He stopped rubbing my shoulders. "Why? What did I do?"

"You told that Pig Gazza about what you saw that night."

"I never, Miss." He held out his open hands to prove his innocence, sounding wounded beyond belief.

"Well, he found out somehow. He said some revolting things to me."

"He talks revolting to everybody so don't feel special on that account. But, truly, Miss, I never said nothing. But everybody who sees you two together knows something's going on."

"How? Mr Warren never even speaks to me."

"Exactly!"

I harked back to Grade Six again. Everybody knew that Apollo had kissed me when we started ignoring each other. I gave up on the argument, apologized for the misunderstanding, and went to find a shower and clean clothes. Anyway, I liked Jason and wanted to believe he hadn't betrayed me. It was our last morning in camp which meant that we had plenty of packing to do. Mary got up early (for her) to give us a big cooked breakfast.

"Mr Warren brought heaps of bacon and eggs back with him last night."

"Did he go all the way into Kununurra? Whatever for?"

"Dunno. Said he had some business to attend to. Anyways, it'll be the last time most of these kids eat bacon and eggs at the same meal for a long time. They don't even get food like this in the lock-up."

"You think many of them will be in the lock-up soon?" I asked as I dipped the bread in bacon grease and fried it. Once upon a time that would have made me shudder and weep, but this morning it smelled really good and made my stomach growl.

"Not all of them, but it's on the cards for most. It's a dead cert for Timbo. That boy's got history that can't be fixed."

I recalled that his crime of "vagrancy" was probably soliciting. I banished those thoughts from my mind.

"I think you're wrong, Mary. Every one I've talked to has big dreams now. They'll get back to Darwin and find the world's their oyster. This trip really helped them, I figure."

Mary just shook her head. "You are one optimistic lady, Lou, but you still got a bit to learn about the real world."

Once again, my pride was kicked to the kerb and I didn't know why. These kids were so young and positive; why couldn't they be whatever they wanted? I guessed Warren was right. I probably hadn't learned anything that wouldn't be forgotten the moment I re-entered my privileged world. Life sure could be bloody unfair.

I dished up breakfast and couldn't help smiling as I watched my juvies trying to fill the bottomless pits they called their stomachs. I even cheered up enough to eat a slice of my fried bread with a greasy egg on top. Why not? I had another day of this feral life, might as well enjoy it. But my smile faded when I looked around and spotted Pig Gazza sopping up his egg with fried bread as well. He was so gross I lost my appetite and my good humour. He winked at me and I nearly gagged as yolk and grease leaked down his chin. Him I would *not* miss at the end of this trip.

Just then I caught the look on Laurel's face and was, once again, filled with rage. Warren should have gotten rid of him two days into the tour for drinking. I was so angry and swore never to support or believe in a police force that not only kept a pig like him employed but entrusted a busload of young children to his care. That same police force which had arrested me! Malcolm Fraser be damned, this was just *too* unfair. Nothing could be achieved by sitting here and stewing so I buried my frustrations under the congealing lump of lard that I had called my breakfast and went over to give Laurel a hug.

"If you need some help packing up, I'm your gal!" I said which brought peals of laughter from her and Melanie.

"Get real, Miss!" Laurel gasped, hanging around my neck for support. She was laughing so hard she could barely stand up. "If anybody around here's gonna need help packing, it's gonna be you, eh?"

"I like you, Miss," Melanie added. "You are one funny lady."

"Ha, ha, ha," I smiled and tried to join in the mirth but, in truth, I was feeling a bit put down. Was there a conspiracy to highlight how useless I was on this, the last day? And then Jason came over, afraid he was missing out on something good.

"It's Miss, here, gonna help us pack up." Laurel shared the joke and he had a good chortle as well. My fragile ego couldn't take anymore. I stalked off. I'd show them!

I spent the next twenty minutes or so fighting (and very

nearly losing) battles with aluminium tent poles, getting tangled in ropes, tripping over tent pegs and trying to stuff giant-sized sleeping bags into something the size of a child's purse. When my toothbrush finally disappeared into my rucksack, I collapsed, soaked in sweat. Wild cheering broke out and I looked up to see all the juvies, led by Warren and Mary, gathered around me, laughing and applauding.

Suddenly, I could see the funny side of it and gave a sheepish grin. I had to stand up for myself, though, since nobody else was. I heaved my sleeping bag feebly in Warren's direction.

"Here, Boss, you're the expert. Get this stuff into the trailer."

"Gladly." He smiled. "We're running a bit late."

He picked up the sleeping bag and tent and it was then I looked around and saw that everything else in camp had been packed and stowed already. Laurel and Melanie came over and reached down to pull me up.

"That's OK, Miss. We reckon that's stuff they don't teach at Uni, eh? Bet you know heaps of other stuff we'll never learn."

"Never say never, girls. Let's hit the road." As I followed the youngsters onto the bus Mary handed me a cup of coffee.

"Been saving this for you. You looked like you were going to need it. Lord, that was the funniest thing I've seen in awhile!" She punched my shoulder nearly capsizing my drink and climbed onto the bus, still laughing. I smiled weakly. Obviously I had been forgiven my earlier trespasses.

The coffee was lukewarm but it was strong and sweet and thick. It wasn't Starbuck's, but it was just what I needed. I cupped my hands around the tin mug (I think it's what they call a "pannikin"), and sat down on the bench in quiet reflection while the juvies fought over whether or not they needed a last toilet break before taking off.

CHAPTER THIRTY

THREE WEEKS AGO, the day I flew to the NT, Dalby had been busy tutoring and couldn't take me to the airport, but Suzanne and Claudia came, each with a large latte, full-cream milk, hazelnut flavouring, two sugars, as decadent as possible for me.

"Have you thought this thing completely through? You'll be roughing it up there, you know, maybe for three or four days," Suzanne reminded me.

"Yes, Louisa, anyplace that's called a 'territory' sounds pretty grim to me," Claudia added. "I don't know if they even *have* coffee in places like that. Why, I bet everyone still drinks billy tea!"

"I'm doing this for queen and country, girls. Hard-boil my tea over a campfire and, by God, I'll drink it!" It was easy to be courageous sitting in a departure lounge with your two best friends. God help me, I was even allowing myself to feel self-righteous, holier-than-thou, and braver-than-the-brave. I was marching off to war and may not return. "Be careful what you wish for, Louisa," Mum used to caution me. Don't you just hate it when your mother's right?

"Where's Dalby?" One of them had to ask it, deflating my balloon slightly.

"Busy. New students, you know," I answered carelessly. He had been tutoring an eighteen-year-old freshman over the summer. A comely female, but I hadn't told the girls that.

"We know all too well. He must be really good in bed for you to put up with all the grief he gives you." Claudia looked almost envious.

"He's really good at a lot of things," I said defensively. "And you both agree that we make a beautiful couple." There was so much about our relationship I hadn't shared with them. I guess we never want our friends to see what losers we actually are. My flight was called and we stood up.

"Yes, girlfriend, and you certainly do. It's only because we love you and want the best for you." Suzanne gave me a big hug. I set my lattes down so I could return it.

"We're showing our concern," Claudia said. "How can anybody who is perfectly happy be leaving Sydney to go to a place called 'Darwin' in November? It all seems very odd to *moi*." She smiled and held me close. "Maybe you'll find a real hottie up there."

"Hugh Jackman doesn't *really* live in the Northern Territory, Claudia." I squeezed her tight and Suzanne stepped in as well, and then it was time to go. I shouldered my bag, said final farewells, and ran to catch up with the end of the line. As I entered the tunnel and turned to wave, they stood with their arms around each other's waists, looking very worried. A jolt of trepidation shook my body. Not even my best friends knew the true reason why I was going. They thought I was going up there to visit fellow engineers for a tour of the uranium mines.

"Get real, Louisa," I had told myself. "You're going for four days. What could possibly happen?"

"HEY, MISS, LOOK SHARP! We're about leave without you!" Jason called from the window of the bus. I looked up, startled out of my reverie, and realized that the only thing that wasn't loaded and stowed was me. I jumped up and leapt up the steps, trying to avoid Gazza behind the steering wheel but he made a swipe at me and I was forced to look at him.

"I'd like to spend a week teaching you how to camp." He laughed, hissing through his yellow teeth, his little pig eyes disappearing into his fat face and his breath carrying a stink of old grog. There was nothing about this arsehole that didn't make my gorge rise. I knocked his hand away and kept walking. Warren looked up. I shook my head and gave him a frown. He looked away like I'd wanted him to, but really, I'd wanted him to fight for the right to acknowledge my presence because my stomach knotted up so painfully I couldn't even look at his crotch to admire the bulge in his blue shorts as I walked past.

The kids were in high spirits, the boys showing off to the girls, and the girls giggling their appreciation. It might get out of hand later but right now it was just good fun. I left them to it. Feeling pretty lonely, useless, and ignored, I moved to the back of the bus, draining the last of my coffee as I sat down heavily. Mary was deep in her Mills and Boon but I wasn't in the mood for talking anyway. I dug into my rucksack and found my copy of *Even Cowgirls Get the Blues* by Tom Robbins. Maybe he could cheer me up while he was bringing me down. I no longer cared who the murderer was in my crime novel. My personal experience of the judiciary had left me jaded.

"What's up, Lou?" Apparently Mary hadn't been ignoring me after all. "I thought you'd be happy, this being the last day and all."

When I looked into her sympathetic face I realized that I hadn't wanted to be ignored. I closed Tom Robbins and sighed. "Oh, Mary, I don't think I've accomplished a damn thing on this trip."

"Did you want to?"

"Not at the beginning, no, but now we are at the end, for some reason I'd like to think that I learned *something* or helped *somebody*, even if it were only myself." Try as I might, I could only remember all those times I'd gotten it so wrong. Corey and the croc. Sara and the scorpion. Brooke and the sprained ankle...

"Don't sell yourself short, girl. None of these kids are going to forget you in a hurry. To tell you the truth, I never expected them to have this much fun or behave this well. Full credit to Mr Warren for coming up with the idea, but you helped make it a success. There's something about you that makes them all want to be that little bit better."

"Do you really think so?" I was flattered but not convinced. Mary was being kind. "There's that other thing too. How could any police force anywhere put someone like Gazza into a position like this? He smells like he's drunk again today and could kill us all! Warren shouldn't have let him get away with what he did to Laurel. *Why*, Mary?"

Mary took a large bandana out of her handbag and wiped her face. She looked around as if to make sure no-one was listening and leaned over toward me to speak in a confidential whisper.

"First of all, Gazza scared Laurel but he didn't actually get the chance to *do* anything and that *is* thanks to you and that walking stick. Don't you never forget that, Lou. Like I told you before, he's is still on the job because he's the commissioner's brother-in-law. He's never been fit for this or any job. He's only got ten months to retirement on full pension. Mostly they just keep him in the office where they can keep an eye on him. You remember how this trip was originally supposed to be going into the Kakadu? Well, they'd arranged to have a different driver. He was an Aboriginal liaison officer as well. But at the last minute we had to change our plans because of all those Greenies demonstrating against the uranium mining. What with them blocking roads and causing trouble here and there, the higher-ups in Darwin decided it might be dangerous to take our juvies there and chose WA instead. Plus, another thing..." Mary leaned closer. "That Aboriginal driver stole his wife off a fella in Kununurra and he's not allowed to go back there."

"What do you mean, 'not allowed?'" How much weirder could rules in the Top End get?

She pulled a Beedie out of her bag and lit it without offering me one. This being our last day, maybe she didn't worry about the rules. "That's tribal law but it's deadly serious. If he goes back, that other fella's family has every right to spear him. So, anyway, they had to get another driver at the last minute and Gazza was the only one handy with a bus license. Nobody reckoned he'd be this bad, but..."

The blood drained from my face as my jaw dropped.

"Hey, don't take it personal. It's not like it was your fault."

She must have seen my expression and was trying to be helpful, but what would she say if she knew the truth? I remembered Warren saying how a lot of people—whites, to be specific—behaved as though there were no laws in the Outback. Apparently, even some coppers. I took a deep breath and fished around in my bag for some smokes, forgetting that I'd given them all to Mary.

Suddenly I was looking forward to that flight to Sydney once again, grateful that they all thought I had been arrested for acting like a spoiled rich bitch. At the beginning of the trip, my disdain for all things Outback had kept me from revealing the truth. Now it was self-preservation.

The terrible thoughts running around inside my head told me that *I* was partially responsible for The Pig's presence. I sank back in my seat and wanted to die. How could something that had seemed so noble have turned into something so rotten?

CHAPTER THIRTY-ONE

THE SOUND OF A SIREN directly behind me brought me out of my reverie. I sat up, turned around, and stared out the back window. A Western Australia highway patrol car was pulling alongside us, gesturing for Gazza to pull over.

"What the fuck?" he grumbled. "Who do these arseholes think they are?"

We could all hear his swearing over the noise of the air conditioning. He didn't pull over straight away and the honking and the sirens got louder. Warren leaned forward and tapped him on the shoulder.

"Better see what they want. Might be a tire or tail light or something."

"Shit. This mob are so up themselves," Gazza complained but he complied. Once the bus stopped, he grabbed his license from where it was stored behind the visor and opened his window. The cop car stopped in front of us and the guy on the passenger side got out and walked back to where we'd parked. I was oddly relieved to see that police in WA wear the proper blue uniforms. They looked more genuine and less like kids playing safari.

Our kids, well trained in and experienced with police etiquette, remained frozen in their seats and quiet as little mice. They were probably thinking about all those drinks and lollies they'd knicked when we stopped for the fish and chips a few days ago.

"What's up, Officer?" Gazza leaned out the window with a revolting attempt at an ingratiating smile. "I'm a policeman myself, from the NT. Got a busload of juvenile offenders here learning how to be good citizens here in your fine State."

"Could you get out of the bus, please, sir?" The other cop wasn't smiling.

"What for? It wasn't my idea to send these delinquents into WA."

"Could you get out of the bus, please, sir?"

The other cop wasn't even trying to be friendly and I was intrigued. Apparently cop-on-cop camaraderie didn't cross state lines. I settled back to enjoy myself and glanced at Warren to see if he was learning anything.

See? I wanted to tell him. *A pig is a pig no matter what uniform he is wearing!* I turned to catch Mary's reaction, but she had chosen that moment to enter the toilet. Was she hiding?

Gazza said, "Well, fuck me dead." He climbed slowly out of his seat, lumbered down the steps, and stood in the shade of the bus on the side of the road until the other man joined him. Warren followed, shook the newcomer's hand and smiled. I was on the wrong side of the bus and couldn't hear what was said after that but I gasped in shock when the WA cop pulled a breathalyser out of his pocket! I watched Gazza go off the deep end when the other wanted him to blow in it. Gazza looked ready to hit somebody. I had to know what was happening so I hurried up to the driver's seat and leaned my head out the window. Now I could see and hear everything.

I heard a car door slam and looked up to see the driver of the WA car getting out and walking over to others. A woman! She was short but looked mighty efficient. Maybe Suzanne's type. Gazza's sneer turned into a grin. He just couldn't learn. He took the breathalyser, slobbered his lips around it, and blew, winking lewdly at her.

"Wish this was you, sweetheart?"

He reached out and took a swipe at her breasts. She pulled her baton from her belt and snapped it open. Gazza's grin turned to wide-mouthed alarm and he stepped back behind Warren. Her partner retrieved the wet breathalyser, looked at the reading, and whistled.

"Point-one-one-five at 8 a.m. in the morning! This is bad even by Northern Territory standards. Oh man, you are *so* under arrest!"

Gazza turned his slack-jawed face to the male cop in outrage. "You can't arrest me! I'm a Territorian! I'm a police officer! I'm on duty!" He turned to Warren. "Tell 'em, George! Tell 'em they can't arrest me. Tell them who I am."

Warren raised his hands and moved away. "It's nothing to do with me, mate. You're the one who keeps reminding me how you're the boss."

I thought The Pig's jaw would dislocate if it fell open any further. Then he took a swipe at Warren, who deftly avoided it, before stepping up menacingly to the male WA cop with fists clenched.

"You haven't got the balls to arrest me."

"Keep it up, fella. You're digging yourself in deeper every minute." The cop got out his handcuffs as the woman slapped her baton against the palm of her hand. Gazza turned to her.

"Your balls would be bigger than your tits, wouldn't they? You the one with stones in this outfit?"

In a flash that baton slid under his left elbow, across his back, under his right elbow and had his arms pinned behind his back. Handcuffs were clamped tightly onto his fat wrists before he could react. She gave them a sharp jerk upwards and her prisoner was on his knees in the dust. He gave a high-pitched holler.

"You scream like a girl," she said. "Stand up!"

Gazza scrambled in the dirt, lacking the balance to stand upright with her holding onto the cuffs but eventually his feet got under him. As she pulled him sideways to the police car, I thought I saw tears in his eyes.

"Warren, say something. Do something!" he pleaded, needing an ally. I held my breath, wondering if Warren was going to fold, once again.

"Oh, please," I whispered, "Be strong. Don't give in."

Warren smiled and walked over to the car so he could slam the door shut on his former boss.

"He's all yours, officers. As you can see, he was in charge of a vehicle carrying thirteen passengers, nine of whom are children assigned to his care. I know you don't want him loose in your fine State. Lock him up and throw away the key."

"It will be my pleasure, Officer George," the female copper said. "And I thank you for giving us the heads up about his driving yesterday. A couple of women from the caravan park came in last night to complain about his behaviour as well."

"You *what!*" Gazza spluttered against the window. Then a

cunning look came over his face. "You think you're so smart, don't 'cha, George? Well whatcha gonna do now? You can't drive that bus!"

"Actually, I can." Warren pulled his wallet from his back pocket and handed a sheet of paper to the police woman. "I took the test for my bus driver's license a few weeks ago. Just to be on the safe side. You never know when the original driver might become incapacitated, eh? I had the station fax my results to Kununurra Post Office and I picked them up yesterday. So, I am legal. Good-bye, Officer O'Brien."

Slapping the roof of the car, he leaned down to deliver his parting shot. "I'll be sure to tell the commissioner everything."

A few more hand-shakes and back slaps followed before the two WA coppers got into their car, did a U-turn in the dust, and drove off into the morning. The last I saw of Pig Gazza was of his face plastered against the rear window with his mouth wide open. Warren reboarded our bus, taking a small bow as we all erupted with the loudest cheer I'd ever heard.

"All right, Boss!"

"Let's hear it for Mr Warren!"

"Good onya! That's the way to do it!"

Laurel burst into tears, ran to the front, and threw her arms around his neck. "Oh, Mr Warren, thank you so much! Now I don't have to testify!"

Still in the driver's seat, I looked up at him. He looked down at me and smiled.

"More than one way to catch a fish," he said quietly.

I got out of his seat and he sat down and turned the key. "Now, Miss Smith, please look after your charges."

I wanted to grab him and smother him with kisses. I wanted to kneel in front of him and suck his dick until his jism ran down my chin. I wanted to climb on his lap and feel his love pumping inside me while having a million simultaneous orgasms. The more I watched the back of his head, the wetter my panties got. I gave a little wiggle and heard somebody sniggering behind me. That brought me to my senses and I turned around to settle the passengers. I noticed Mary was out of the toilet.

The children (all except Jason who had been watching me

and gave a knowing wink that made me blush) were shouting, hugging each other, high-fiving, and leaping over seats. It was this last business that I put a stop to, but I had to leap over a few seats myself to get their attention. With such an incredible burden lifted from our spirits, we were high as proverbial kites like we'd been snorting lines and smoking njarndi all night long. Hey! I'd learned an Aboriginal word! I looked at Mary and didn't think she'd ever stop laughing. Tears ran down her face until it looked like the Ord River.

"Miss Smith, do your job!" came over the loudspeaker as the bus bumped back up onto the highway, but I could hear the delight in his voice.

"You betcha, Boss, right now, Boss!" I shouted in reply and grabbed the microphone from his hand. "Oi, youse kids!" I was getting right into this Top End lingo. "Sit down and behave the lot of youse, or you'll have me to answer to!"

"Yes, Miss!"

"You betcha, Miss!"

"Hope the Boss don't wreck the bus, Miss!"

Answers flew back at me as the kids divided into twos and threes and took their seats. I stayed up at the front in Warren's former place of authority and, gradually, individuals came up to sit with me and chat for awhile. The time flew and by lunchtime, we were back in the Northern Territory.

CHAPTER THIRTY-TWO

I DIDN'T EVEN KNOW which National Park we stopped in. The Northern Territory is lousy with them, which is good, actually, because the majesty and heritage of the Top End is nothing to be taken lightly. The southeast coast is wonderful too, but this up here gets into your blood and turns you a bit feral. I could easily understand how Warren's mother had got hooked and—damn and blast!—I could just as easily understand his reluctance to get involved with me. I thought I was different...but how would I know for sure?

Mary and I cut sandwiches and sliced fruit. It wasn't like we were missing a worker with Gazza gone because he'd never lifted a finger that wasn't feeding his own fat gob.

Where were these words coming from? I hadn't used language like this since kindergarten! I could just imagine the look on my mother's face if she were to hear me speaking like this!

Warren had the mob off on yet another educational exploration. They all went with him, boys and girls alike, Brooke even hobbled along on her crutches and Sara hung back to help her. On this, the last day, they'd all become best mates and stuck together, throwing soft punches, hugging, giving secret handshakes and giggling. They had turned into a real little family. Did that make me their mum? I shuddered with horror and delight at the thought.

"Feeling better there, Lou?" Mary asked between bites of a cheese and pickle sanger. *Sanger? Jeez, I'm even thinking in NT slang!* Mary had learned to get a feed in before the youngsters arrived to vacuum up every crumb in sight. I grabbed a sanger for myself and sat beside her.

"There was one thing I fully expected to happen that didn't, Mary. I was so certain these teenagers would be going at it like rabbits, but there's been no sex at all this week."

"None at all, Miss Louisa?" she said meaningfully and, once

again, I had the grace to blush furiously.

"You know what I mean," I mumbled. She laughed and took another sandwich, ham and pickle this time.

"I know what you mean and I also know you're wrong."

"I'm wrong?" I was shocked! "Who? When? *Where*? Are you sure?" How blind had I been?

"Laurel and Timbo. They been having it off since that first night we left Darwin. I can't believe you didn't notice."

I hadn't. But then, I'd left Darwin with the full intention of noticing *nothing* about *anybody*. "Laurel and Timbo. Well I'll be damned. So that's why they avoided each other in the daylight. I'm surprised *he* didn't kill Gazza."

Mary laughed again. She thinks the strangest things are funny.

"Wouldn't be the first time a white man took a blackfella's woman," she said.

With no idea how to respond to that remark, I returned to talking about the kids. I wanted to know what else I'd missed. "I know Melanie's already got a boyfriend in Darwin. Caleb and Andreas are still young enough to be more interested in men's business than girls. Corey too, by the looks of him. But what about Brooke, Jason, Sara, and Spider? Do any of them have partners back home?" I refused to count the vagrancy/soliciting as even being real, let alone describe it as a relationship.

"You're right about them young boys," Mary agreed, "although they might act a bit different when they get drunk on a Saturday night. I don't know much about Caleb, of course. The Indian community pretty much keep themselves to themselves, but I bet a sweet young boy like Caleb might be popular for reasons I don't want to think about. Could be why he acts out so much. I wouldn't be surprised if Jason and Brooke start hanging around now, but I reckon they've both got too much of the wrong attention from too many of the wrong people. They won't to move too fast with each other. Spider mighta liked Sara but Sara isn't into boys so no luck there." Mary poured and drank a cup of red cordial. "Actually, Jason and Sara might end up having a little tug-of-war over Brooke. I'd favour anything that got her away from her old man."

I was stunned–"gobsmacked," as the kids say–by her insight. "Mary, you are amazing." I held out my own cup for her to fill. "My best friend in Sydney is a social worker, has a university degree and all, but she doesn't know half of what you do about human nature!"

"Bet she's only half as old too! Life experience, girl. Anybody who pays attention can learn plenty."

"All I'm saying is that you should be working at a Juvenile Centre, dishing out tea and scones and advice. That would clean up Darwin's mean streets in no time."

She laughed and slapped my back. "Watch out, Lou, here they come!"

I heard them before I saw them, and then they were there, inhaling the food we'd prepared. As I watched I couldn't help noticing how healthy and normal they all looked. Most were still skinny as, of course, but their bodies had a wiry alertness. They gave off a glow that should always be associated with youth. I caught Warren's eye and smiled. He smiled back and my knees went weak.

I sat down, but looked away, scolding myself. "*Louisa Mayflower Smith, you stop that right now! The moment you return to Darwin you are going straight to the airport where you will catch a flight home to Sydney and a good job and Dalby and the rest of your family and friends and you will forget that this place even exists! Face it. You are no different than Warren's mother. Do you hear me? This whole experience was nothing more than a flash-in-the-pan and will be forgotten the moment you return to civilisation!*"

Then, of course, the romantic school girl had to argue. "*You are never going to forget this man, girl. He's the best you will ever meet!*"

"*There are plenty of good men in Sydney,*" the woman of the world replied. "*Just because you are going back doesn't mean you have to settle for Dalby.*"

"*As if you ever could! Your eyes have been well and truly opened this week. The Top End is where you belong and Warren George is the one you should be with.*"

"*Not if he doesn't want to be with you. Have you learned nothing? Love isn't real without respect. Does he respect you?*

And don't forget, Miss Louisa, that this entire experience has been only three weeks out of your entire life and you've only know him for one *of those weeks."*

"Yes." The romantic schoolgirl sighed. *"Three weeks of feeling more alive than I have in twenty-three years of living. And what about those juvies? They are amazing! Mary says they need me but, I'm pretty sure I need them."*

Oh, God, I didn't know what to do. Warren was a stubborn man and not about to change his mind. I was pretty sure he'd forget his "rich bitch" far sooner than I'd forget my "Indigenous experiment." Just then Andreas and Corey came running up and plopped down beside me.

"Look at this, Miss!" They excitedly thrust dirty hands full of sharp pieces of ivory into my face. "Crocodile teeth!" Andreas's grin split nearly his face in two. "True, maybe a million years old! Just like they got at the museum, eh?"

Darwin had a *museum*? Maybe there was more to that city than had met my jaundiced eye. I stuck the last bite of apple into my mouth and picked up a couple of their treasures to inspect.

"Wow! How do you know they're so old?" I asked, talking with my mouth full. What a primitive! "They look new to me."

"Duh, Miss," Corey teased. "Ivory don't break down. It'll stay in the earth like forever and crocs *are* prehistoric creatures. Mr Warren said. We're gonna start collecting stuff like this and put it in our shop. I reckon tourist's pay top dollar for prehistoric croc teeth." Young Corey was giving me lessons in history and commerce.

"Wow, you know so much about this." My chest swelled with an absurd pride.

"You're not wrong!" Andreas added. "And there's more! We're gonna make videos of us like fighting the crocs and sell those as well." Both boys smiled and sighed as they dreamt of their rosy futures. I smiled too, and gave them each an impulsive hug.

I looked over at the picnic table where all four girls sat, doing each other's hair and nails, applying make-up, and chattering away like the beautiful birds they were. Jason and Timbo had a book of native animals Warren must have given them and were arguing over whether some tracks they'd found belonged to a wallaby or a kangaroo while Caleb and Spider tossed around homemade boomerangs. Mary and Warren were relaxing over mugs of tea. I knew, in that instant, that I never wanted to leave this place. Australia's Top End was my vocation. I wanted to stay but how could I? My heart was ruling my head and I was powerless to stop it.

"Come on, everyone, it's time to go!" Warren jumped up and clapped his hands for attention. It was another half hour before we finally went, but the magic spell had been broken. It was also time to quit kidding myself. I didn't have the strength to remain up here without Warren at my side. By this time tomorrow I'd be in Sydney, drinking wine with my old friends and trying to convince my parents that I could still be seen in polite society.

And giving Mr Dalby the boot.

That was the only thing I was really looking forward to.

CHAPTER THIRTY-THREE

SUDDENLY, SOMEHOW, we were pulling into the parking area behind the Delta Tours offices. It was after dark but the place was floodlit illuminating a few miscellaneous adults hanging about, waiting to retrieve their respective juvies.

Was it really just about to be over? I had prayed/counted the hours for this moment but my heart bounced around inside my chest, looking for a way out. The kids disembarked first, slowly for once, and not like caged animals being set free, but reluctantly. Mary followed them and I did my job, walking through the empty bus, checking for forgotten items. I found that chunky bracelet of Melanie's stuck between seat cushions and a large crocodile tooth on the floor. I picked them up and got off the bus, too filled with emotion to know what I was feeling.

The kids, orange T-shirts reflecting the street lights, had accepted that the trip was over and they were hugging each other and promising to keep in touch while the spectators hung back in the shadows. It looked like one of those American TV movies. I was amazed and touched when Jason took my hand, leading me to where all my juvies had formed a line to give me hugs and kisses and, most surprising of all, to thank me for the time I'd given them.

"Don't forget, I'm one of the crims," I joked, struggling to hold back the tears.

"Aw, you ain't no crim, Miss," Andreas reassured me. "You mighta broke the law like us, here, but that don't make you a criminal!"

So much wisdom from one so young. I gave him his lost tooth.

Brooke's father was waiting for her, and the way he rubbed her back in greeting made my skin crawl, but his concern over her injury appeared genuine enough. He shot an angry look over toward Warren in the bus, but his daughter worked hard to placate him and apparently succeeded because he never made an issue of it. Brooke's younger sister was having great fun with the crutches and looked so happy and carefree that I chose to conclude that there had been no close encounters with her dad during Brooke's absence. I, of course, had no real idea how an outsider could determine whether or not something like that was going on, but I bet Mary would know in an instant. I walked over and shook the man's hand, murmured reassurances about Brooke's ankle, and then Melanie dragged me away, pulling me over to the light to meet her baby.

He was in a stroller the size of a small car that must have cost the earth, but I didn't go there. Her friend, who looked about fifteen herself, had brought him to the bus to welcome his mum home. He had thick, curly, black hair, light brown skin, and a toothless grin so wide I was worried for the flies he might catch.

"Oh, Mel, he's gorgeous!" I gushed. Handing her the bracelet, I then made the mistake of picking him up. His paper nappie had well surpassed its absorbency quota.

"Yeah, he's not bad for a boong!" his mother agreed. I tried not to look shocked while everybody else laughed.

Sara watched Brooke and her family, started to join them, and then hesitated. She left with Melanie and her friend, pushing the stroller and chattering away, but before they reached the street, Brooke ran over and gave Sara a hug. I looked across at Mary and we shared a smile.

Corey, Spider, and Caleb had people waiting for them as well and Mary and Jason, as adults, volunteered to walk Andreas and Laurel to their respective homes.

"Laurel can come with me," Timbo said.

"We'll all go together. Wouldn't do having youse booked for vagrancy again the same night you get back, eh?" Jason joked, but I could hear the warning in his voice. Was it too much to hope that he had matured a bit? Timbo grabbed him in an affectionate head-lock and Jason threw a well-intentioned punch into the other boy's gut.

I ran over to hug Mary. "You've been my rock," I said. "I hate to say good-bye."

"Don't, then," she said simply. "I reckon you're one of the

stayers—and I'm not often wrong about people. You said so yourself, didn't you?"

I glanced over at Warren. He'd remained on the bus, filling out paper work. He had merely shaken each juvie's hand as they had exited the bus, admonishing them to be good. I hung my head like a lost child, feeling foolishly abandoned. "I don't think I'm wanted here, Mary."

"You are wanted here, Lou, by all them kids and by plenty more you might care to take under your wing." She nodded in Warren's direction. "And I reckon that man there wants you more than he's willing to say."

My heart leapt into my throat. "Do you really think so?"

"Go to him and find out. Now, we gotta get these kids home. So long, Lou, and don't you be a stranger, hear?"

"You go for it, Miss." I looked up into Jason's foolish grin. He wriggled his eyebrows and hips. "I reckon you already know how, eh?"

I punched him. "You behave yourself or I'll find myself a stout walking stick and sort you out."

He responded by grabbing me in an enormous bear hug, lifting me right off the pavement. His coat still ponged, but his hair was clean and smelled like apple shampoo, and he no longer had a single zit on his face or neck. I wondered whether Warren had noticed what a success story our Jason had become?

Our Jason. Mary was right–he belonged to everyone.

"You are one fine lady, Miss," he said when he put me down. "Now, Mary, where's them kids?"

A few more hugs and kisses, and then, suddenly, the parking lot was empty.

Empty except for me and the guy on the bus.

CHAPTER THIRTY-FOUR

WARREN LOOKED OUT THE WINDOW and saw me standing on the tarmac, lit up like Christmas by the million-watt security lights that supposedly kept cars and drivers safe at night. I looked at him, in the driver's seat, ubiquitous clipboard balanced against the steering wheel, a stern and efficient expression on his face. My knees trembled so badly I thought I'd fall down, and my heart thumped so loudly he must have heard it. I was hot and flushed with fear—of rejection? This particular Smith woman was sweating, big time, and wiped her brow with the sleeve of her none-too-clean T-shirt.

"You'd better get going," Warren called to me gruffly out the window. "There's a taxi rank on the street there. I've signed off your CSO and you can come by the station tomorrow and pick up your copy. We open early. Plenty of time to catch your flight home."

I hesitated, trying to read his expression but he had turned back to his paperwork so his face was in shadow. "Everything I brought with me is in my rucksack," I answered. "I'd planned to go straight to the airport and see if there was a red-eye available, but if I need to hang around 'til morning..." *Please ask me to stay!*

He paused, shuffled his papers, but still didn't look at me. "So, you're bugging out for real, eh? Can't say I'm surprised. The Outback is too much like real life for most people."

Damn him! It was all because of *him* that I was leaving! *His* lack of interest, *his* eagerness to see the back of me. Without even thinking about it I knew in my heart that a single gesture or word from him would keep me in Darwin until the next millennium. Mary could see that. Why couldn't he? All those feelings of anxiety and fear turned into a flood of anger. My shot nerves turned to steel as I stamped my foot and marched up the steps and onto the bus. My pupils were still constricted from the glare of the lights around the parking lot so he was nothing more than a silhouette but I could feel his surprise as I let fly.

"Why, you...you pompous, overblown, holier-than-thou, pompous—"

"You said that."

I raised a hand to slap him but he reached up and caught it in midair.

"You know nothing about me!" I spluttered, struggling to free myself. "The only thing that you do know about me is that I remind you of your mother and I make you hot. Those two facts together are a bit sick and I don't want to go there, but you have no right to just *assume* I'm like her!"

He wiped my spittle off his face with his free hand. "What about the small but important fact that we only met because you committed a crime?" he said calmly. "What was it? Speeding your expensive car through the bush, not caring what you hit? Or maybe driving drunk? Why worry? You're at the end of the earth in the Top End, eh?"

I jerked my hand free. I couldn't step back without falling down the steps so I was forced to remain close enough to feel his heat. His voice might have remained calm but mine rose several decibels.

"And just what is it that makes you so damn superior? You never had a drink? You never drove too fast? Am I being punished just because I can afford a decent car? For your information, mister." I shook my finger in his face. "I was arrested for demonstrating against uranium mining. I was out there risking my neck trying to save your precious Outback!"

"You were *what*?" My eyes had finally adjusted to the darkness by now and it was easy to discern his look of confusion. "You...were one of the *Greenies*?" His brows came down and his lip curled up as he tried to catch me out. "Hang on, Louisa. As you keep pointing out, I work for the police. You don't get arrested and threatened with jail just for demonstrating."

"Well." I relaxed a little, hands on hips, and couldn't help grinning at the memory. "Actually, it was my paint balloon that burst on that CEO's desk. He was pretty pissed off about that."

"*Your* balloon?"

"Balloons plural, if truth be known. Filled with paint in the colours of the Rainbow Serpent."

Warren tossed his clipboard onto the seat behind him, stood, took hold of my shoulders, and bent to look me in the eye. His smile was balm to my wounded soul. "But, Louisa, that's fantastic." He laughed his delightful little giggle and put his arms around me. "Oh, I wish I could have seen that."

We moved to a middle seat and sat beside each other. Taking his warm hand in mine I clutched it tightly, never wanting to let go. He didn't resist but moved closer and I thought my heart would burst.

"Tell me more. I want to know everything," he said.

"To be perfectly honest, it was like it happened by accident. You see, I was doing the final year of my engineering degree, and during my last semester at uni I got involved with these people who were really concerned about the environment. They made a lot more sense than most of my university lecturers. Those guys were sending the message that our jobs would be to conquer the natural world and, I'm ashamed to admit it, I never gave any thought to the contrary. Until I met these Greenies, I'd never thought of nature as something that needed to be protected so when they invited me to join them in this protest around Jabiru, well...it was like I had a lot of lost time to make up for. And that was before I'd even seen the Top End or could appreciate what I was actually demonstrating to save."

I saw no need to confess to Warren that my original interest in the Greenies had been a strong sexual attraction to their fearless leader. After all, he's only a man. Warren held me close, sighing happily.

"This place *is* pretty deadly." He pulled back and gazed into my eyes. "I wanted to join in with that mob too, you know," he explained seriously, "but I was just finishing up at the police academy. I don't think they would have approved. I thought that the good I could do my people as a police officer outweighed the need for one more demonstrator."

"So you're a proper copper, now, not just a liaison officer?" I fingered the embroidery on his badge. "No longer a tour guide?"

"I get inducted next week. And, for your information, there

is nothing 'improper' about a liaison officer. Anyway, they'll be needing new recruits now that Gazza's gone."

I shuddered at the memory of that pig. "And not a moment too soon." I looked up at Warren, wanting to touch him but frightened again. He looked away and I was afraid that meant it was time for me to go. "I guess I better find that taxi if I'm going. You can mail me any forms I need." I stood up and looked at him one last time, giving him a chance to protest. "I wish you'd gotten to know me better, Officer George."

He reached out and took my hand. "Louisa Smith, we got off on a very wrong foot, but, in my defence, you were pretty up yourself in the beginning. I definitely want to get to know you better, but you're going back to Sydney. You can't expect me to follow you, not when my career is getting started."

His hot hand in mine warmed my blood, but he was reading me wrong again. What is it with men? Don't they even try to understand women? I threw my rucksack onto the floor and grabbed my hand away so I could shake my fist in his face while giving him the evil eye.

"Mr Warren George, I have never 'expected' anything from you except respect!"

He grabbed my fist and laughed. "Oh, lady, you have my respect. I've seen what you can do with a stick. I wouldn't have the nerve to disrespect *you!*"

My shoulders drooped and I shook my head wistfully. "Well, maybe I wanted a bit more than just your respect. The truth is, Warren, my gut tells me that I should stay up here. I really love this crazy place, but I'm afraid my heart would break if I didn't have you by my side." There, I'd said it. "I'm reverting to my natural cowardice and running home to Mummy."

"I don't think you're a coward, Louisa." He lifted my hand and kissed it.

My heart in my throat, I reached out and touched his face. "Say my name again."

He stood up. "Louisa, Louisa, Louisa," he repeated until his mouth covered mine and neither of us could speak. His tongue searched my mouth eagerly as his hands combed my hair and his pelvis ground into mine.

His cock grew thick and hard against me as my vagina

swelled, almost painfully in its need to be filled with him. My hands stroked down his back and pulled his shirttail out of his shorts, sliding my palms down over his warm, firm buttocks. Then those same hands came around to the front, struggling to unbuckle his belt, unzip his shorts, and free the most marvellous dick in the world so I could hold it close. I dropped to my knees and kissed it, licked his balls, and then put the huge, throbbing thing into my mouth and sucked.

He groaned, hands kneading my shoulders, legs buckling. He pulled me up. His hands grabbed my waistband, pulling open my belt, pushing my shorts to my ankles and, while he was down there, he stuck his face in my fanny. With his fingers inside me and his tongue licking my clit I almost came.

"No," I cried, pulling him up. "I want you inside me.

We were beyond reason, at it like animals, this time on the filthy floor of the bus. The moment he entered me I came, crying out in ecstasy as I pulsated around his cock. His first spasm followed soon after, but when he tried to pull out to come onto the floor, I locked my legs around his thighs and wouldn't let him. He released all his love juices inside me where, I am hoping, a little environmental activist is now taking shape.

We were spent, engulfed in our love, lying there among the stale chips, cello wrappers, and empty drink bottles. Another prehistoric crocodile tooth stabbed my back but I didn't care. When I could talk sensibly again, I peered at my lover through the darkness. Digging grit from my knees I asked, "Am I being a rich bitch if I say I can't wait to fuck you between clean sheets?"

He laughed. "Oh, Louisa, I do love you."

We stood up, brushed the dirt and pebbles from our bodies and departed the Love Bus, hand-in-hand. Warren's Nissan Ute waited, dusty but unmolested, where he'd parked it seven days—a lifetime—ago. We drove to his flat where there was blessed air conditioning, a private bathroom, ceramic mugs, an electric kettle and, I am most pleased to report, crisp and clean bed linen. We shared a shower first of all, and didn't sleep much. Making slow, languorous, love was a pleasure we couldn't get enough of.

NEEDLESS TO SAY, I didn't fly back to Sydney the next day. In fact, I have cancelled my return ticket. In the morning Warren left early for work, despite his lack of sleep and I didn't complain. Both of us were eager to get that report filed on Officer Pig. Warren hadn't taken the time to shave and I hope I can talk him into keeping that sexy stubble. I fell in love with his kind and compassionate nature, but blokes who look all blokey are totally hot and turn me on.

After he was gone I had wallowed around in the soft bed for a bit longer; so much better than a sleeping bag on the ground, even if the air doesn't smell as exotic. Eventually I got up, enjoyed a leisurely breakfast for one (not fourteen) consisting of Earl Grey tea and designer muesli. Warren's pantry was awesome!

I then checked out the rest of his flat and discovered a computer room full of gadgets and games of vengeance that my brother would adore, and a bookcase full of Wilbur Smith novels, but considering recent activities that room might have to be changed into a nursery. From the front window I saw that the whole neighbourhood was up-market, full of high-rise flats with water views, coffee shops, and book stores. I looked forward to learning a whole lot more about Darwin...and my man.

I rang my mum. She's planning a trip to Darwin and will arrive later in the week. I might have neglected to fill in some of Warren's details–like race, colour, and profession–but I'm certain none of that will matter once she meets him and sees how happy we are. She always said that she could forgive her children anything, even murder, and, God, I hope she was telling the truth! I'm not saying that my mother would consider my living with Warren anything akin to murder, but I am afraid that my decision to stay in the Top End might be the greater sin. On the other hand, she did admit she's over the moon that I finally dumped that "officious boor" (her words), Dalby. Why did everybody know but me?

While she was blubbering about her happiness, Dad got on the phone and I firmly informed him that I would get my own credit cards. I was prepared to argue the point but he agreed so readily that I suspect he'd been about to suggest it himself. And that was before I told him the full story of my arrest. I think he will come to terms with my Aboriginal partner long before he accepts having a radical Greenie in the family.

Next, I called the girls. Claudia was sad that I wasn't coming home but it was Suzanne who cried the hardest. "What am I going to do?" she wailed. "With you in the Northern Territory and Claudia in Queensland, I'm going to need a passport just to visit—not to mention *shots*!"

I promise to phone and have a long (or short) talk to Dalby soon. I tell myself that remaining in Darwin wasn't just a cowardly way of disentangling from that sorry mess, and most of the time, I believe it. I'm not worried about him. I should worry about the next wealthy co-ed he snares.

I don't think I'll have any problem getting a good job around here—there can't be *that* many beautiful young women with university degrees—but it definitely won't be with any mining company. I can't imagine Warren's copper's salary going too far and I do like my creature comforts.

Once the phone calls were out of the way, I got dressed in my least-dirty clothes while leaving the others to soak for three days—at least—and went into town. First, I signed up to volunteer at one of the local juvenile centres Warren had recommended. I didn't see anybody I recognised. They're probably all still sleeping off their seven days of healthy living. I'll find Mary and take her to the Coffee Club one day very soon. They make great lattés, but I'm predicting that their scones won't hold a candle to hers. So much to do and so much space to do it in way up here in Australia's Top End.

The second thing I did was go into the cop shop to sign off on my Community Service Order. The same skinny guy with the fly-specked glasses was on the desk.

"How'd it go?" he asked sceptically. "Did it change your life?"

"It did, Officer Joe," I answered with a huge smile. "It most certainly did!"

GLOSSARY

For those of you who thought Australia was an English-speaking country...

Abo – slang for Australian Aboriginal
Akubra – iconic Australian felt hat; cowboy hat
arvo - afternoon
Beedies – slim, aromatic Indian cigarette
billabong – a small lake
billy tea – tea boiled up in a can over a fire
biscuits – cookies in the USA
blackfella – Aboriginal/Indigenous person
blackfella's camp – areas where Indigenous people live "out bush," often for long periods of time, comprising of makeshift shelters, tents, etc., usually without power or running water
boab – uniquely shaped giant trees found in Western Australia, used for food, shelter, medicine and impromptu prison cells
boong – derogatory term for Australian Aboriginal
Bradley John Murdoch – truck driver and drug runner who murdered an English backpacker in the Outback in 2001
Brett Whiteley – Australian Artist, 1939-1992
brumby – Australian wild horse
bunyips – mythological Outback creatures
bush bus – bus that travel from larger towns to isolated communities in the Outback
caravan – camper trailer
caravan park – trailer park
Coffee Club – restaurant chain, specializing in coffees
college – high school in the USA
cordial – drink mix similar to Kool-Aid
crook – sick
cuppa – cup of tea or coffee

damper – bread made from flour and water, often cooked over a campfire

dero – derelict person

Dettol – an antiseptic

drover - cowboy

emu fart – crack of dawn

Ernie Dingo – popular Indigenous actor

Esky – large, insulated food/drink container for picnics, etc.

fanny – pussy (or vagina), **not** the buttocks like in the USA

First Fleet – First British settlers of Australia, came in 11 ships of convicts in colonials in 1787

fronted up – turned up, showed up, approached

gammon – fake, not genuine

Gough Whitlam – Australian Prime Minister from 1972-5, fired from that position, born 1916

grey nomads – retired people who constantly travel, especially by **caravan**

Guides – Girl Scouts

Home Brand – the generic store brand

housing estate – public housing

Humpty-Doo – a small town in the Northern Territory

Jabiru – site of a uranium mine in the Northern Territory

jocks (underwear) – short for "Jockey shorts"

kerb - curb

kookaburras – Australian bird with a unique call or "laugh"

Lifeline – charity organization with shops of second hand clothing, etc.

Lisa Ho – Australian fashion designer, born 1963

littlies – little children, opposite to "oldies"

Macca's – slang for McDonald's fast food

Mary and Frederick – Crown Princess Mary (formerly Mary Donaldson of Hobart, Tasmania) met Frederick, Crown Prince of Denmark, in a Sydney pub during the 2000 Olympic Games

min-min lights – nocturnal lights that hover above the ground, appearing and disappearing, in Western Australia

mossie - mosquito

Myer – My Store, department store chain, one step up from Target

Never-Never – the vast Australian Outback

NIDA – National Institute of Dramatic Art, Sydney, New South Wales

njarndi – Aboriginal name for marijuana – also spelled "yarndi"

NT – Northern Territory

Paddy Pallin – store, suppliers and outfitters of campers and bushwalkers since 1930

paracetamol – an over the counter drug like Tylenol

Patrick White – Australian author, 1912-1990

pong – smell, stink

QANTAS – Queensland and Northern Territory Air Service–leading Australian airline

Rainbow Serpent – mythological creature associated with Aboriginal creation stories from the "Dreamtime"

rank – very unpleasant, angry

road train – large truck hauling multiple carriages–a road train going 80 kilometres an hour needs one mile to stop

Rum Rebellion – in 1808 was the only successful armed takeover of the Australian government, deposing New South Wales governor William Bligh

slope – derogatory term for Asian

sly grog – illegal liquor

smoko – coffee/cigarette break

snag - sausage

Spinifex – a type of grass

sprog – semen, cum

Sunday Session – drinking and entertainment at pubs on Sunday afternoons

Sydney Heads (The Heads) – entrance to Sydney Harbour

TAFE – Training and Further Education schools throughout Australia

thongs (footwear) – also known as flips-flops or sandals in the USA

Top End – the Far North of Australia

torch – flashlight

tucker - food

uni– slang for "university"

Ute – small utility truck

WA – Western Australia

willy-willies – small whirlwind or dust devil

ABOUT THE AUTHOR

One of nine siblings, **Maggie Brooke** was born in Kansas but has lived in Oz (aka "Australia" to the uninitiated) since 1982 when she immigrated as a single mum with two children, one white and one black (for contrast) who are now grown and successful. She is the proud grandmother of two grandchildren and indulges in them and in her love for writing.

As a nurse/midwife/nurse practitioner, Maggie has worked in hospitals, public health, prisons, schools, institutions, remote Australian Aboriginal communities, in Liberia with *Médecins Sans Frontières*, and All Points East. Through her writing Maggie hopes to share the knowledge she has gained from living in this marvellous world and meeting its very varied, yet amazingly similar people.

With her writing often described as "gritty," Maggie wrote first short story at age ten and, yes, the little boy died. She is not conventional with her writing—or her sense of humour. Her other credits include short stories, poems, and articles published in anthologies, journals, ten national magazines, and various newspapers. Maggie's writing rejections, however, could make a full-length novel.

Visit her website "From the Pen of Miss Brooke" at
www.maggiebrooke11.webs.com

ABOUT THE PUBLISHER

"...taking the reader down a different path."

Logical-Lust Publications was established in 2003 and is the erotica and erotic romance imprint of **LL-Publications** based in Scotland, UK and produces books in paperback and in multiple ebook formats. Our talented authors represent both sides of the Atlantic.

We are proud to be a small, independent press providing **quality** over **quantity**. Our motto is "taking the reader down a different path" because the titles we publish are not recycled, formulaic plots with predictable characters in uninspired settings. We publish books that readers will remember.

We do not follow trends.

With that in mind, we invite you to take a short Reader Experience Survey to get your feedback on this book and your reading experience. To participate, please go to the following web page:

www.ll-publications.com/88976.html

Your opinion is truly appreciated!

Best wishes,

LL-Publications/Logical-Lust Publications
www.ll-publications.com
www.logical-lust.com

OTHER TITLES BY LOGICAL-LUST PUBLICATIONS

Tight Women in Hard Places
By Alicia Night Orchid
ISBN: 978-1-905091-75-1 (print) / 978-1-905091-45-4 (ebook)

Although told from a woman's point of view, don't expect mushy, romantic, happy-ever-ending stories here. Instead, meet real women making tough choices and getting on with imperfect lives. These women don't always get what they want, but they usually get what they need, both in life and in bed.
These are tight women in hard places.

Pilgrim for Love
By Anna Austen Leigh
ISBN: 978-1-905091-46-1 (ebook novella)

This enchanting erotic romance features Alys, a strong, clever, middle-aged heroine with a sharp, witty voice who goes on a medieval pilgrimage after five varyingly successful marriages. The arduous journey proves enlightening in more ways than one and Alys is broadminded enough to make the most of her opportunities. But when the young squire Parys falls in love with her, she finds life becoming more complicated than she bargained for.

The Cougar Book
Edited by Jolie du Pré
ISBN: 978-1-905091-56-0 (print) / 978-1-905091-57-7 (ebook)

Cougar women are smart. Cougar Women are sexy. Cougar women are *hot*.

Read this scintillating collection of Cougar stories edited by Jolie du Pré and featuring the best erotica writers around.

Includes an introduction by the original *Cougar* – Valerie Gibson.

Land of a Thousand Dances
By Evelyn Applegate
ISBN: 978-1-905091-62-1 (ebook novella)

Land of a Thousand Dances is a modern-day lesbian fairytale about a librarian hooking up with a mysterious stranger in a bar and getting much more than she bargained for...and enjoying every moment.

Evelyn Applegate writes romance and erotic fiction. She lives in Brisbane, Australia, with two cats, Heinrich and Butternut, and a ridiculous number of shoes. Her veins frequently contain more coffee than blood.

Messalina: Devourer of Men
By Zetta Brown
ISBN: 978-1-905091-11-9 (print) / 978-1-905091-19-5 (ebook)

Eva Cavell is a woman with an embarrassing secret...

A tenure-track instructor at a private Denver college, despite desperate attempts to maintain control, Eva's world is spiralling into chaos. As emotional pressures build inside her, an explosion is imminent. Will she ever be able to live her life how she wants and without shame?

Scouts – The Orgone Chronicles Book 1
By Nobilis Reed
ISBN: 978-1-905091-68-3 (print) / 978-1-90509-1-69-0 (ebook)
2011 EPIC eBook Award™ finalist for Best Sci-Fi Erotic Romance
An overpopulated space station threatens to separate two young loves. At any moment, Challers Dizen could find himself conscripted by the Fleet and forced to become one of their lethal, over-muscled Marines, while Valka Parl could be taken away by the gluttonous Merchants. Their only hope to stay together is to join the mysterious Scouts. However, they soon learn that exploring space as a Scout means exploring their sexuality in ways they never imagined.

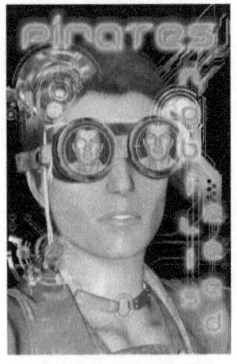

Pirates – The Orgone Chronicles Book 2
By Nobilis Reed
ISBN: 978-1-905091-91-1 (print) / 978-1-905091-92-8 (ebook)

Challers and Valka are safe, protected aboard the Pirate city-ship known as "Port." The scars of their ordeal among the Scouts remain, however. The only way for them to raise money is for them to join the Worthies—reality-TV celebrities who are always on camera. In an environment where loyalty is dismissed and betrayal is rewarded, their love suffers its greatest test yet.

Future Perfect – A Collection of Fantastic Erotica
By Helen E. H. Madden
ISBN: 978-1-905091-20-1 (print) / 978-1-905091-21-8 (ebook)

Speculative erotica at its best from author Helen E. H. Madden, from the adventures of a sexually obsessive superhero to the best orgasm you'll ever have – at the end of the universe.

Helen takes erotica to a whole new level in this astounding collection!

www.ingramcontent.com/pod-product-compliance
Lightning Source LLC
Chambersburg PA
CBHW020941180626
46814CB00003B/884